AND DON'T FORGET
THE CANDY AND FLOWERS . . .

"LOOPY" by Ruth Rendell.

A wolf's costume from a "Little Red Riding Hood" production comes alive in this grisly tale that teaches us what can happen when we don't tame the beast within.

"NINE SONS" by Wendy Hornsby.

A poor Midwestern farm wife can't seem to wait for the doctor to deliver her babies who keep dying at birth . . . or so everybody thinks.

"RUBY NELL'S ORDEAL" by Jan Grape

When Ruby Nell's old mom is found smothered in her nursing home bed, the police naturally suspect her long-suffering daughter. But they may be dead wrong.

"IRON FROG" by Rich Hautala

A mother and child reunion starts with a heart-to-heart talk and ends up with some chilling revelations about family secrets.

"AND NOBODY CARES FOR ME"
by Christina McPhee Benight

Ellen Cargill, head of Cargill Construction, is one tough lady, but she's also alone . . . except for her .357 magn̶u̶m̶ ̶a̶n̶d̶ ̶t̶h̶e̶ ̶m̶a̶n̶ ̶s̶t̶a̶l̶k̶i̶n̶g̶ ̶h̶e̶r̶.

MURDE

MURDER
FOR
MOTHER

~

EDITED BY

Martin H. Greenberg

A SIGNET BOOK

SIGNET
Published by the Penguin Group
Penguin Books USA Inc., 375 Hudson Street,
New York, New York 10014, U.S.A.
Penguin Books Ltd, 27 Wrights Lane,
London W8 5TZ, England
Penguin Books Australia Ltd, Ringwood,
Victoria, Australia
Penguin Books Canada Ltd, 10 Alcorn Avenue,
Toronto, Ontario, Canada M4V 3B2
Penguin Books (N.Z.) Ltd, 182–190 Wairau Road,
Auckland 10, New Zealand

Penguin Books Ltd, Registered Offices:
Harmondsworth, Middlesex, England

First published by Signet,
an imprint of Dutton Signet,
a division of Penguin Books USA Inc.

First Printing, May, 1994
10 9 8 7 6 5 4 3 2 1

REGISTERED TRADEMARK—MARCA REGISTRADA

Printed in the United States of America

PUBLISHER'S NOTE
These stories are works of fiction. Names, characters, places, and incidents either are the product of the authors' imagination or are used fictitiously, and any resemblance to actual persons, living or dead, events, or locales is entirely coincidental.

BOOKS ARE AVAILABLE AT QUANTITY DISCOUNTS WHEN USED TO PROMOTE PRODUCTS OR SERVICES. FOR INFORMATION PLEASE WRITE TO PREMIUM MARKETING DIVISION, PENGUIN BOOKS USA INC., 375 HUDSON STREET, NEW YORK, NEW YORK 10014.

Contents

Introduction to
Murder For Mother

Mom. Just savor that word for a few moments. M-O-M. For most of us that monosyllabic word evokes feelings of warmth and security and love. The tender breast. The gently hummed lullabies. The sentimental laugh.

For most of us.

Gathered between these covers, however, are some writers who have elected to take slightly different views of M-O-M.

You see, it's very possible for mother love to be a little *too* much sometimes. Just ask Norman Bates about that.

It's also possible that Mom doesn't fit the Mom profile.

For instance, there was the gangster Ma Barker, not a lady who spent her time knitting little booties or changing diapers.

And there was—if you're aged fifty or so—"Ma Kettle," a very irascible Mom whose children lived in basic terror of her (as did the endearing lumpen Pa Kettle).

You see what we mean.

While it's nice to think that all Moms are the kind, attractive, dutiful Moms we have—well, unfortunately, some of them just don't make the cut.

And that's the kind of Mom you're about to meet here.

Good reading.

And Nobody Cares For Me

by Christina McPhee Benight

It had been a long hard day for Ellen Cargill, but then all her days were long and hard. She planned it that way.

The stainless steel clock on her desk glowed 10:37 as she added the final column of figures on the yellow pad in front of her. She rechecked the total, underlined it with two slashing pencil lines, swept back a stray lock of strawberry blond hair, and rose from her chair.

One other office in the Cargill Construction suite showed a light. Ellen entered without knocking. Sam Capeletti, her construction manager, sat hunched over a mound of papers like a benign troll.

"We've got the SOBs," she announced triumphantly.

His eyes narrowed as they met hers. "Are you sure?"

"Of course. I've pushed those numbers around for the last three days. As long as the information you got me is good . . ." Her chilly green eyes challenged him.

He folded his arms over a substantial paunch, leaned back, and returned her stare. "They're good all right. They sure cost us a bundle."

"It was worth it. The civic center will be the most profitable project this city has ever seen. What we spent to buy information on the competing bids is chicken feed compared to what we'll make." Her face glowed with satisfaction. "Come on into my office, Sam. Let's have a drink to celebrate."

"Best offer I've had all night," he replied.

A few minutes later they sat in Ellen's office sipping a fine single malt Scotch. Sam glanced at the clock and wiped his mouth with the back of his hand. "I've got to leave pretty quick. I'm picking up my boy and his wife and the new baby. They're surprising Theresa for Mother's Day on Sunday."

"To Cargill Construction," Ellen said raising her glass as if she had not heard. "This will show them once and for all who's number one in Denver." Her lips curved in a smile that almost reached her eyes. Then she spoke in a flat empty voice. "On Sunday, I'll be thirty-seven, Sam. It's been ten years."

A chasm of silence yawned between them as each remembered that raw spring day a decade earlier. They stood in the icy sleet staring helplessly into the depths of a muddy foundation. At the bottom of the hole the body of Steven Cargill, Ellen's husband, lay smashed and broken in a freak crane accident.

That was the third time someone she loved had been torn from Ellen. As hot tears mingled with the freezing rain, the new widow swore she would never let it happen again.

The next morning at seven sharp, she entered the office of Cargill Construction and took charge. She was competent, clever, and utterly ruthless. Over the years she had won respect if not affection from her men and her competitors.

"Time to head to the airport," Sam said. He rose stiffly from his chair and pulled on a heavy jacket. "God-awful weather for May, more like November. This stuff's supposed to last through the weekend."

She drained the last drops from her glass. "That's springtime in the Rockies for you."

"Let me walk you to your car. After this morning's trouble, I'd feel better," he said.

Earlier in the day a foreman had reported a stranger hanging around the job site. Ellen and Sam had spotted him behind a pile of lumber remote from the center of activity. He was tall, dressed in a bulky navy down jacket and blue jeans. A knit watch cap pulled low over his ears and forehead shadowed his features. As soon as he saw he was observed, he turned away. Sam dispatched two husky carpenters to warn him off, and he left immediately without a backward glance.

"I can take care of myself," she answered sharply.

The office was located in a warehouse district that was deserted at night, but that had never bothered her.

"Okay, you're the boss-lady. See you tomorrow." As he stepped through the door, he turned. "Happy birthday," he said.

Ellen did not answer. She sat for a few minutes as the sound of Sam's footsteps faded down the hall, then she locked the incriminating papers in her safe.

Her mouth twisted in a parody of a smile. Thirty-seven. Wasn't seven supposed to be lucky, she asked herself. Not for her it wasn't. In her seventh year, her mother's rheumatic heart had failed. At seventeen she had fallen in love. Nine months later her lover was gone and so was her newborn son. She had seen him for the last time as a triumphant social worker lifted him from her arms and bore him away to his new and worthier parents. At twenty-seven Steven had died.

"Some lucky number," she murmured half aloud. Well, to hell with them all. She had survived, and in style. And she had made sure her heart could never break again.

Moments later the outer door of the building clicked behind her. She hesitated in the doorway, glanced up and down the dingy street, then started for her car. The tapping of her high heels on the damp cement echoed from the brick walls of the dark old buildings. As she pulled her keys from her coat pocket to unlock the car, a sudden movement seen from the corner of her eye warned her that she was not alone. A tall figure loomed in the sickly glare of a mercury vapor lamp not fifty yards distant. She recognized the silhouette instantly. It was the man who had been loitering around her building site.

She unlocked the door, slid behind the wheel, and jammed the key into the ignition. Nearly two hundred and fifty horses under the Corvette's hood rumbled to life. She checked the mirror. The man was gone.

The city was behind her in a matter of minutes. She hummed along with a country singer, a song of love and loss, as she rolled along winding suburban lanes. Suddenly a flash from her rearview mirror almost blinded her.

"Jerk!" she muttered. "Turn off your brights."

She tapped the pedal to flash her brake lights, but the other driver did not back off. She jammed the accelerator to the floor, and her car leaped forward with a screech of tires. The other car matched her speed.

Her stomach squeezed in a spasm of fear. She was somebody's target. She sorted through a lengthy list of potential enemies. During the last few days at work and at home her phone had rung at odd times, but when she answered the line was dead. She had dismissed it at the time. Now those calls seemed part of a threatening pattern.

She hurtled down the placid streets, wrenching the car around corners. The other car followed as if connected by an invisible cord. She choked on a nauseating mixture of fear and fury. Finally she rounded one last curve and saw the twinkling lights of the municipal building that housed the village police station. Just let him try to follow me there, she thought. She skidded into the parking lot, and the other car roared past. She peered into the blackness. The license was not the familiar forest green and white of Colorado plates. There was nothing to identify her pursuer, only the taillights of an anonymous medium-sized sedan disappearing into the darkness. Her heartbeat slowed, and she breathed normally again as she hurried to the police entrance and jabbed the night buzzer. An officer appeared in seconds.

"Can I help you, ma'am?" he asked.

Ellen surveyed his pink cheeks and eager blue eyes. My God, she thought. They're hiring cops right out of high school.

"Officer, someone's following me."

She tried to sound reasonable as she told him of the phone calls, of the stranger on the building site, of the car chase. No, she did not get a license number. No, she could not tell the color of his hair or eyes. He was tall, about six-two or -three, she guessed. Well no, she could not be positive that he was driving the car. He hadn't threatened her, not in so many words.

The young policeman nodded as he recorded her answers. He yes ma'amed and no ma'amed until Ellen wanted to scream. His bored voice told her plainly, he had written her off as just another neurotic woman with too little excitement in her life. At last he snapped the lid of his notebook shut. The sharp click of his ballpoint pen signaled that he was through listening.

"Don't worry, ma'am," he said soothingly. "We'll keep an extra eye out. I'll be sure to let the patrol know about your problem."

She was too drained to argue. "You do that," she said in a sarcastic voice, then turned on her heel and marched out the door.

She was still fuming when she arrived at home a

few minutes later. Just outside the door she hesitated. The alarm panel was dark. She gasped, then relaxed once more. That morning she had been running behind and neglected to set it. She unlocked the dead bolt, entered the front hall, and froze. Her skin prickled in apprehension. Something was wrong.

Slowly she moved from room to room, every sense hyperalert.

First the entry. No trace of dust or dirt marred the gleaming polish of the black marble tiles. As she moved from living room to kitchen to bedrooms she scanned every object and every surface. All was as she had left it.

At last she entered the bedroom she had converted into an office after Steve's death. She kept the room and its contents in meticulous order. Every object was functional and utilitarian, every object but one.

In a life purged of sentiment she clung to one souvenir, a photograph of herself and Steve. She had enshrined it in an ornate sterling silver frame, and it occupied a place of honor on her desk. Now the frame lay facedown on the floor. She turned it over. The glass was shattered, and the photograph gone.

That night she checked the locks and windows twice, and reset the alarm before sinking into a troubled sleep.

The next day began badly. The cleaning woman called to explain she could not come before noon. One of the kids was sick, and she was going to borrow her cousin's car, but it had a flat. The whining litany of domestic disaster droned on.

"Yes, sure. Okay, Susan." Twenty-four years old and four kids already, Ellen thought with disgust. Her boyfriend takes off and spends more on beer than he does on the kids. She's not much better, popping babies out like shelling peas. You'd think she didn't know what caused them.

On her way to work she allowed herself to consider the past, something she disciplined herself to avoid. Unbidden questions plagued her like a swarm of stinging insects. Could Steve and I have made a decent home for a child? We never got the chance. What if I'd kept my baby? Would I have ended up like Susan?

The blast of a horn jerked her back to the present. She raised her middle finger at the offending driver and turned up the volume on the radio.

Later that morning, she related the previous night's events to Sam as they inspected one of the Cargill projects. "I know that dumb cop tossed away my report before I was out of the parking lot," she grumbled.

Sam took one last drag from his cigarette, then ground it underfoot. "Weird," he said. "Especially about the picture."

"It's getting to me. I feel like something awful is going to happen." She hunched deeper into her coat and turned up the collar against the spring wind. "And listen, if that guy comes around again, call the cops. Have them throw his butt in jail."

Sam glanced around. None of the men were close enough to hear them. "What you need is a gun. Have you got one?"

"I've been kicking myself since all this started," she answered. "I got rid of all his guns after Steve died."

"I've got a .357 magnum locked in my desk. It's yours if you want it."

"Thanks. I was wondering how to get hold of one. I guess it beats Valium any old day." She grinned at him. Things were definitely looking up.

Ellen drove home that evening with the cloying aftertaste of bakery icing in her mouth and an ache at the base of her skull. Her well-meaning secretary had arranged an impromptu birthday party, but wine in a paper cup and supermarket cake was not Ellen's idea of a festive occasion. She endured forced smiles and made artificial chatter. The others were there from duty. Nobody wanted to offend the boss. She knew they were anxious to get home; so was she.

The cold rain pummeled the early spring flowers into submission. A soggy mass of ruined pink crab apple blossoms spread across the driveway and lawn and plastered themselves to her shoes as she dashed to the door. Heavy clouds brought early darkness. Damn that stupid Susan, she thought. I told her to change the bulb in the outside fixture. Frigid gusts of wind eddied around her as she fumbled with her keys on the darkened porch. Once inside, she snapped on the light and tossed her dripping coat into a corner. The gun felt heavy in her purse.

"Don't use this unless you mean it," Sam had warned. "This thing can blow a hole in someone's gut big enough to drive a truck through."

"If I have to use it, I won't be kidding around," she had assured him.

She removed the weapon and inspected it methodically. It was loaded and ready to fire. For the time being it could stay in the hall. She opened the drawer of a dainty antique table. The weapon looked incongruous as she laid it on a pile of silk scarves and neat leather gloves. She caught sight of herself in the mirror hanging above the polished surface of the table. Her skin was chalky. Shadows stained the hollows beneath her eyes and cheekbones like bruises. She stared at herself. God! I look like a corpse, she thought. She flicked a switch on a small brass lamp, and its glow dispelled the illusion.

Ellen idly riffled through the day's mail, which Susan had left on the table. There were no birthday cards, but she expected none. The rest was junk with one exception. She squinted at the return address on the thick pink envelope. She had grown up in New Mexico, but the name and Albuquerque address meant nothing. Curious, she reached for a letter opener.

Suddenly the telephone shrilled. She flinched, and the envelope and opener dropped from her hand. "Hello." No answer. "Hello," she repeated, angrier this time. The sigh of someone breathing rasped through the line. "Leave me alone, creep!" she shouted, and slammed down the receiver.

The adrenaline from her anger warmed her momentarily, but soon it faded leaving her restless and apprehensive. She picked at a few cold leftovers, then toured the house double-checking every lock.

Sleet drummed at the windows as the storm intensified. Now and then the weather stripping moaned like an animal in pain. She drifted into her office. There was always work to distract her. In minutes she was absorbed in a black-and-white world manipulating the numbers she could always trust.

Several hours passed. She raised her head. Had she heard the throb of a car engine and the crunch of tires on gravel? She tensed and strained to detect alien noises over the rush of the wind and splattering of rain. She hurried to the living room window that commanded a partial view of the driveway. Had she just seen the dying glow of a pair of headlights?

A legitimate caller would soon ring the doorbell. Seconds slogged by, then minutes. Nothing. She strained to pick up any strange noise. Nothing. The lights dimmed, and she gasped. The glow intensified, and her breath escaped in a shuddering sigh.

She reached for the phone. No. The police had condescended to her before, she would not make a fool of herself. She moved quickly to the hall, opened the drawer, and snatched up the gun. She gripped it tightly as she hurried from room to room peering out each window into the storm. Then from the kitchen she caught sight of a figure rounding the corner of the house. The dark blue jacket and knit cap pulled low were all too familiar.

She released the safety on the gun and padded silently across the marble floor of the hall toward the front door. Her hand trembled as she slipped the dead bolt and slowly turned the knob.

She jerked open the door. Not two feet away a figure loomed huge dark and featureless against the night. She screamed. Her finger jerked. The gun roared and with a wet sucking gasp the stranger toppled to the floor.

When she had recovered enough to examine the man's face, her first thought was, he's so young. The dead features were twisted in an expression of idiot bewilderment. Dulling green eyes stared at her while droplets of rain meandered down his cheeks from reddish-blond sideburns. Ellen covered her mouth as her stomach heaved, then turned and staggered to the phone.

The body was gone. Two sullen attendants cursing at the night, the storm, and the corpse, hustled it into an ambulance. Mud streaked with rusty splotches stained the porch and smeared the marble entry hall. The scent of wet leather and damp wool mixed with stale cigarette smoke filled Ellen's office. Two police officers both overfamiliar with the aftermath of sudden death were finishing their questions.

Ellen could not seem to concentrate on their words. At last, from her daze she realized one of the policemen was holding something out to her. It was a New Mexico driver's license.

"It was in his wallet. Scott Allen Bonfils. Does the name mean anything to you?" he asked.

"No." She examined the photo. *His hair looks*

lighter in the picture, she thought as she absently
pushed a coppery strand of hair from her own forehead. The bony young face was the face of a stranger,
but there was something familiar she could not define.
The name was strange, too, or was it?

"Wait," she cried. "That was the name on the
envelope."

"What envelope?" asked the officer as Ellen dashed
from the room.

She pawed through the stack of mail on the hall
table until she retrieved the envelope she had almost
opened earlier that evening. "This came today," she
said turning to the officer who had followed her into
the hall. "I never got a chance to open it."

She ripped open the flap, and drew out a greeting
card. The front showed a lush bouquet of roses over-
laid with gold lettering.

"Is that a Mother's Day card?" asked the detective.
She slowly opened the card. On one side a note had
been printed with painstaking neatness.

Dear Ellen Cargill,
   It is hard to write to somebody you have never met,
but I feel like I have always known you. I always
hoped I would meet you some day, and I hoped that
you did not forget me.
   I looked for you for a long time, but when I finally
found you I got scared. I've been trying to see you. I
even called you a few times, but I lose my nerve when
I hear your voice.
   I hope it will not be too big a shock for you to meet
me after all this time. If you don't want to know me
after we meet, just tell me and I will go away and not
bother you again.

                         Your son,
                         Scott

World's Greatest Mother

by Barbara Collins

Mark Twain once came to town. He wrote about seeing the most magnificent sunsets here. Nestled serenely on the Mississippi River, our little city offers its citizens good quality life.

But all life ends, eventually. Sometimes abruptly.

My name is Joan Munday. My partner is Frank Lausen. We make up one-third of the six man—actually, five man, one woman—detective unit of the Port City Police Department.

It was Saturday, June 18, a day so perfect I could have killed to be out with Dan and the kids on the river; but instead, Frank and I were called to a new housing addition on the north side of town.

The homes in Mark Twain Meadows were expensive—by small-town standards, anyway—with manicured lawns and well-tended flower gardens. The streets had quaint names—Samuel Clemens Road, Tom Sawyer Drive, and Huckleberry Finn Lane.

We pulled up in front of 714 Pollyanna Place, and got out.

Walter, our crime lab technician, met us at the door. He was pushing fifty, balding, and looking tired.

"This way," he said, turning.

We followed.

The living room was tastefully decorated—perhaps too tastefully; it could have been the showroom of a pricey furniture store: couch and chairs matching in fabric, pictures and knickknacks coordinating in color, all working together in harmony to produce somebody's idea of wonderful. Not mine. I couldn't imagine anyone "living" in this living room.

And there was one person who obviously agreed with me.

He was stretched out on the floor, on his face, in front of the fireplace, like a big bear rug. About six feet, two hundred pounds, he wore black cowboy boots, blue jeans, and a worn white T-shirt. His hair was blond—except on the left side of his head, where it was now a blackening red.

Walter broke the silence. "A single blow to the head. His name is Travis . . ."

"I know who he is," I cut in.

Every town has a bully. Travis Wykert was ours. As far back as junior high, his penchant for pounding those smaller than him had got him in trouble with the law. As an adult, he'd been brought up several times on assault charges, but no one would testify.

"That the weapon?" asked Frank. He was a sandy-haired, husky man in his late twenties—ten years younger than me. He gestured toward the couch, where a trophy lay encased in a clear plastic bag.

Walter nodded. "Wiped clean."

"Went there," Frank said, pointing to the mantel above the fireplace. "See the spot in the dust?"

I looked, and caught my reflection in the large mirror over the fireplace; should have spent a little more time on my hair this morning.

I crossed over and picked up the bagged trophy, a heavy bronze statue of a woman holding a baby. A plaque on its base read: "WORLD'S GREATEST MOTHER."

"Where's the owner?" I asked Walter.

"In the kitchen," he said, "down the hall."

The kitchen, in the back of the house, was a bright,

spacious room, so clean the cabinets gleamed. But like the living room, it too didn't look lived in. There was nothing on the counters, not even a toaster. Lace curtains framed the windows, while flocks of country geese roamed the walls.

At a round, oak table sat three women. The one on the left, smoking a cigarette, was middle-aged. She wore dark slacks and a black turtleneck top. Her brown hair, streaked with gray, was short, mannish. She wore no makeup.

The woman in the middle, in a white skirt and a blouse with kittens on it, was also middle-aged. Her hair was dark blond, shoulder-length; her face was obscured, buried in her hands as she sobbed.

The one on the right was young and slender, with long, ice-blond hair. She wore jeans and a sweatshirt with a Port City Community College logo on it. The girl sat motionless, in apparent shock, staring, her face a mask.

A uniformed cop, who was first at the scene, stood behind them taking notes on a pad.

"This is Louise Harris," he said, pointing to the woman in the middle. "She owns the house. And this is her daughter, Laura." He gestured to the young girl. Then he nodded to the woman on the left. "That's Pamela Schultz. She's renting a room."

I approached them. "Who wants to tell me about it?" I asked.

Pamela Schultz threw her head back and blew out smoke, then stubbed her cigarette out in an ashtray. "He was hurting Laura so I hit him," she said, matter-of-factly, like she was giving me the weather report.

Louise Harris looked up from her hands. Her eyes were red, swollen, her face puffy. "Don't try to protect me, Pam," she said. "*I* did it."

Now the younger woman, Laura, turned her face toward me, slowly, robot-like. "They're both lying," she said softly, and then announced, as if ending a game of *Clue,* "I killed Travis Wykert in the living room with the trophy."

It was 4:35 in the afternoon when we got back to the Public Safety Building—a big, modern, red-brick affair we shared with the fire department.

We were faced with a unique problem: usually it was hard enough getting *one* confession; now we had three.

The women had each been Mirandized; all three declined an attorney.

I waited with Frank in the interrogation room.

"Because the suspects are female," I said to him, "we might do better if I take the lead. But jump in when you want to."

He nodded.

"But no good cop, bad cop crap," I warned.

"Got ya."

The interrogation room door opened, and Pamela Schultz was brought in. I nodded toward a chair. She sat, sullenly, legs crossed, one hand resting casually on the table.

"I called your probation officer in Colorado," I said. "She said she couldn't understand why you left friends and a good-paying job to come here."

"I had permission," the woman shrugged. "Maybe I just wanted to do something different."

"Like work at McDonald's?"

She looked away.

"What's your relationship with Louise Harris?" Frank asked.

She looked over at him. "I'm renting a room from her," she said.

Frank smirked.

Pamela's eyes narrowed. "We're not *lovers* if that's what you're getting at. God, you *men* are all alike."

Then she looked at me. "And *you're* just as bad . . . I can tell what you're thinking."

No she couldn't—but I let it go.

"How well did you know Travis Wykert?" I asked.

"I've never met him before today," she said. Then she leaned forward, spreading the fingers of the hand that lay on the table. "Look—I've already given you people a confession. What more do you want? That creep was beating on Laura, so I stopped him. If you ask me, I did the world a favor."

I leaned in. "Then why are *both* Louise Harris and her daughter taking credit for your good deed?"

"How the hell should *I* know!" she said. "I mean, do you *really* think either of them could have done it? Louise is afraid of her own shadow, and Laura was obviously under the spell of that sadistic bastard."

"So *you* stepped in," Frank said.

"I've done it before."

I looked at Frank; he raised his eyebrows.

I walked around the table and stood next to Pamela Schultz, placing a hand on the back of her chair. "And paid twenty long years for it," I said, putting compassion into my voice. "But it doesn't hardly seem right," I continued, "considering how that man abused you."

Her body stiffened.

"Back then," I said, moving closer, "rights for abused women weren't in fashion." I whispered in her ear, "Today you would have *walked*."

A look of agony passed over her face, then sudden rage.

"I *told* you I killed the bastard," she snapped back. "Now quit wasting my damn time!"

"If you did kill him," I said, "you'll be doing plenty."

"Plenty of what?" she smirked.

"Time."

* * *

Louise Harris sat fidgeting—a bundle of twitches and tics. I couldn't make up my mind whether to come on strong and watch her dissolve into a puddle of protoplasm, or take a more humane approach.

I chose the latter.

"Just relax," I said to her, reassuringly. "That's right, take some deep breaths. Now, I want to know exactly what happened this morning."

She signed. "It was about eleven," she said, her voice quavering, "Pam—she's renting a room from me—and I were in the kitchen having coffee when I heard the front door bang open. Somehow, instinctively, I knew it was him, and I was frightened for Laura ..."

"Why?"

"He's hit her before. A few weeks ago she came home with a black eye. Said she'd run into something. But I knew who did it. I told her I was going to call the police ... but she said she wouldn't cooperate."

Louise Harris looked at me with sad, swollen eyes. "Do you know what it's like to have to sit by and watch your child throw her life away?" she asked. "Ever since her father walked out on us five years ago, it's like she wants *every* man in her life to treat her badly."

Mrs. Harris buried her head in her hands and sobbed.

I took some Kleenex from a box on the table and handed it to her. She wiped her eyes and blew her nose.

I waited for her to compose herself.

"Getting back to this morning," I said. "where was Laura when Travis Wykert entered the house?"

"Laura was in the living room, reading," Louise said. "By the time I ran out of the kitchen, that man had her cornered in front of the fireplace. He was shouting at her, slapping her."

"What was he shouting?" Frank asked.

Louise looked at Frank, then turned her head, avoiding his gaze. "I ... don't remember," she said haltingly. "Obscenities. Things ..."

"Then what?" I asked.

"Pamela—she was standing next to me—tried to pull him off Laura, but he threw Pam onto the davenport. That's when I picked up the trophy and ..."

She lowered her head, crying softly into the tissue.

"Come now, Mrs. Harris," I scoffed gently, "you don't have the stomach to commit murder, now, do you? Stop covering up for Pamela Schultz. The most she'd get is manslaughter."

Louise Harris looked up angrily. "May I ask you something?"

I nodded.

"Do you have any children?"

I nodded again.

"Then you can understand how a parent feels when their child is in danger. You would give your life for that child, you would do anything ... even kill."

The woman was right.

"And I *hated* that man!" Louise Harris said viciously. "I wanted him out of Laura's life!"

I looked down at her. "I'm afraid you've got that wrong, Mrs. Harris."

"How's that?"

"He isn't out of her life yet."

"I'd been seeing Travis for about six months," said Laura. She seemed composed, but her eyes were haunted. "Could I please have a glass of water?"

I looked at Frank, who left the room.

"I know what people thought of him," Laura said, "but I saw something different: a frightened, abused little boy. His father beat him. I guess I thought I could help him—which was a laugh, considering what my *own* father did to me ..."

Frank returned with the glass of water and set it on the table in front of Laura, who took a drink.

I waited.

"A while back," she continued, "I came home with a black eye. Travis and I had an argument." She paused. "Well, actually, I won't lie ... he hit me for no good reason. My m-mother was furious. She wanted to press charges against Travis, but I told her I loved him and I wouldn't cooperate."

Laura took another sip of water.

"Shortly after that, she rented a room out to that woman. At the time I couldn't understand why—we didn't *need* the money."

"Did you know the Schultz woman was convicted of murder?" I asked.

She shook her head, then she nodded, "Not at first. But I found out later."

"Your mother brought this woman in to kill Travis Wykert," I said flatly.

"No!" Laura said sharply. "That's not true!"

"Then what *is*?"

She took a deep breath and exhaled. "Pamela Schultz is my m-mother."

"What?" Frank and I said.

"My natural m-mother."

Frank and I exchanged wide-eyed glances.

"How did you find out?" I asked.

"I think I always suspected. But I knew for sure the moment I saw Pamela Schultz ... and my own eyes looked back at me."

Laura told us that she had confronted her adoptive mother, who said that she and Pam were best friends in high school. After graduation Pam got married and moved away. A year later when Pam came to visit Louise—who herself had gotten married—she had a

new baby. But Pam didn't seem happy. Pam asked
Louise to take care of the newborn while she visited
another friend. It was a few days later that Louise
heard Pam had killed her husband.

"So my m-mother ... Louise Harris ... kept me as
her own," Laura said, "and never told me about any
of it ... until my *real* mother came around."

The room fell silent.

"Why did she come around?" I asked, finally.

"To try to talk some sense into me."

"About Travis abusing you?"

"Yes."

Frank asked, "Why was Travis so pissed off when
he came to see you this morning?"

Laura winced. "He wanted me to get an abortion.
I told him I wouldn't."

"Did your mother know you were pregnant?" I
asked.

"Which one?"

Frank rolled his eyes.

"Either," I said.

"Well, they *both* knew after he started yelling
about it."

"Then what happened?" I asked.

"When Travis hit me, Pamela attacked him. But he
threw her off. Then Travis looked back at me with
such hatred that I was really frightened ... I was
scared for me, and the baby! I grabbed the nearest
thing I could get my hands on, a trophy I had given
my m-mother ..."

Laura stared at her hands. "Funny," she said, "a
decision you make in a split second can change the
rest of your life ... or somebody else's ..."

She looked up at me with eyes that pierced me.

"Don't you see?" she said, pleadingly, "I had no
choice. I *couldn't* get an abortion."

She shook her head. "No ... there was just no way

I was going to do that. After all ... that would be murder."

It was 8:45 that evening when I stood with Frank on the steps of the Public Safety Building, watching the three women get into the backseat of a squad car.

We let them go. For now.

"I have a feeling," I said slowly, "that we may never solve this one. Hell. Maybe I should have been tougher on 'em."

The car door slammed shut.

"Know what I think?" Frank said.

"What?"

"I think that each of those women *thinks* that *she* really did it ..."

The car pulled away from the curb.

"... That for one moment, in front of the fireplace, the urge to kill Travis Wykert entered all of their minds ... and then it didn't matter whose hand actually held the trophy."

I looked at Frank. "But if you had to pick one, who would it be?"

He looked at me, shrugged. "Who cares who killed Travis Wykert?"

We watched the squad car, until it disappeared into one of those magnificent sunsets Mark Twain wrote about.

"Not me," I said.

Then we went back into the station.

Pressure

by Douglas Borton

"Happy Mother's Day." Darryl lifted the tarpaulin with a theatrical flourish.

Annie Goddard gasped. "Oh, Darryl, you shouldn't have. This is too much, *far* too much."

He knew she was already computing the cost with preternatural accuracy. Many times he'd sat with his mother in this room, on the overstuffed sofa under the velour draperies, watching her favorite program, *The Price is Right*. She outmatched every contestant.

"It's Samsonite," he told her proudly. He patted the largest suitcase in the set. "Good tough stuff. Your luggage needs to be tough, the way baggage handlers treat it these days."

"I'm sure that's true. People have absolutely no respect for property anymore. I don't know what the world's coming to." She sighed. "But, dear, I really don't travel very often, you know. It's so awfully expensive."

"Mother," he chided. "To travel is to live—Hans Christian Andersen said that."

"Did he really?" Annie said vaguely, sounding uncertain about the name, as if perhaps it belonged to some friend of hers from the old days, one of the ones who were always turning up on the obituary page.

She was increasingly vague each day, Darryl noted. Her mind was clouding, no question about it; but at seventy-six her physical health was still damnably good.

"Yes, to travel is to live," he repeated. "In fact, I had such a good time on my trip to Europe last month that I decided you deserved a similar adventure."

He plucked an envelope from his vest pocket and handed it over.

"A weeklong, all-expense-paid vacation in San Francisco, just for you. Accommodations at the Meridien, the best hotel in the city."

"Why, Darryl, you can't afford this." She gazed at the envelope with dazed, greedy eyes.

No, I can't, he answered silently. You can, of course—you could buy a round-trip ticket to the moon and never notice the cost—but not me. Still, that won't stop you from going if I foot the bill.

Aloud he said, "Naturally I can afford it, mother dear. I'm more than happy to do it for you."

He heard himself slipping into the pretentious quasi-British mode of speech he always felt compelled to use with her, a consequence of years at private schools that turned out mincing ninnies of the sort Annie preferred. His sharpest childhood memory was of her voice shrilling boastfully, "Look at Darryl, isn't he just the perfect little gentleman?" And the other rich besotted ladies at the cocktail parties and luncheons murmuring, "Yes, what a darling, a fine boy, you and Henry must be so proud."

A gentleman, yes, that was what he was, nothing less than that, and nothing more. Those stifling all-male schools had taught him manners but no skills, professional, athletic, or sexual. Now, at thirty-nine, he was underemployed, unmarried, and unhappy, but still polite, always polite. For a long time he had politely contemplated suicide, considering various genteel methods of which his teachers would doubtless have approved.

But suicide was not what he wanted. What he wanted was a way out of the trap that was his life, a way to màke something of himself, to be somebody. In short, money—his mother's money, the vast piles of it Henry Goddard had left her when a coronary toppled him ten years ago. The money she stubbornly refused to spend on herself or others, the money she hoarded in international bank accounts and obscure tax shelters, the money that brought joy only to bankers and accountants.

He was her only close living relative. All he needed in order to get hold of her fortune, to sink his hands into those heaps of crisp green treasure, to run his fingers through loose bills as another man might caress a sex goddess's hair, to be rich and free and *important*—all he needed was for his mother to die. That was not such a large request to make of God, now, was it?

"San Francisco," Annie said, marveling. "It's been so many years since I was there." She put on her glasses and squinted at the ticket. "First class, too. You are *such* a thoughtful boy."

"Nothing's too good for my mother."

She noticed the departure date. "I leave in a week. So soon!"

He had made it soon because he could not wait. But of course, he couldn't let her see that.

"Is it too early?" he asked. "I can have the tickets exchanged. Although, there might be some additional expense . . . and I'm not certain I could cover that."

"A week will be fine," she said hastily.

"Wonderful." He smiled at her and at the luggage. "Well, Mother, I'd suggest you start packing."

Darryl Goddard had not actually enjoyed his trip

last month, nor had he gone to Europe. He had traveled to Pakistan, of all the forsaken places. A bus had taken him to Peshawar near the Afghan border; via jitney he had been transported, jouncing and swearing, another twenty miles to Darra.

In Darra you can buy anything. What is not immediately available can be obtained.

The Afghanistan war has been good to the Pashtun tribesmen who ran the Darra bazaar. The armament of many nations is for sale in generous quantities. Antiaircraft guns are rolled out to tempt visiting customers. Tribesmen playfully aim Stinger and Javelin missiles at the empty sky. Nearby, their children crawl amid scrap from Soviet tanks rusting in the weeds.

What Darryl wanted was not there. But he had money, money hoarded in his mother's miserly fashion for well over a year till it reached the critical mass necessary for his purposes. He bargained, speaking slowly in his clumsy Pashto. Then he waited.

The Pashtuns are far from unsophisticated in matters of international commerce, especially those pertaining to the black market in arms. One of the vendors made a deal with somebody in Turkey, who talked to a friend in Rome, who had connections in Ireland. A week later Darryl had what he'd come for.

He encountered no trouble carrying it home. His luggage was X-rayed at the airports he passed through, naturally, but Semtex is invisible to X rays. That was the whole point of getting the stuff.

Back in Worcester, he purchased the five-piece luggage set. The largest suitcase was the one he chose to use.

Semtex, like other plastic explosives, can be modeled by hand, cut with a knife, flattened by a hammer, and otherwise mistreated with no ill effect. Pass an electric current through it, however, and you have a hell of a blast.

Working in his spare time and on weekends, just as one would pursue any other hobby, Darryl first cut the Semtex into thin sheets, then lined the largest suitcase with it. He coated the plastic with a special glue obtained from a hardware wholesaler. The product is known as conductive glue, because, like wire, it conducts electricity. Unlike wire and quite like Semtex, it does not show up in X rays.

When the glue had dried, Darryl sewed new fabric lining into the bag to conceal the explosive beneath.

During his tedious stay in Pakistan, when there had been little to occupy him but *buzkashi* matches and an occasional fight to the death, he had reviewed the various methods he might employ to detonate the bomb.

A timer mechanism had been his first thought, but subsequent analysis dampened his enthusiasm for that plan. Airlines were notorious for delayed or even canceled flights. Suppose the bomb went off while the jetliner was still on the ground, before the passengers had even boarded. No, he had to be certain the explosion took place only after the plane was aloft.

Research led him to the answer.

Shortly after lining the suitcase, he purchased an aneroid barometer from a scientific-supplies company. He paid in cash, ensuring that the transaction would leave no traceable record.

The aneroid barometer is a remarkable instrument. The heart of the device is the aneroid cell, a thin-walled metal box enclosing a partial vacuum. Changes in atmospheric pressure cause a slight contraction or expansion in the cell, inducing a metal pointer to creep across the calibrated dial.

As pressure rises, the pointer inches toward the right. As pressure falls, it jerks bug-like to the left.

In an airplane, pressure drops as the craft ascends.

Darryl taped a small dry-cell battery to the barometer. Thin wires ran from the battery's positive and negative terminals. He soldered the negative-terminal wire to the barometer's adjustable reference pointer, which he then fixed permanently at 28 on the left end of the dial.

To the active pointer, the one free to move in response to changes in pressure, he soldered a short length of wire that was unattached, for now, to anything.

The positive-terminal wire was also left unattached for the time being. On the day of the flight, he would cut a hole in the fabric lining and use the conductive glue to bond this wire to the Semtex. Then he would glue the active pointer's wire to the plastic. The explosive would be connected "across the battery," as electricians say.

Then, just imagine:

When the active pointer swung to the low-pressure side, it would touch the reference pointer affixed there. The two soldered wires would make contact, closing the circuit. Electrons would stream from the negative terminal, through the wire to the reference pointer and from it to the active pointer, then along the wire to the Semtex, through the Semtex, and finally along the positive-terminal wire into the battery again. The Semtex, destabilized by the voltage, would detonate. Boom.

It was the thought of that boom, loud and clanging and final, that made Darryl postpone the final connections till the last minute. He had no intention of having the damn thing go off prematurely for some ungodly reason.

He reviewed his plan a hundred times and found it good. The greatest danger was detection during the loading of the baggage. Though the Semtex and the conductive glue were transparent to X rays, minimizing the risk, the battery, barometer, and threadlike wires might be picked up on the screen. But the bundle of equipment was quite small, and once it was nestled in a corner of the suitcase, surrounded by other junk, it should not call undue attention to itself. At least he hoped not.

Most likely the bag would pass the cursory inspection that luggage generally received. Then it would be loaded into the baggage compartment, and a short time later the jetliner would lift its nose into the sky as its landing gear retracted. The plane would climb, the pressure would fall, the active pointer would creep inexorably to the left . . .

He lay awake for many nights, his imagination running an endless loop of images and sounds: the sudden shuddering eruption in the belly of the plane, the disintegration of the fuselage, the aircraft's screaming, spiraling descent.

"Happy Mother's Day," he would whisper to his pillow, his teeth bared in a smile.

It was a shame so many others would die with her. Hundreds of innocents. Children, some of them.

When Darryl thought about that part of it, he did not feel like a perfect little gentleman at all.

A week after Mother's Day, he was back at Annie's house, his car parked in the long driveway with its trunk lid popped. The morning sky, translucent as a pond, cloudless and blue, smiled down on him in forgiveness and benediction.

"All set, Mother?" he asked brightly as she came down the big staircase, dressed in her traveling suit. She moved spryly and her eyes were alert; the excitement of the trip seemed to have peeled away some of her years.

"Absolutely, Darryl. And I do want to thank you for all this."

"It's nothing." Which is precisely what you'll be, soon. "Where are your things?"

"Upstairs, in the master bedroom. Some of those bags are awfully heavy, I'm afraid."

"I'll manage. You sit tight." He glanced at his watch. "Isn't *The Price is Right* on now?"

"Why, yes, it is. Thanks so much for reminding me."

She settled on the sofa and happily immersed herself in all the things she was too frugal to buy. Darryl headed up the stairs, pleased that he had remembered the show. It was nice of him to give his mother one last chance to watch it.

The five suitcases stood near her king-size canopied bed in a wedge of white sunshine. He had known she would use all five bags. She had never learned to travel light.

He placed the largest suitcase flat on the floor and opened it, then pawed at the stuff in the bag, a raccoon digging in a garbage can, till he had made a niche in one corner. From his coat pocket he removed the barometer-battery unit; he put it carefully in the space he'd made.

A spool of electrician's tape and a Swiss army knife came out of his other pocket. He taped the barometer and battery in place, then slit the suitcase lining with the knife. Quickly he dabbed conductive glue on the ends of the active pointer's wire and the positive-terminal wire, then pressed them both to the Semtex. He waited impatiently for the glue to dry.

Everything was connected now. The bomb was armed. His heart kicked, and he felt a chilly trickle of sweat under his shirt.

Breathing hard, he replaced some of the stuff his groping hands had dislodged. He was relieved to see that there was a TravAlarm in the suitcase, along with a pocket calculator, which Annie used for computing interest on her various investments, a daily and sometimes hourly preoccupation. The presence of other electronic items would make the battery-barometer package less noticeable.

It was an effort to lug the bags down the stairs and heft them into the trunk of his car. He was careful how he handled the big suitcase

The Price is Right was ending in a blare of applause and canned music when he said to Annie, "Well, I think we're ready to go."

"I would have beaten every one of those players," Annie said, switching off the TV. "Every one."

"You always do."

"Ridiculous how much things cost these days. Do you know what a coffee maker retails for?"

"Mother, we don't want to be late."

"Oh, of course. Of course."

She checked the lights, all hooked up to timers meant to scare off burglars, then locked and bolted the huge front door. He let her into his car on the passenger side and pulled the shoulder belt over her bulky fur-collar coat.

Then he was behind the wheel, guiding the sedan out of the driveway, down country roads, onto Route 90, east to Logan International Airport. Annie chatted but he hardly listened. He was thinking of the bomb in the trunk.

If something were to go wrong ... if it were to detonate now ...

Again he imagined a fireball, a cry of ruptured metal, but this time the fantasy was not quite so pleasant as it had been when other people were involved.

Twenty minutes into the trip, he hit a traffic jam on the highway and came to nearly a dead stop.

"Oh, *hell*," he breathed.

"Don't swear, Darryl," Annie said automatically.

"Sorry, Mother. It's just ... well, I'd hate to see you miss your flight."

"We've got plenty of time."

They didn't, though. It had taken him longer to load the luggage and hustle Annie out of the house than he'd expected. Their margin of error was small and shrinking rapidly as the traffic crept along at ten miles an hour.

"Goddamnit, what's going on up there?"

"Darryl, *please*."

This time he didn't apologize. He switched on the radio and tuned in an all-news channel.

A traffic report came on. Major accident on Route 90 near the Route 140 junction. Traffic slow in east-bound lanes, clearing past the Grafton exit.

"That's only a few minutes from here," Annie said calmly.

Darryl looked at the dashboard clock. They were behind schedule. The plane was leaving in an hour, and he was a good forty minutes from Logan right now. This was going to be tight, very tight.

Then it occurred to him that his original intention had been to detonate the bomb via timer. If he had built it that way, every tick of his watch would be bringing him closer to the explosion. Thank God he had opted for a barometric bomb instead. Thank God.

"Thank God," he murmured.

Annie glanced at him. "What?"

"Nothing, Mother."

The maddening crawl continued. Ahead he could see a flicker of dome lights and the waving blue sleeve of a cop directing traffic. They had nearly reached the scene of the accident. Good.

He checked the clock again. Just forty-five minutes till takeoff. His only chance of making it would be to drive like hell, exceed every speed limit, once the traffic thinned.

"Darryl, I don't think I've ever seen you so nervous. We'll get there. And if I miss this flight, they'll book me on another."

He didn't want her on another flight. He didn't want to wait in the airport lounge for hours, knowing the bomb was armed. He didn't want his plans altered in any way.

Savagely he said, "The ticket was nonrefundable. If you try to exchange it, you'll be charged a penalty. I can't pay for that."

"Oh." Annie paled. "Oh, I see."

Got you where you live, you penny-pinching old bitch.

He felt a smile struggling to be born under the smooth mask of his face, and stifled it.

Finally they were alongside the accident. A big diesel truck had skidded and turned turtle, crushing a Japanese econobox like a snail. Bodies were being pried from the wreckage.

"How horrible," his mother whispered.

You're next, Darryl told her voicelessly. Only in your case, there won't be enough left to zipper into a body bag. You'll be more like . . . pâté.

This time he could not smother his smile; but Annie, intent on the carnage visible through the side window, didn't see it.

Then they were past the crash site, and with amazing swiftness the highway opened up again, traffic bulleting down the lanes. Darryl laid his foot on the gas and watched the speedometer needle climb. He thought of the plane's altimeter registering an increase in altitude, while in the luggage compartment the barometer's pointer dipped toward the low end of the scale. He drove still faster.

"Please, Darryl, don't get both of us killed."

"I won't." Not both of us. Just you.

The drive was a race with the changing numbers on the dashboard clock, the sweeping second hand of his watch. Time was his enemy. He counted the hard, regular beats of his pulse in his ears, each beat another unit of time, single and discrete, lasting for an instant, then gone forever.

Fifteen minutes before takeoff, he emerged from the toll tunnel under Boston Harbor and saw the Logan tower rising in the near distance.

"We're going to make it," he breathed through gritted teeth.

His mother said nothing. She was white-faced and trembling. The ride had been too much for her, it seemed. Well, she would be taking an even wilder ride before long.

With ten minutes to go, he pulled into the airport and searched frantically for the terminal. There it was.

All he had to do was stop the car. Every curbside space was taken. To hell with it, then. He double-parked and got out.

A line of traffic was halted behind him. Horns blared. Darryl ignored them. He lifted the trunk lid and began hauling out suitcases. Hurry, hurry.

Annie appeared, having struggled free of her seat belt without his assistance. "Darryl, all these people are honking at us."

"Fuck them!"

She recoiled, shaken. "That's . . . that's not very polite, dear."

"I'm not polite!" he screamed at her. "I'm not a gentleman! *I'm not your little gentleman!*"

A hand seized his arm. Darryl's head jerked up, and he came face-to-necktie with a burly porter, all big shoulders and square jaw.

"Hey, pal," the porter said, without friendliness, "what exactly do you think you're doing?"

Darryl drew a fluttery breath and fought for calm. "My mother's flight is leaving in five minutes."

"You can't park here."

"She's going to miss her plane."

"Double-parking's illegal in this zone."

Cars were pulling around him, now, the drivers giving him the finger as they passed.

"Look," Darryl said, easing the man aside, searching for whatever diplomatic skills he possessed, "my mother, as you can see, is quite elderly." He lowered his voice. "She's got cancer. This is going to be her last trip. To see her grandchildren. I just don't want her to miss it."

He put a pleading look on his face and waited.

The porter softened. "Oh, hell, all right. Five minutes, you say?"

"Maybe less, now."

"Well, let's go!"

Then the big man was piling the unloaded suitcases onto his baggage cart. Darryl hustled Annie to the curb.

"I'm sorry I yelled at you, Mother," he said. "It was the strain of the situation, that's all."

"One must not lose one's manners in an emergency, Darryl," she said primly. "That is precisely when one needs them most."

"I'll remember that."

She relented. "Oh, I can't be mad at you, not after you've given me all this. You're such a good boy." She hugged him, her thin arms surprisingly strong. "I've always loved you so much. Perhaps I haven't shown it. I should have, but ... well, you know us New Englanders—flinty and hard."

Her lashes beat feebly at a sting of tears. Standing on tiptoe, she kissed his cheek.

"I love you, Darryl," she whispered.

He felt a tightness in his throat. For a moment,

just one moment, he wanted to hold her there, to tell the porter not to check the bags, to forget the whole thing.

An instant later the luggage cart was gliding past them, the tiny wheels squeaking. The porter guided it through the sliding doors into the concourse.

"Looks like I have to go now," Annie said, as if in prophesy. She stepped away from him and raised a white-gloved hand with a smile. He thought of a ghost's salute. " 'Bye, Darryl. And don't worry about me. I'm sure I'll have a *wonderful* trip."

Then she was gone, hurrying after the big uniformed man, merging with the crowd.

Darryl returned to the car, numb and shocked, oblivious to the cacophony of horns. He drove slowly away.

Originally he'd meant to park near the airport and watch the planes ascend. He had hoped to catch a glimmer of the distant explosion and hear the crack of sound.

Now he just wanted to get away, far away. Guilt was chasing him; he felt the need to outrun it.

He turned the radio off. He didn't want to hear about the crash, the bodies. He didn't want to hear anything.

The drive home passed in silence and stillness. The blur of the road outside his car seemed unreal, a movie image, flickering and grainy. The sun died as the sky clouded over. A gray pall settled over his world.

He parked in the driveway of his house in Brookfield and walked slowly inside, shoulders stooped, feet shuffling in an old man's gait.

The blank picture tube of his TV taunted him: Turn me on, see pictures of the strewn wreckage, the reporters breathless as they babble into their handheld mikes.

He left the set off. Tried to eat lunch, but the food had no taste and he could not seem to swallow it, no matter how thoroughly he chewed.

For a long time he stared out at the window at the premature dusk. He thought of Annie watching *The Price is Right*. That last hug. "I love you," she had said.

He didn't want the money anymore. He had been crazy to want it. But it was his now.

His eyes closed. He slept.

The ringing of the telephone woke him.

This was it. This was the call they always made. When he had charged the round-trip ticket to his credit card, he'd anticipated that the airline would phone him, some time after the accident, to express sympathy and regret.

He had expected to be happy about this call. He had been a fool.

The phone rang seven times before he found the strength to lift it from its cradle. "Hello?"

"Darryl?"

His stomach clenched. His head spun. "*Mother*?"

"Yes, I'm calling from San Francisco. I just checked into the Meridien. A lovely place, so elegant ..."

He couldn't comprehend what she was saying. "You're in San Francisco?"

"Yes, of course I am. Where did you think I would be, the French Riviera? But listen, Darryl, there is one problem. I think I've lost one of my bags."

He gripped the wall to keep from falling. "Which one?" But he knew already.

"The largest suitcase. It's not here. I didn't notice till I was at the luggage carousel. I asked the airline people, and they swear they have no record of checking it through."

"No record," he echoed stupidly.

"So what I think is, we must have left it in the car.

In all the confusion, with the people honking and the porter and everything, we just forgot it. It was the biggest one, so it was probably at the bottom of the pile."

"I ... I see." His voice was flat, distant. It had that quality of foreignness he associated with hearing himself on tape.

"I can do without those items, I suppose. If I need a few things, I'll just have to buy them here." Nothing flat in her voice. She sounded young and buoyant, a girl on a spree. "Imagine me, buying duplicates of things I've got at home. But I don't care. It's time I started living a little."

"To travel is to live," he said pointlessly.

"Yes, didn't some friend of yours say that? Well, he's right, and so are you. Thank you so much for this wonderful trip, for all your generosity. You've made a new person out of me. Oh, there's room service. Must be going. Ta ta."

Click, and a dial tone hummed.

He set down the phone and stood motionless for a long stunned moment. Gradually he became aware of laughter in the room. He thought it was odd that someone should be laughing here. Then, with a small shock, he understood that the sound was coming from his own mouth.

I'm happy, he realized. I'm ... so ... *happy*.

It was more than happiness. He was giddy with relief and with gratitude toward some unknown and previously unsuspected goodness in the world.

Was this how it felt to have a reprieve? He supposed it was. And maybe there was a God up there, after all. A God who looked after children and drunks and ... and fools.

Then he remembered the suitcase in the trunk, the bomb still wired to explode. Better defuse it before anything went wrong.

He left the house, whistling. A mist of rain peppered his face like fairy kisses. He inhaled dampness and smelled the ozone odor of approaching rain.

The trunk lid popped up, the interior light came on, and yes, there it was, the suitcase. He reached for the handle, then froze, stopped by a thought. A bad, stomach-sinking kind of thought.

What was it the weatherman was always saying on TV as a storm moved in?

Barometer's falling.

"Oh," Darryl said, looking down at the suitcase, his back measled with the first patter of raindrops. "Oh . . . *shit.*"

He almost turned to run, and at that moment the barometer's pointer, which had been easing steadily leftward throughout the afternoon, shifted one final fraction of an inch; the wires touched; the circuit closed; and Darryl registered a bloom of white heat, beautiful as the unfolding petals of a rose, expanding to fill his field of vision in a heartbeat. His last heartbeat.

Later, combing the scorched yard, the authorities could find no remnant of Darryl Goddard larger than a silver dollar. There was so little left of him that burial seemed almost beside the point.

Even so, his mother tearfully insisted on purchasing the very finest casket money could buy.

Keepsakes

A Koko Tate Tale

by Peter Crowther

(for Kathleen Crowther)

The man stared at me, checking me over.

He looked like he'd been made by a poorly coordinated kid who got bored easy and had no sense of design. He was carrying about thirty pounds more than he should, stood around six foot in shoes, and his general demeanor was a complex mixture of hard and soft, aggression and compassion, warmth and coolness. His disarming and yet authoritative air probably made people forgive him almost anything. Almost.

The face itself was straight from *Sesame Street,* shaped over time by fist, blackjack, occasional knives and razors, and other assorted objects. It was a thick wedge of tan skin-colored modeling clay with two bushy, almost-Neanderthal brows—a bullet had burned a gap in the right one—and large green-brown eyes, bordered by lines and underscored with overnight bags. Right now, the eyes were narrowed tightly, appraising me. This was a cautious man.

Above the eyes was a thick tuft of sagebrush hair, cut unfashionably short and so black it was almost purple. On one cheek was a small dark circle that looked like stubble missed by the morning razor. It was actually a healed-over bullet hole. Below it, and to the side, his lips looked like they were welded together so they'd never smile. But that was just a pose, and one of many. Perfectly on cue he allowed a small smile. This was not a man to do what was expected of him.

He wore a brown Polo shirt beneath a light green tweed sport coat, beige canvas pants, and a pair of lace-up sensible brogue shoes, thick-soled and bearing the soft look that shoe leather can only get over years of painstaking cleaning and polishing. He lifted one leg so that the sock became exposed. It was bright yellow with green vertical flashes. This man was not a slave to fashion.

We'd known each other a long time, him and me. I was used to him, familiar with his ways and always comfortable with his decisions. I bent down and hoisted up my travel bag. He did the same. He also copied me when I checked my side pocket for my car keys, my inside pocket for my wallet, and my holster for my .38. What else does any man need?

I checked behind me in the room to see if I'd left anything. I hadn't. I turned back in time to see him turning back from checking *his* room. It looked a lot like mine. He looked a lot like me. I had one advantage, though: when I looked at him, I saw only what I wanted to see. When he looked at me, he saw the truth.

But we did have one very important thing in common. Our mom loved us. And we loved our mom.

It was only three weeks since Easter, but already the threat of New York summer hung heavy in the air; its muggy ninety-degree days sending out an advance guard of thin wispy tendrils of heat, snaking along the sidewalks by the delis and the art shops, and in the park beside the bushes and around the band shell.

I felt a mixture of excitement and apprehension. The excitement came from leaving the city for a few days, the apprehension from spending those few days with my mom. When I looked at him, I saw that the guy in the mirror showed only the apprehension, carved deep in a long line across his forehead. As I watched, he relaxed. Gave me a smile that said, *It'll be okay*. Maybe it would. I took a final look around the apartment and walked out, slamming the door. Hard.

Out in the street, my Toyota waited breathless, ready to move. I threw in my bag and my jacket, unclipped my holster and tossed it onto the passenger seat, climbed in behind the wheel. We set off, man and machine—both sluggish at first—heading for Broadway and parts beyond.

It was one of those days when I wished I had a convertible, but I made the Toyota into the next best thing and rolled down all the windows. The finishing touch was a cassette of Vivaldi's *The Four Seasons* ... all I needed now was Alan Alda sitting beside me, and we'd be fine.

Broadway parallels the Hudson River and, if you ever want to go north out of New York, it's the best route of escape ... straight, colorful, and interesting. I crossed the Harlem into the Bronx, drove past Cortland Park into Yonkers and the start of Westchester County. Somewhere over left of me, fortunes were being made and lost, and reputations manipulated, along the lush tees of St. Andrews. Golf had never been a game I could come to terms with, but it ranked second against big business. Maybe the two of them deserved each other.

Along the way, Broadway changed its name a few times—Albany Post Road and U.S. 9 being the most common—but it was always Broadway to me. The Toyota had got its wind now, and it gulped both the oncoming countrified air and the endless blacktop with impressive ease. I leaned my arm out of the window and enjoyed the flattening landscape and the lush compositions of Vivaldi as we moved through small towns whose names ended with -on-Hudson, then Hastings, Ardsley, and Croton, and over the Tappan Zee Bridge and into whimsical Tarrytown, onetime home of Washington Irving.

From there into Ossining where, glancing across at the ghost town of Sing Sing, I turned down the sound to see if I could hear the spectral echoes of metal mugs on steel bars that so characterized the old pris-on-break movies. But all there was was wind and the smells of defeat, failure, and incarceration.

Before long, following State 9D, we drifted through Garrison, Boscobel and Cold Spring. For old times' sakes, I stopped the car in Cold Spring and, amid the heady perfume of roses—maybe more imagined than real—I thought of Mom and Dad and, more recently, of Philippa Tamidge and Rodney Millerchap. I made a mental note to bring Ella Thornley out here some-time. When I got back to the car, I had butterflies in my stomach.

Back on the road, we rejoined U.S. 9 into Rhine-beck before branching off onto State 9G, less traffic, nearer the river and air redolent with the smell of apples. I stopped at a little road stand and bought a bag from a towheaded kid, dressed in faded denims and sporting the biggest booger of dried snot on his top lip that I'd ever seen. "You ought to see about getting that amputated," I said. Who needed Alan Alda?

"Huh?" he said.

"Doesn't matter," I told him, taking the apples. I held out a five-dollar bill and he snatched it, keeping his eyes on me all the time. Those same eyes looked set to fall right out of his head when I waved away his offer of change. Koko Tate, Big Spender.

Munching my McIntosh, I drove on through Hudson

itself, switched to State 9J to keep next to the river, and onward to Kinderhook, Resselaer, and the dusty state capital, Albany. Out of Albany and into Troy—where, sparing a thought for Herman Melville, I bellowed "Thar she blows!" out of the window, scaring an old man, who was busy scything his lawn, out of any growing he still had left to do—we took U.S. 4 back over the Hudson into Waterford and across the Mohawk to Cohoes. By this time, the butterflies in my stomach had put on boots and were busy working out to Michael Jackson.

Crescent Road followed the Mohawk through Crescent, Vischer Ferry and Rexford, then it became State 146 and took us on into Niskayuna and Schenectady.

Our destination.

Schenectady is home to two formidable institutions: General Electric's research and development center and my mom.

Although New York's heartland is generally considered to begin west of the industrial triangle of Albany, Troy, and Schenectady, north of the Catskills and south of the Adirondacks, there's still a lot of small-town soul in Schenectady itself . . . along with some of the prettiest picket-fenced smallholdings you'll see this side of a Rockwell calendar or the pages of an old Archie comic book. Eleanor Alice Tate lived at one of them, 421 Fenimore Street.

I pulled the Toyota up against her front lawn and turned off the engine. The car breathed a clink of relief and began to settle itself onto its chassis for a well-earned rest. I got out and stretched, winding my head around to bring some feeling back into my shoulders, breathing in the heady scent of roses and night stocks that wouldn't even begin doing their real work until the sun went down and the air cooled off. Just as I was thinking of opening the back door and getting my jacket, the little old lady that used to protect Tweety and smack Sylvestor with a broom walked out onto the step of the house, holding the screen door ajar with her shoulder and wiping her hands on a blue-and-yellow floral apron. Shielding her eyes with her right hand, she stared at me across the grass. "Koko?"

"Hi, Mom," I shouted. The butterflies had tuned in to a metal-rock station. I walked toward her, the years falling away from me with every step, the sounds of the Toyota's hot metal ticking behind me, the gentle breeze lifting the branches of a huge sycamore that probably looked down in the same benevolent way when the American Locomotive Company opened for business back in 1851. Two houses along, a guy in a Hawaiian shirt stopped mowing his lawn and leaned on the machine handle.

The smell of freshly cut grass drifted across and around me and, by the time I got up to her, I was fourteen years old, knees scuffed and hands dirty, looking behind her small frame for a sign of Dad standing in the doorway, rolled-up copy of *The New York Times* grasped firmly in one hand. But he didn't appear. I hadn't seen him—except in my dreams and one time during a scary hypnotism session with Jim Garnett—since 1972 when we'd laid him to rest in a small graveyard in Lawnswood where, on a still clear night, you could hear the shouts of kids reaching for the brass rings on the Palisades rides and smell the sweet, cloying drift of cotton candy.

My mom took hold of my arms and held me there, eyes moistening. Behind me, the guy in the shirt started up his mower. She shook her head, and when she spoke it was with a mixture of pride and loss, her voice shaky and unsure. "Koko," she said, "it's real good to see you."

"You, too, Mom," I said, and I bent forward and

hugged her to me and bit my lip to stop from crying, squeezing my eyes tightly closed and breathing in her smells so that I could call on them those times when I felt scared or lonely. She patted my back and shook her head again, pushing me back to arms' length and taking another look. "My, but you're so *tall*," she said with just a hint of a smile.

"Six feet is all, Mom," I said. "Same as ever."

She nodded her head and then lifted a hand to tuck a strand of hair beneath a silver clip. "It's me, I guess. Shrinking," she said. Then, with a dismissive wave, "Go get your things, now. I've got hot blueberry muffins and a fresh pot of coffee."

"Hot dog," I said, immediately wondering where the words had come from, and I jogged back, up through the years, to the disappointment of adulthood and the promise of decay and obsolescence offered by my slumbering Toyota.

As the afternoon drifted into early evening and the first night flies took to the airwaves, my mom and I brought each other up-to-date with news and stories, rediscovering each other again after long months of unnecessary separation.

I told her about "Lonesome" Pines—missing out the shooting—and Philippa Tamidge, and about the Bible murder and my trip down to Louisiana with Jeff Sandusky. She liked that story a lot, always having been partial to cats. I didn't tell her about the little old ladies from last Christmas. Too close to home.

And as she stood at her sink, washing our plates and cups and staring out into the colors of the evening, I told her about Ella Thornley, and about how much she'd like her. My mom told me that Ella sounded just fine and that I had to bring her up to visit. In her voice I could hear her silent prayers that God should keep me well and make me settle down and marry and, maybe, just so's she could see them one time, bless me and this Ella Thornley with kids that could run bare-assed through the long grasses that she still thought existed off the main roads of New York City.

Sitting in Dad's old chair, smoking a stale Pall Mall from a pack that Mom kept around for emergencies, I flicked through an old copy of *Vogue*. Mom turned on a side lamp and settled down into the chair next to me, picked up her sewing. I felt like I was in an off-Broadway play, maybe something by Arthur Miller, set back in the mid-Fifties. We were building up to moving into the second stage of our conversations when the knock on the door interrupted the thought flows.

"Just hold on a minute," Mom said, straining out of the chair. "Now who could that be at this time?" she muttered, aside to me. I watched her walk to the door, arthritis pulling her knees outward, and wondered where all the time had gone.

She pulled the door open and gave a small yelp of delight. "Tyrone Daniels, what are you doing out here at this time?"

A tall, thin man in his late fifties ambled through into the living room, nodding to Mom and smiling over at me. "I couldn't get out here until now, Eleanor, and I truly am sorry."

Mom waved him nevermind.

"We had all manner of things going on today, and I did promise I'd get out here and talk to you about the missing hose and . . ." Tyrone Daniels let his voice drift and fixed his eyes on me the way any lawman would.

"This is my son, Koko," Mom said grandly. "Koko, this is Tyrone."

I nodded and held out a hand. "Tyrone, how you doing?"

He took it and shook it hard. "Doing just fine," he said, "just fine." He removed his hand and jammed it into his jacket pocket. "Koko you say?" he said to Mom.

"It's short for Kokorian," I explained over Mom's nod. "Mom always wanted me to be a ballet dancer, but I never did make it."

"Oh, Koko!" she said with a laugh, and struggled back to her chair, landing with a *plump* and a sigh into the cushions.

Tyrone Daniels gave out the kind of smile that people reserve for when they don't know what the hell's going on. I shook my head and waved him free.

"Sit down, Tyrone," Mom said. She turned around to me and said, "Tyrone works out at the sheriff's office."

"Oh?" I said, like I hadn't already guessed. The big man nodded and sat on the edge of a high-backed chair. "What you been doing, Mom? Not speeding again?"

Mom shook her head, allowed her beaming smile to spread still farther across her face, and pushed her glasses farther back on her nose.

"There's been a whole spate of burglaries along this road, Mr. Tate," he said.

"That's Koko," I corrected.

He smiled and gave a quick nod.

"Burglaries? You didn't mention this to me, Mom?"

"Didn't see that I needed to, son. They didn't get away with much at all, just some old hose I had curled up outside the back porch."

"Any ideas on who was responsible?"

"Kids most likely," Daniels said in an easy voice that covered up his strength and sharpness admirably. I was impressed. "Stole junk and bric-a-brac mostly," he went on. "No offense, Eleanor."

Mom shook her head and resumed her sewing. "None taken, Tyrone."

"Junk? Like what?"

"Well, your mom's hose, some barbecue equipment—tools and the like, you know—a couple of garden pixies from Mrs. Berryman's place..." Mom sniggered, and Tyrone shot her a glance before continuing. "A garden fork left out overnight ... that kind of thing. Nothing important, but it's just the fact that there's someone prowling around that ... well, it just causes folks some discomfort."

"When was this, Mom?"

"Couple of nights ago, now. It's not all that important, now, so stop your worrying," she said, patting my arm. Then to Tyrone, "I'm really grateful you came around, Tyrone, but everything's all right now Koko's here."

I flexed my muscles and put on one of my toughest expressions. "Koko Tate, scourge of pixie thieves!" He laughed dutifully.

"So what line of business you in?" he said, getting to his feet. "Seeing as how you didn't make the Bolshoi."

"Same as you," I said, "but private."

"A pee eye, huh." He didn't sound impressed. Nobody ever did. "How's it pay?"

I shrugged. "I eat every other day and sleep at the Y on Saturdays. What was it the animals used to say on *The Flintstones*? 'It's a living!' "

"Yeah, right," he said. He didn't know what the hell I was talking about. He turned to my mom and gave her the big warm smile he had so successfully kept from me. "You let me know if you hear anything now, Eleanor," he said, "and keep those doors locked." Mom started to get out of the chair, but stopped when he placed a firm hand on her shoulder. "I'll see myself out." He turned around and walked to the door. "Good meeting you Mr. Tate," he said.

"You, too, Tyrone," I answered. I walked over to him, pulled open the door, and walked out onto the step with him. He paused and looked up into the steadily darkening sky. "Gonna be another hot one," he said.

I followed his gaze ... Fredric March and Spencer Tracy out on the front porch in *Inherit The Wind*. "Yep," I said, fighting off the need to hitch up my pants. "Looks that way."

"You staying long?"

"Over the weekend," I said. "Mother's Day."

"Right. My mom died few years back." I nodded and just managed to stop from telling him I was sorry to hear that. "Well, gotta get along now." He ambled off across the grass toward a waiting Dodge Rambler with its sides on. "Be seeing you."

I waited until he got into his car and gave a wave as he pulled off. Somewhere up behind the night-time clouds, a god that must've had a soft spot for Stephen Spielberg sent a comet searing across the treetops on the other side of the road, flying high enough to make Toledo. Its trail flashed bright and then disappeared, leaving a dark scratch, like a kid's uneven scrawl or an old woman's signature, etched on the blackness.

When I looked down and turned around, the guy in the Hawaiian shirt was watching me, standing out on the sidewalk smoking a cigarette. I nodded to him. "Hello there."

"Hello yourself," he said. "You Ellie's boy?"

"I guess so"—I laughed—"but 'boy' might be a bit ambitious." I held out my hand and walked over to him. "Koko Tate," I said.

He took the hand, limply, held it for a second or

two, like it was fresh dog turd, and then let it drop. "Jerry Parmenter. So how's she doing?"

"My mom? She's doing just fine far as I can make out. But maybe it's me should be asking you."

"Me? Hell, we never hardly see hide nor hair of Ellie. Keeps herself to herself," he said, pulling on his cigarette. "And that's just fine with me's, what I say." He raised his eyebrows and nodded at me, as if to say it was a pity more folks along the street didn't follow my mom's example.

"Yeah," I said, mainly because I couldn't think of anything else to say, and looked around at the street and my Toyota. "It sure is quiet along here."

He pulled again on the cigarette and threw it to the grass, ground it in with his foot, and blew out a cloud of smoke. "We were worried about her awhile back, me and Doreen—Doreen's my wife."

I smiled. "Worried?"

"Yeah, she didn't seem herself."

"How's that?"

"Oh, I don't know." He pulled a bent-looking pack of Kool out of his shirt pocket and shook one out. I didn't even know they still made menthol cigarettes. He put the cigarette in his mouth and said, "Walking around the lawn late at night, muttering . . . like she was talking to somebody." He looked sheepish, embarrassed to be telling me this about my mother.

I glanced back at my mom's house, saw the curtain twitch at the window. "How late is late?"

"This time, maybe a little later. I always come out 'round about now. For a smoke, you know. Doreen, she doesn't like me smoking in the house."

"She do it often?"

"Every night," he said emphatically.

"When was the last time?"

He frowned. "Night before last, I think."

"Well, I'm grateful for you telling me, Jerry. I don't

see how there's a whole lot I can do about it, but I do appreciate you telling me."

"Where're you from . . . Koko?"

"New York City. Born and bred. Mom moved out a few years after Dad died."

"You staying long?"

"Just over Mother's Day, going back Monday morning."

He threw the cigarette down on top of the first one, ground it in the same way. "Well, gotta be getting back. Only supposed to have the one." He slapped the pack of Kool through his shirt pocket like a teenager checking his trusty Trojans. "You give her my best, now," he said as he walked across the grass to his house.

"Will do," I shouted after him. When I turned around, the curtain twitched again.

Back inside the house, Mom was making a fresh pot of coffee and there was a plate of cookies all laid out on the table. "Who was that?" she said.

"One of your neighbors, Jerry Parmenter."

She sniffed her disapproval. "He's new. Been here around four months, never speaks to me, neither him nor Doreen—she's his wife."

"I know."

"You shake his hand?"

I laughed. "Like a dog's paw."

She joined in with the laughter. "He's out there every single night, smoking those mint cigarettes." She tutted and stirred the coffee. "You'd never catch anyone who was anyone smoking those things."

Mom had always been the ad man's dream come true. For most things, but particularly for cigarettes. She smoked Chesterfield because Ronald Reagan said he sent all his friends a box at Christmas and then Luckies when Marlene Dietrich advertised them in the early Fifties. It was Camel when John Wayne told the nation "It's kind of gratifying to see that *my* cigarette is America's choice, too," then Philip Morris when Lucy Ball told everyone to "Call for Philip Morris." She kept with Philip Morris right up until Lucy and Desi got their divorce, then switched back to Chesterfield when they advertised that they were actually airsoftened and because the ads said that two out of every three smokers smoked them. Now she smoked hardly any at all, and she only bought what was cheapest in the store.

"He say anything about me?" She handed me a pot of steaming coffee that smelled strong enough to climb right out and walk around the floor.

I took the coffee and frowned, shook my head thoughtfully. "Oh, he said for me to give you his best." I sipped.

"Mmmm." She flopped into her chair and winced in pain.

"Bad?"

"They're always bad around nighttime, honey. There's not a single thing you can do about it." She rubbed her swollen knee joints tenderly, and I felt suddenly sorry that she had to do it for herself. No one around to give her sympathy, show her affection, tell her she looked nice.

"You look great in that dress, Mom," I said.

"This?!" She took hold of the collar like it was an old sooty rag, and laughed a short sharp snort. But deep down, I knew, she liked me saying that.

I never sleep late.

So it was a surprise to find it was almost ten o'clock when I came downstairs in the morning, the house silent and empty, a bowl and packet of Cheerios left out on the table for me. A note in Mom's careful hand said she'd gone out to church and would be back around eleven-thirty.

The slowed-down country air had furred my head cogs and left me feeling thick, couldn't-care-less, and young. I wandered around the rooms rediscovering pieces of my youth, all preserved just the way I remembered them. My heart ached with the memories and the silence. I felt like I was waiting for something to happen.

I went down to the Toyota and brought up the flowers and candies I'd bought before I left New York, put them out on the table so she'd see them as soon as she walked in the house. Then I decided to cut the grass. Out in the garage, jammed down behind the mower, is where I saw the hose. To one side of it were two brightly colored pixies that could have been identical twins. Behind an old washtub cabinet that I remembered Dad taking the mechanical guts out of I found the pitchfork. Everything else was there, too. It seemed like I could solve cases without even trying.

By the time she got home, I'd finished the grass and used the telephone. The first thing I said to her when she walked in was, "Happy Mother's Day, Mom." The second was, "Cute move stealing your own hose. The last person to suspect is a victim."

Her mouth dropped open, then snapped shut. Years tumbled down out of the ceiling and landed squarely on her shoulders, bending her almost double by the time she'd made it to the chair.

I lifted the flowers and placed them on her lap, gave her a big kiss on the cheek, and knelt beside her. "You want to tell me about it?"

The world has a lot of sights that just take hold of your heart and wring the life right out of it. One of the worst of those is seeing your mom cry. Only seniority can truly console and when you get on up toward seventy years old, there's not too many folks left around who qualify for the task. She sobbed and shook her head, holding onto her flowers like a mother with her baby. Which made an awful lot of sense.

"You feeling lonely out here?"

The tears subsided a little, and she nodded. "Very," she said, making such a short simple word into a huge weight of despair.

"So you took the things to draw attention to yourself."

She looked at me in horror. "No! I did no such thing. I didn't want people to know it was me."

I stroked her arm and shook my head. "No, I know you didn't want people to know it was you, but, deep down, maybe you thought they'd find out. Then wonder why you did such a thing."

"No, it wasn't a cry for help, son." She gave the phrase a dose of disdain and licked her lips. "They were keepsakes."

"Keepsakes?"

"Yes, mementos of life, I suppose."

I watched her face, waiting for it to make some sense to me.

"The pixies and the barbecue things . . . they're all things that people have, that people make a noise around. I guess I just wanted to bring some of that life inside." Her face was bright now, animated with trying to make me see. "There's no life around me anymore. Everything's so still and so slow, everybody treats me so soft and gentle . . . I don't want that, Koko. I remember the days when . . . when everything was so active around me." Her eyes misted up again, and I held onto her hand tighter now. When she spoke again, it was so soft I almost couldn't hear her. "I miss him so much, son," she said. "I get so lonely."

"I know, Mom, I know."

The knock came right before the door opened, and

Tyrone Daniels stood there, a sky-gray Stetson Whippet clasped tightly in his hand, a big beaming Sunday smile on his face. When he saw Mom, his smile dropped.

"It's okay, Tyrone," I said, "she hates it when I give her things."

Tyrone looked a little confused and cleared his throat. "I just came to say I got all the things back to their owners, Koko."

I squeezed Mom's hand twice. "Glad to hear it. You figure you'll ever catch who left the stuff over in those bushes?"

He shook his head. "Kids. Like I said. Leastways nothing was broken."

"Yeah, nothing was broken." I stood up and moved toward the door.

"I just came around to thank you again, Koko," he said, following me. "Seems like we country folks could learn a thing or two from you big city clickers."

I smiled awkwardly and slowly pushed the screen door open.

"Well, you take care now, Eleanor," he said over his shoulder, and I saw Mom's eyes twinkle in surprise. "I'll be in touch Monday or Tuesday. There's a recital at the church on Thursday, thought you'd like to go. I'll give you a call. Thought you might be lonely when Koko goes back."

Mom nodded in amazement.

I followed Tyrone outside where it had started to rain. I'd cut the grass just in time. Halfway down the path, he said, "How was I?"

"Don't give up the day job."

He sniggered.

"You laid on the country bumpkin act with a trowel," I said. "And what the hell are city clickers?"

"Huh?"

Maybe he hadn't laid it on all that much.

Waving him off, relishing the refreshing coolness of the rain on my head and shoulders, I felt undeniably good. The first warmth of the year's summer. Mom would never know that I had told Tyrone Daniels the truth, told him what she'd done, and what I believed had caused her to do it. That was the *real* present right there. Real presents aren't always things you can see or buy, like candies and flowers ... they're things you *know*, and things you *do*.

I turned around just in time to see the garish strains of a Hawaiian shirt disappear into Mom's house.

When I got back inside, she was pouring hot water into three mugs. The cookies were already laid out on a plate, and Jerry Parmenter was halfway through his first Kool.

Before I got the chance to say anything, Mom said, "Jerry asked if he could duck in here for a cigarette. Doreen doesn't like him smoking in the house."

"Yeah," I said.

"It's raining," Jerry Parmenter said.

"Yeah," I said again.

"I told him it was okay to call in any time, particularly when it's raining. I love the smell of tobacco."

I looked across at the man with the dullest handshake this side of a cemetery and saw him wink at me. Some neighbors are like that. They don't miss a trick. He'd seen Tyrone Daniels and me loading the things into Tyrone's trunk, put two and two together.

Mom handed out the mugs of coffee and plopped into her chair. She looked as fresh as mountain air. "We'll just drink this down, and then I'll fix us some lunch," she said, taking a sip.

"And I'll just have another cigarette," Jerry Parmenter said. "You want to try one of these?" he asked my mom, holding the pack of Kool out to her.

Mom reached for them and looked up at me with

that old mischievous gleam. "Don't mind if I do, thank you."

Jerry Parmenter lifted his mug toward the ceiling. "Here's to mothers . . . everywhere," he announced.

Thornton Wilder . . . Edgar Lee Masters . . . Sherwood Anderson . . . John Howland Spyker—eat your hearts out!

The Disappearance
of Edna Guberman

by Wendi Lee

I leaned back in my chair and tried to put my feet up on the desk, the way I'd seen so many private eyes do it in the movies. When the chair tipped so far back that I thought I'd slide out of it and through the open window onto the unforgiving pavement below, I tried to get my feet off the desk. But the heel of my running shoe was snagged on a tack that, in a moment of boredom and stupidity a few days ago, I'd stuck halfway into the desk surface. So I tried to make myself as comfortable as possible and, phone clamped to my ear, listened to the voice on the other end of the receiver. It was my mother, and she was talking about my upcoming visit to her.

"Aunt Sarah will want to see you girls when you and Rosa get here," she was saying as I tried to figure out how the hell I was going to get myself out of this pretzel position.

"No one likes Aunt Sarah, Ma," I replied. "And I don't think she's too crazy about our family. Besides, how come Sophie or our brothers never have to come along?"

"They all have their own families, darling," Ma explained to me patiently. Once again, in that subtle motherly way, she was reminding me that I hadn't gotten married and produced any grandchildren for her. But I outsmarted her—I ignored the dig. My little sister Rosa would have completely lost it and confronted Ma on her outmoded notions.

Aunt Sarah was this creepy old lady who is distantly related to us by marriage. Although she never seems to appreciate it, Ma insists that we go visit her several times a year, always bringing casseroles and desserts. The inside of Aunt Sarah's house was lined with old newspapers that were stacked to the rafters, creating a surrealistic maze for visitors that rivaled some of the best British garden mazes. It was a fire hazard, and whenever I tactfully brought this up to Ma, she would just say, "She's thrifty."

The place was also thick with cats. During our visit, Aunt Sarah would spend half the time carrying on silly one-way conversations with the sullen felines who were draped over the furniture, the mantelpiece, and every other square inch of space in the living room. The cloying, musty smell of old cat litter hung heavily in the air, and cat hair was everywhere.

"Anyway, you and Rosa will be here tonight, right?"

I managed to extricate one foot from the lip of the desktop. My chair did a crazy tilt to the left, and I reached out to steady myself, dropping the phone receiver in the process. My office door opened at that precise moment, and a worried woman walked in. I must have looked pretty silly with one foot on the desk and the receiver dangling from its cord over the desk, Ma's squawking coming from it. "Angie? Angie? Are you okay? Are you there?"

Trying to maintain as much dignity as possible, which wasn't much, I pulled my other foot off the desk and righted my chair. Somehow I managed a businesslike gesture to the only empty chair in the room as I picked up the receiver at the same time.

"Ma? I have to call you back. Someone just walked in."

"Angie! Don't you dare take a case this time. You missed Mother's Day last year." Ma sounded like she was going to cry.

I winced, remembering how I had come up with some lame excuse for not visiting her on Mother's Day a year ago. Something about car trouble and paperwork. I enjoy visiting Ma, but not on holidays when my older sister Sophie is there. We don't get along, and I don't think it adds to the festive atmosphere when the two of us—the three of us, actually, because lately my youngest sister Rosa has been joining in the fracas—start arguing at the top of our lungs.

Frankly, I think Mother's Day is Ma's way of getting back at us kids for all the trouble we gave her during our formative years. There's never any question that her single children will be spending Mother's Day with her. Since my brothers are all married, they can get out of it. They get to skip the feast once in a while—and all the fighting and backbiting and guilt trips that go with it—to visit their mothers-in-law. It almost makes marriage sound appealing.

"I promise I'll be there, Ma, but I have to eat, too." I threw an ingratiating smile at my potential client, who looked through me as if she was thinking of something else. When I had hung up, I turned my attention to her. "Now, what can I do to help you?"

She was about forty, but her elfin features, framed by a shiny dark cap of hair and large gray eyes, made her look younger at first glance. She was thin to the point of anorexia, but was well-dressed in designer business attire. I guessed that she either worked as a stockbroker or ran her own company. She started to say something to me, but before she could get a word out, her chin trembled and she tried to gulp back great big sobs. I pushed a box of tissues across the desk, and she grabbed a fistful, pushing it to her face to get control of herself. It's a weird experience to see a career woman in tears.

"I-I don't kn-know where to begin," she began with a huge shuddering breath. After blowing her nose, which had turned a shiny red from the crying, she introduced herself. "My name is Carol Zakowski, and my mother's missing."

Bingo, I thought. This is how I can get out of driving down to Providence to visit Ma tomorrow. "When did you discover she was gone?" I asked, grabbing a pencil and paper.

"I came home from work early, about an hour ago." That would be about three o'clock, in my brilliant estimation. "I live, we live, a few blocks from here," she continued, dabbing at the flow of tears in the corners of her eyes. "My mother's name is Edna Guberman, and she's lived with me for almost three years. Ever since my divorce became final, it just seemed convenient to share an apartment. Neither of us are interested in getting married again."

It turned out that Edna Guberman was sixty-two years old and widowed, according to her daughter Carol. I was given a picture of the two of them sitting on the sofa next to last year's Christmas tree. Edna was a sweet-faced woman with a halo of fluffy, curly white hair. She looked like the perfect mother.

"I was planning on surprising her tonight with a trip to Hawaii. She's always talked of how much she wanted to go back—my parents honeymooned there in the 1940s—and I thought how nice it would be to take her." Boy, did that make me feel guilty for wanting to postpone the inevitable family event at Ma's tonight.

"How do you know she's not coming back?" I asked.

Carol dug into her purse and produced a hastily

scribbled note on the back of a grocery receipt that said: Carol, I know what you're planning and I can't let it happen. Don't worry about me. Love, Mom.

"I had packed her bag and left it in my bedroom this morning, but it was gone, too," Carol explained. "We were supposed to leave tonight on an eight-thirty flight from Logan Airport. I know she's not fond of flying, or traveling of any kind really. When we flew to Chicago for my grandma's funeral last year, Mom had to down two glasses of white wine before I could get her on the plane."

"Do you have any siblings she might drop in on?" I asked.

"Jane, my sister in Tulsa. But I checked all the flights out, and she's not on any of them. I also called Jane to find out if she knew anything, but she hasn't heard from Mom either."

I let out the breath I had been holding. "What about anyone local?"

Carol gave me the names of several people her mother knew: her beautician, the local grocer, the neighbor, Edna's best friend, her bridge partners, and her brother, Carol's uncle. But no, Edna couldn't go to Uncle Harry—he lived at the YMCA. Besides, Carol had called him, and he'd told her he hadn't heard from Edna. They weren't all that close anyway.

"Okay," I said. "What about this best friend, Marilyn Strickland? Have you called her?"

"I couldn't reach her," Carol said. "Maybe she's out or something. I can keep trying." She got up. "I only have a few hours before the flight. It's worth hiring you for these few hours if you can find her quickly."

"You haven't had a disagreement with your mother lately? It seems strange that she would leave so suddenly."

Shaking her head, Carol said in a puzzled voice, "She must have found out about the trip, but I can't believe she would be this upset about going to Hawaii."

I didn't say anything because there was no use in alarming my client over nothing, but I was wondering if Edna Guberman had left of her own accord.

I called my mother to tell her I would be late. At first she yelled at me, but after I explained that this was about a vanishing mother, she said, "Disappearing daughters happen all the time, but a disappearing mother? Something's fishy. Take all the time you need." I thought she was being sweet until she added, in the tone a drill sergeant uses with his men, "Just be here tomorrow at noon for dinner."

Maxie's Cut 'n' Curl was right down the street from my office. I walked into the perm-and-shampoo-scented salon and asked to speak to Maxine. While I waited, I checked the place out. The walls were painted yellow, and the chairs were pink.

Maxine came over to me. She was a large woman in a pink smock and bright yellow hair was pinned up in an elaborate do. She went with the decor. I introduced myself.

"So you're a private eye," she said with frank curiosity. "Just like in the movies, right? Wow! Never met one before, but to think I've met a female P.I." She eyed my hair. "What can I do for you?"

I got straight to the point. "I'm looking for Edna Guberman. She's moved out of her daughter's apartment, and Carol only has a few hours to find her." I explained the circumstances. Normally private eyes don't discuss their cases with the people who are being questioned. But with the limited amount of time we had to find Edna Guberman, I figured that the gossip circle could spread the information in about half the time it would take me to question everyone.

"I saw her early this afternoon, about one o'clock, for a touch-up perm. She'd just come off of her hospital volunteer work at Brigham's." Maxine reached out and felt my hair. "You really need a hot oil treatment. It shouldn't be this dry. And you could use a trim, too."

I smiled. "Thanks. Maybe I'll make an appointment with you after we find Edna."

Maxine smiled and nodded. "I think one of Edna's bridge partners is here. Lori," she called over her shoulder. A shapely nineteen-year-old girl with lots of hair and thick black eyeliner completely outlining her eyes came up. She was chewing and cracking a wad of gum. "Lori, is Louise Harris still here?"

"Yeah," Lori replied before popping her gum. "She's under a dryer."

Maxie led me back and introduced me, raising her voice above the sound of the dryer. "It's an emergency, Louise."

Louise Harris was a dumpy, middle-aged woman with bright red lipstick. Her hair was all done up in small pink rollers with a big strip of cotton keeping the perm solution from running into her eyes. We had interrupted her reading. "Eh?" she replied.

Maxine repeated herself, and Louise shook her head. "Haven't seen Edna since last Tuesday," she said loudly, then looked at me and shrugged. "Sorry," she shouted before going back to reading her copy of *People* magazine.

I thanked Maxine and left.

Since Marilyn and Edna and Louise were three of the four who played bridge every Tuesday night, I headed for the home of Phyllis McKay. We had agreed that Carol would stay at home and keep trying to get in touch with Marilyn while I tracked down and questioned the others.

Phyllis McKay, the fourth bridge partner, lived a few blocks north of my office in a high-rise. She let me in only after I explained my mission over the intercom in the lobby. Once inside her apartment, it was obvious that Phyllis lived well. I'm not good with antiques, but I recognized a few things, French chairs and Italian commodes and a nice tapestry hanging on the wall in the foyer. I wondered what she was doing hanging out with dumpy Louise and widowed Edna. I hadn't met Marilyn yet, so I had no way of knowing just how out of place Phyllis was in the group.

"I'm afraid I haven't heard from either Edna or Marilyn since—"

I finished her sentence for her, "Last Tuesday. Tell me, has she seemed depressed lately?"

Phyllis wrinkled her perfect forehead, which I suspected of having been worked on, and brightened. "I remember a few months ago, she was a little upset when she came to bridge night. Carol had discussed putting her in an old-age home. At least, that's what she told me." She shook her head. "But that wouldn't help you, would it. Edna was her usual self the next week, and it was never mentioned again." Phyllis turned her attention to flowers in a large vase and started to arrange them. "Would you like some coffee?"

I told her coffee would be very nice. Before she went out to the kitchen, I asked permission to use the phone, then called Carol at her home.

"I haven't heard anything," she said in a sad voice. "And Marilyn still isn't home." There was a moment of silence, then she said in a whisper, "You don't think anything . . . bad has happened to them, do you?"

I assured her that she was probably blowing it out

of proportion. "I'll go over to Marilyn's place as soon as I finish questioning Phyllis." We hung up.

Phyllis and I talked a few more minutes, but when I finished my coffee—a dark, aromatic Italian blend—and looked at my watch, it was already six o'clock. I had only two and a half hours to go. I thanked her and left. The only place left to go was that of Edna's best friend, Marilyn Strickland.

Marilyn's apartment was only a few blocks away, but the neighborhood wasn't as nice as Phyllis McKay's. The apartment building was still fairly well-maintained with the smell of lemon-scented ammonia in the hallways and all the hall lights working. I knocked on her door, but there was no answer. A woman balancing a bag of groceries in her arms came down the hall and stopped at the door of the apartment across the way. I thought she hadn't taken notice of me, but as she pulled her keys out, she said, "Looking for Marilyn Strickland? I don't think she's back yet."

"Do you know when she'll be back?" I asked.

The woman opened her door and put her groceries on a table just inside the apartment, then turned back to me. "I don't know that, but I do know she went out earlier today about four-thirty. There was a woman with her who was carrying a suitcase. Looked like she was going somewhere."

I nodded and pulled out the photo of Edna Guberman. "Is this the other woman?"

Marilyn's neighbor nodded. "That's her. She looked real upset as they were leaving. It looked as if she had been crying."

I couldn't believe my luck. "I don't suppose Marilyn told you where they were going."

The woman thought for a moment, then said, "I think I heard Tulsa in their conversation, but I couldn't swear to it."

Well, if Edna wasn't taking a plane, there were only two choices—the train station and the bus terminal. I called Carol and told her what I had just learned.

"Oh, she probably wouldn't take the train," she replied. "She doesn't like trains. All forms of travel involve either Dramamine or a good, stiff drink. Buses stop more frequently so she can get off and walk around, have a drink."

Edna Guberman was beginning to sound less like the perfect mother and more like a lush, but I kept my thoughts to myself. I hung up the phone and took the subway to Arlington Street. The bus terminal is the very definition of a pit. Gum wrappers and spilled soft drinks littered the sidewalk outside, and inside was a haven for the homeless, the hopeless, and the insane. I scanned the apathetic faces of those who would soon be boarding the departing buses, but Edna was not among them. I checked the rest room downstairs, but there was no one at all down there. Somehow, an hour had already gone by and I only had a little over an hour to find her and pop her in a cab headed for Logan.

I pulled out the photo of Edna and went over to the counter. When my turn came, I went up to the first open window. "Has this woman bought a ticket in the last few hours?" I asked.

The clerk gave me an exasperated look. "Lady," he said, "you gotta be kidding. You expect me to remember? Geez, I've only seen a couple hundred people since my shift began at four."

I was relentless—and desperate. "She bought a ticket to Tulsa. Probably within the last two hours. And she was with another lady about her age."

He looked at me for a minute, a disgusted look on his face. But when he saw that I was not going to leave without some information, he sighed heavily and checked his computer monitor. A few minutes later, he said, "Three people have bought tickets to Tulsa since five o'clock. That's all I can tell you. We don't require names or anything like that."

"Can you tell me if a bus has left for Tulsa since then?"

"No," he replied, "we only have two heading out that way each day—one at twelve-forty-five, and one at eight-oh-five tonight."

I felt a surge of hope. "Thank you," I said before turning and scanning the faces of the crowd one more time. There was still a possibility that she was here in Boston, here in this very terminal, or she was very close by. I looked at my watch. It was seven-fifteen. If she had bought a bus ticket, she and Marilyn had gone out, maybe for a cup of coffee. The coffee shop! There was one attached to the terminal that was just as greasy and depressing as the bus station itself. I entered it and looked around, but there was no Edna Guberman sitting at a booth, sipping java with her good friend Marilyn.

I supposed I could wait until eight, but I was restless. I started to walk out of the coffee shop when I had a thought—Edna wasn't going to be drinking coffee right before she boarded a bus for a long ride to Tulsa. She'd find a bar, something close by.

Outside, I looked around. There wasn't much choice in the way of bars. You'd think in an area like this, there'd be a dozen seedy joints surrounding the bus terminal. But the weird thing about the area was that across the street from the terminal was one of the more elegant hotels, Park Plaza. Of course, these days, it was a bit worn around the gilt edges, and there were an awful lot of businesses occupying the first floor, but it still had Trader Vic's and a few upper-class shops for the discriminating traveler. Then I spotted a likely place: The Wishing Well Lounge.

It was dark inside, but then, it was dark outside,

too. A steady beat throbbed in the main lounge area, and colored lights flashed on and off. What kind of place was this? I asked myself.

"Five dollars," someone said. I looked around until I found a woman sitting at a small table just inside the door. As my eyes adjusted to the darkness, I talked to her. "I'm not here for a drink, I'm trying to find someone." I started to pull Edna's photo out of my pocket, but she waved it away.

"That's what they all say," she said in a flat voice. She stuck out her palm again, and I paid up, making a mental note to bill it to my client.

"Woo, woo!" some woman screamed. Another squealed. Then I saw why they were shrieking—a man was doing a bump and grind on the stage, wearing only a sequined G-string. Women crowded each other along the foot of the stage. It was a truly frightening spectacle to watch. Anonymous hands waved dollar bills at the stripper, and his G-string kept getting pulled and tugged in various ways. My eyes traveled up to his face, which wore an expression of phony rapture, presumably at the touch of these women's dishpan hands.

As the music wound down, he bent down and kissed a few of his admirers. Then he slowly turned around so we could see his muscled ass, and picked up his costume and left the stage. The lights came up, and the women drifted back to their seats. I picked my way through the milling crowd in search of Edna and her friend. I found them at a table near the stage.

"Edna Guberman?" I said. She had a pleasant smile on her face and when she didn't respond right away, I realized that her pleasant smile was the result of being totally sozzled.

The woman seated next to her, Marilyn, I presumed, was a little taller than me with pale blond hair braided and wrapped around her head. Some of the pins that were holding it in place had come loose, and her normally sharp face was flushed. She answered me readily. "Yeah, that's Edna." Her eyes were too bright from drinking, but at least she wasn't incoherent. She leaned across the table and shook Edna's arm. "Hey, Edna! Someone's here to see you."

Edna shook her head a little and took a sip of some concoction with pieces of fruit and little umbrellas decorating the edge of the fake coconut. Edna perked up a little and looked my way as if she were seeing me for the first time—which she probably was. "So who're you? Do I know you?" She sucked the dregs of her drink and managed to signal a passing cocktail waitress. "You drinking?" she asked me. I shook my head.

"Actually, your daughter sent me."

"Who, Jane? I haven't even tol' Jane I was comin' to Tulsa."

"No, your other daughter, Carol."

"I ain't got no other daughter," a surly Edna snarled at me.

Marilyn leaned toward me and patted my arm. "She don't like to talk about the other one."

I must have looked mystified because Marilyn explained it to me. "She came home this afternoon and found her bag packed in Carol's room. Doesn't want to be shipped off."

Didn't want to go to Hawaii? That was the first time I'd ever witnessed anyone go to such extremes to avoid the sunny islands. Besides, how did Edna find out about Carol's surprise trip? Maybe an unsuspecting travel agent called to confirm the plans, and Edna took the call. I was about to ask the by-now-almost-comatose Edna about this, when the lights went down again.

"And now, ladies," a disembodied Barry White-type voice announced, "here's the man you've all been waiting for, the one, the only, White Lightnin'!" The women rose as one big mass. I put my hand on Edna's arm, still trying to get her attention, but she shook it off. "Gotta see Lightnin'," she said before staggering off toward the stage with a fistful of dollars in her hand.

I turned to Marilyn, who seemed about the only one in the room who wasn't insane with misplaced lust. "Is she really going to Tulsa?" I asked.

Marilyn shrugged. "Who knows? She bought the ticket, but if she keeps drinking at this rate, we'll be lucky to get her across the street to a room in the Plaza." She shook her head and lit a cigarette. "I'll tell you, I always thought Carol was a nice daughter. But she turned out to be a real piece of work."

"What do you mean?" I was still mystified.

Marilyn looked at me sharply and put out her match, taking a deep drag of her cigarette. "You mean you don't know? She's planning to put Edna in a nursing home. They talked about it a couple of months ago. Carol was worried that her mother didn't have enough to do, not enough friends and all. So Edna took up hospital volunteering at Brigham and the bridge club. I'd been wanting her to join us for ages. I guess that wasn't enough for Carol."

"You think Carol packed that bag to put her mother in a nursing home?" I was screaming now, not because I was mad, but because I was competing with some disco dance number to which White Lightnin' was gyrating and peeling off his costume. "Carol planned a surprise trip to Hawaii for Edna. The plane leaves in a little under an hour."

Marilyn's mouth dropped open, and she stood up, her cigarette falling onto the table. She had the presence of mind to grind it out, then turned to me, businesslike. "We'd better get Edna on that flight before she passes out." Together, we battled the crowd of women, most of whom thought we were trying to elbow our way to the front to tuck a tip in White Lightnin's white sequined G-string. We found Edna waving five-dollar bills at the stripper, her hair a wild mass around her head. Marilyn grabbed one elbow, and I got the other side. Together, we carried Edna out of the place.

"Wha's goin' on?" Edna asked, her forehead puckering up in concentration. As Marilyn explained, Edna started to come out of her self-induced stupor. By the time she had the full story, Edna's face was crinkled up in disappointment. "I'll never make it. I've ruined Carol's surprise."

"We can salvage this," I replied. I ordered Marilyn and Edna to get the suitcase, which was in a locker at the bus terminal, and meet me out front. Then I found a pay phone and, over the body-vibrating beat of the music, I shouted instructions to Carol.

Outside the terminal, I hailed a cab and stuffed the three of us inside, ordering the cabbie to get us to Logan as fast as possible. Boston cabs are vehicles of wonder and terror combined. No one can get you anywhere in Boston faster than a cabbie. They know all the streets and all the back roads. Our cabbie was especially fearless, passing a slowpoke driver to the right of a merge when exiting for the tunnel that took us to East Boston. We were at Logan Airport in under fifteen minutes.

Edna was fading fast. We hustled her inside the terminal and looked up the gate number on the departure monitor. I'd had the foresight to ask Carol what airline and flight number. While I moved Edna along, Marilyn gave the bag to a skycap.

Once at the gate, we waited for Carol to arrive fifteen minutes later and out of breath, just in time for the boarding announcement. Edna was peacefully snoring in the seat between Marilyn and me.

"What the—?" Carol exclaimed, looking at her mother, then at Marilyn and me.

I shook my head. "Don't ask. No time." I bent over Edna and shook her. She snorted and mumbled something, her eyes still half-closed. "We're getting on the plane now, Edna."

"Is she all right?" Carol asked, looking worried.

Marilyn patted her arm. "Don't you worry about your mother, dear. We've never done this sort of thing before."

"What sort of thing before?" Carol asked, a befuddled look on her face.

"Let's just say that I think the bridge club has a new hobby, and leave it at that," I said dryly.

Carol and I hoisted Edna between us and waited in line. By the time we got to the airline employee who took the boarding passes, Edna was walking under her own steam, with a little help from Carol.

Carol sniffed the air. "She smells like—"

I shot her a sympathetic look. "She's had enough to last her till you get to Honolulu."

"Thanks," she said, with a grateful look.

"Oh, don't worry," I replied cheerfully. "You'll get my bill." I wondered how I would explain the five-dollar cover charge from The Wishing Well.

Marilyn and I shared a cab out of Logan, and I was dropped off at my apartment in East Boston. She went back to wherever—maybe the Wishing Well Lounge. Who knows?

Rosa was waiting for me. "So I thought you'd never get here. Ma called and told me you had a last-minute case. She didn't sound too put out over it, which was surprising."

"I'll tell you all about it on the way down to Providence. You all set?"

Rosa grimaced. "As set as I'll ever be." She hoisted her overnight bag over her shoulder, I picked up my bag, and we headed out the door, ready to do the Mother's Day battle.

Violence, Strong Language, Sexual Situations

by Ron Goulart

His aim was bad.

The moment after he accepted the golden award statuette, Leonard McGill rushed to the edge of the platform and hurled it at someone who was sitting at a nearby banquet table. But he missed and beaned a prominent, balding playwright two tables to the right of his intended target.

Leonard hadn't wanted to attend the Hobart Foundation Broadway Achievement Awards dinner at all. Even though Molly had been dead for nearly six months, he desired to continue in mourning and avoid all public festivities. But their agent had persuaded him that, since *Murder Won't Out* was up for the best mystery play award, he owed it to his late wife's memory to show up. And if their damn play did happen to win, it would give the sagging theater box-office sales a boost and probably cinch the impending Hollywood movie deal.

Leonard had been moping around the vast glass and redwood living room of their vast hilltop home in Brimstone, Connecticut, when Max Bowman had phoned him on Monday morning.

He was bogged down on the first act of *Murder Repeats Itself*, a mystery play he was attempting to write on his own, and had been pacing, staring out at the surrounding woodlands, gazing into the vast stone and metal fireplace. He was a tall, wide man of fifty.

"Should Dr. Brewster enter stage right or stage left?" Leonard was asking himself as the phone on the blond coffee table commenced ringing. "Should he say, 'I have bad news for you, Alicia?' or 'I'm afraid I have some bad news, Alicia?' Is Alicia a dumb name?"

After the phone rang five times, the answering tape began speaking, "Hi, this is the residence of Molly Crane McGill and Leonard McGill. We can't come to the phone right now, so leave us a message and we'll get back to you soon. Bye."

"How many times have I told you to scrap that tape?" demanded the voice of their agent. "Molly's been dead and gone since last December, and it's morbid to keep running her voice. Are you listening, jerk?"

Sighing, Leonard turned to stare out the vast view window, following with his eyes the winding road Molly had driven on her last night.

"I know you're there, Lennie," continued Max. "Probably wrapped up in black crepe. Okay, so listen. Fogelman is set to buy *Murder Won't Out* for Achilles Pictures, but only if you let him change Daphne to a hooker. It seems to me, my boy, considering that he's talking $250,000, that we can—"

"Have some respect for the dead, Max." Leonard grabbed up the phone.

"Ah, I knew you were lurking there someplace in that chill mausoleum you—"

"Daphne is based on Molly, so there is no way I—"

"You're coming to the Hobie awards dinner this Friday night," his agent informed him.

"No, nope, I'm not. But let's get back to Fogelman's dumb suggestion. I absolutely will not—"

"Fiction," said Max, who was a senior partner at the Creative Services International agency.

"What?"

"You're not the only inventive one, my boy. I made up that crap about changing Daphne to get your attention. Now, here's the real purpose of—"

"That's rotten, Max. Using my affection for—"

"She's dead," reminded the agent. "Six months dead, Lennie."

"I'm in the middle of a new play. I don't have time for dumb banquets."

"How far into the middle?"

"Well, the first act actually."

"What portion of the first act?"

"Well, scene one."

"How far along into scene one?"

"Not very."

"Has the curtain risen?"

"Sure, of course."

"I love you, Lennie. We've been together for six happy, fruitful years now."

"You and I and Molly, right."

"But trust me, it was Molly who was the brains in your team."

"She was better at plotting," he admitted.

"And dialogue."

"That, too."

"Not to mention characterization and stage business."

"She couldn't type very well, though."

"Which is where you came in," said the Manhattan-based agent. "What I am getting at, Lennie, is that you may never be able to come up with a hit mystery play on your own."

"I learned a lot from Molly. I'm damn certain that with—"

"So it's very important that we keep promoting the plays that already exist. *Murder Won't Out* is likely to win a Hobie this Friday," continued Max. "Not because it's especially great, and certainly it's nowhere near as successful as your *Murder Most Fair* five seasons ago—but all the dimwits on the Hobart Foundation awards committee are sentimental. Except for Reisberson—so screw him. The point, my boy, is that a dead author almost always has a hell of a good chance to cop the dingus."

"Molly wouldn't want to get an award because of sentiment."

"Listen to me, schmuck. I'll explain this yet again," said the agent. "Molly is dead. You are alive. Is that clear?"

"Sure, Max, but I wish you wouldn't sound so callous when you—"

"Picture this scene, Lennie my boy. Your play cops the best mystery award. You, visibly shaken, stand up, wipe a few tasteful tears from your eyes, and then go tottering up to the dais. People all across America—not a lot, a few million who are stupid enough to watch the Hobie telecast—they see this touching tableaux. It touches them where—"

"It can't be a tableaux, Max. Not if I'm moving."

"Be silent. These yahoos, as I was saying, witness a scene so touching that it causes them to sob and moan along with you as you receive the gold-plated dornick. You wipe away the flowing tears on the sleeve of your tux—you still have that tux Molly made you buy, don't you?"

"In a closet someplace. I haven't worn it since she—"

"You sniffle, clutch the Hobie to your chest—not to your burgeoning stomach—maybe slobber a little more. You gaze upward, straight up at heaven. 'I'm only sorry that my dear, departed wife couldn't be here to share this great honor with me.' Pause. 'But I'm sure she knows that we've won it.' Pause. 'This is for you, my dearest.' "

"I never called Molly 'my dearest.' That's hokey and—"

"Who knows what the hell you called her? You, me, a few others. But all those half-wits will be touched. They'll sob into their beer and popcorn. And, when *Murder Won't Out* tours the hinterland, they'll remember and go flocking to their local playhouses."

"What do you mean by *others,* Max?"

"And I'll tell you something else, my boy. Fogelman is sentimental, too. Your tearful acceptance speech will hit Fogelman hard, and I can twist $300,000 out of him for movie rights."

"Others," repeated Leonard.

"Eh?"

"You implied that there were others who might know what intimate names I called my wife. I asked you the morning after she died who the other guy was. You said then that there was no other guy, but now you're implying there was more than one."

"Look, Lennie, she was fooling around some," said the agent. "That didn't affect your plays. Although *Murder Won't Out* wasn't quite as socko as *Make Mine Murder*. But age, rather than distraction, would also account for that. You're forty-nine, and she was—"

"I'm forty-eight."

"Forty-eight, and she was forty-three."

"You knew about affairs?"

"Some of them."

"You never told me."

"Not part of my job, Lennie."

"Who was the man she was on her way to see that night?"

"I've already told you—this makes sixty-seven times—that I have no idea."

"He's responsible for her death. If I ever find out who—"

"Can we, please, return to reality? It's absolutely essential that you attend this Hobie thing."

"You really figure we'll win?"

"Sources, reliable sources, have hinted as much."

"Well, you can accept for us, as our agent. Say that I'm still much too—"

"No, that won't play as well," insisted Max. "With you up there in person and heartbroken—we'll get coverage in *People, Time, Mammon,* and the rest. And I'll be able to jack Fogelman up to $400,000."

"That's very crass."

"Exactly. Now start making notes on a heartrending acceptance speech," Max told him. "What's the title of the new play?"

"Murder Repeats Itself."

"That's a terrible title. I'll see you Friday night."

Actually, Leonard had to admit to himself, Molly had pretty much shared their agent's evaluation of his abilities.

The morning they'd completed the first act of *Murder Won't Out,* nearly two years ago that was, Molly had inquired, "You own a dictionary, don't you, dear heart?"

"Two," he replied. "A paperback and that big fat one I picked up at the St. Norbert's Church Yankee Doodle Fair the first year we—"

"Maybe you weren't aware of this, Len, but in most dictionaries they include the correct spellings of a great many words." Molly was a slim, pretty woman and, at the moment, red-haired. She liked to wear, when they were working, faded jeans and a loose sweatshirt.

"Did I misspell something again?" He was sitting in his favorite chair, the white wicker rocker, at the far side of their vast glass and redwood studio.

Molly was reclining on the low white sofa, the manuscript resting on her lap. "I bought you that computer months ago, but you refuse to learn how to use it," she said. "A computer, so I've been told, doesn't allow anyone—even someone like you—to commit spelling errors."

"I do better on my old portable."

"Better than what?"

"Why not just tell me what word I got wrong?"

"Never mind, Len, I fixed it."

"Do you recall my mentioning that the only person who called me Len in my youth was my Aunt Marie?" he asked. "She was not my favorite relative."

"You have mentioned that, yes. Several times." She riffled through the pages of their first act. "I'm not especially happy with the initial encounter between Inspector Emerson and the maid. Or would you rather I refer to him as what you've typed—Inspectator Emerson?"

"I have trouble with that word sometimes."

"So I notice, Len." She tapped the middle of a page with one crimson fingernail. " 'Where exactly was Mrs. Rodney during the electrical storm, young woman?' That doesn't seem to ring quite true."

"We could drop electrical."

"Electrical is the one word I'm content with."

"Sure, but in real life people don't usually refer to electrical—"

"Let me worry about what people say in real life." She turned over a few more pages. "And I really do not care for the scene between Sir Dana and Miss Trowbridge. It sounds vulgar to me now."

"I thought up most of that one, but we agreed at the time that it established him as a—"

"Wait." She rose up and, very carefully, placed the play manuscript on the sofa. Crossing to a cabinet, she picked up a copy of the current *TV Week*. "It's scenes like this one of yours that can damage our reputation." She snapped the magazine open. "I noticed this in here the other night and meant to mention it to you. It's their comment on the movie version of our *A Bad Case of Murder*. They warn potential viewers that it contains, and I quote, 'violence, strong language, sexual situations.' I don't like that. It can scare a lot of people off."

"We didn't write the screenplay," he reminded her.

"Nobody ever said 'violence, strong language, sexual situations' about a movie adaptation of an Agatha Christie play or novel."

"They don't say it about my social life either," he muttered.

"What's that, dear heart?"

"Nothing, not a thing."

"We agreed a long time ago—agreed quite amiably, I had thought—that we wouldn't sleep together while we are working on a play."

"And since then, it seems like we're always working on a play."

"Which is why," she said, gesturing at the big room, "we can afford to live so very well."

"If this is your idea of—"

"I've no time for another of your arguments now." Returning to the sofa, Molly grabbed the manuscript. "This scene has to be mended right away."

"It's only that I love you," he said quietly.

She apparently didn't hear him.

* * *

They had a real argument the night Molly was killed.

That was in the middle of last December with a sleet storm raging.

Just before dinner, she'd walked into their vast kitchen, where he was dicing carrots.

"I think I'll skip dinner." She was wearing a tweedy skirt and a candy-stripe blouse. Her face was unusually pale.

"You okay?"

"I'm splendid, dear heart."

"You look pale."

"I'm just fine, Len. You'd probably spell that *f-e-i-n*."

"Did something happen while you were out this afternoon?"

The trees rattled outside, pellets of ice came hitting at the kitchen windows.

"I was home all day." Molly crossed to the refrigerator. "This hasn't been the kind of day for going out."

"No, but when I phoned you from Max's office in the city, I got the tape."

"I simply didn't feel like answering the damn phone."

He frowned, setting the knife down on the cutting board. "The engine of your Porsche was still warm when I got home."

Molly lifted out a bottle of spring water. "Ah, I'm living with Hercule Poirot now," she remarked. "Do you do that sort of amateur sleuthing every day, Len dear? Yank up the hood of my car, feel the motor to—"

"I happened to slip as I was getting out of my car, Molly. I put my hand against the front of yours to keep from falling."

"That accounts for the greasy handprints I've

been noticing." She carried the opened bottle over to the cupboard next to the sink and selected a glass.

"So where did you go?"

"I stayed home all afternoon."

"Was somebody else using your car?"

"The Porsche was also home all afternoon." She filled the glass. "I'll be in my bedroom."

"C'mon, what's going on? There's no need to lie to me. We've been married too long for—"

"Mostly what we've been is very successful writing partners. That's not the same as—"

"What the hell are you talking about? We both love each other, don't we? That means we have to be honest and—"

"Geeze, I can see why I don't trust you with much of the dialogue in our plays." She set the bottle on the sideboard, hard, and started for the doorway.

"Molly, I want to know where you were." He followed her, catching hold of her arm.

"Let go," she requested evenly.

"Not until you tell me—"

"Let go." Swinging out with her free hand, she slapped him across the face.

His eyes watered, and he released his grip.

Molly ran along the hall and up the staircase. A moment later he heard the door of her room slam.

Then the wall phone in the kitchen made the odd beeping noise it always made when one of the other phones in the house was being dialed.

Leonard did something he'd never done before. Very cautiously and quietly, he crossed to the phone and lifted it from the hook. Covering the mouthpiece with his hand, he listened.

". . . Sorry we had that quarrel, darling," she was saying to someone.

"So am I, Molly." The man had a lazy New England drawl. It was a voice Leonard had never heard before.

"Can I come over there?" she asked.

"Tonight? Didn't he come home?"

"He's here, but I don't give a damn. I have to see you."

"Fine, come right over," he said. "We won't quarrel this time."

Leonard kept holding the phone until the dial tone came back.

He wanted to confront his wife, tell her he wouldn't allow her to go see someone else.

Warn her, too, that this wasn't the sort of night to go driving around on the quirky back roads of Brimstone.

But instead he simply hung up, went over, and sat on a kitchen stool. He heard her come downstairs and go into the garage.

Her Porsche came to life, then went squealing out into the cold, stormy darkness.

Forty-five minutes later the police called to tell him that Molly'd had an accident.

Her car had skidded on an icy road and slammed into a stone fence.

She was dead.

He never found out who the man was she had been on her way to see.

He did go as far as checking their next phone bill that came in for the number his wife had called that night. But that turned out to be a hotel in Stamford, a dead end.

But he knew that the man was responsible for what had happened to Molly.

"You're overdoing it," suggested Max Bowman, gesturing with his steak knife.

Leonard was sitting forlornly at the table, both

elbows resting on it, ignoring his London broil. "Hum?"

Leaning closer, his agent said, "Don't act so sad yet."

"I'm not acting, I am sad. I should never have come to this fiasco."

After eyeing the other six guests sitting around their table, Max lowered his voice even further. "You're not playing this scene right," he advised. "You ought to be looking brave at this point, stiff upper lip, keeping your heartbreak and sorrow firmly in check. Then, when they announce you've won the knickknack, you start to let loose with the gloom. It'll wow 'em."

Leonard gazed absently around at the seventy-some tables that were packed into the central ballroom of the Ritz-Manhattan Hotel. "Why would I want to wow these idiots?"

"Not the idiots here, although it couldn't hurt. I meant the idiots in the TV audience." He used a thumb to point at the television crew hovering around the bright-lit dais far across the big room.

Up at the podium a plump man in a tight dinner jacket was speaking into the microphone. "This next award is for the best comedy of the season," he announced. "The nominees are *Bring Me A Danish, Isn't It A Drag?, Bottoms Up in the Catskills,* and *Charley's Aunt For President.*"

A stunning blonde in a glittering green dress stepped forward to hand him an envelope.

"And the winner is . . . hold on while I get this damn thing open . . . the winner is *Bring Me A Danish* by Walter Truett and Maurice Esalen," announced the plump man with a gratified chuckle. "Walt and Maurie, as you probably know, are basking out in Hollywood. But their able agent, Jack Stratton-Porter will be doing the accepting for the boys."

"A schmuck," muttered Max.

Stratton-Porter was seated at a table up near the dais. Grinning, he hopped to his feet and hurried up to the podium. He was tall, deeply tan, vaguely handsome, about forty.

He waited for the enthusiastic applause to die, then hoisted the Hobie statuette high over his head with his left hand. "Wally didn't think they had a chance," he began. "But all along Maurie and I have had a hunch that this . . ."

Leonard sat up straight, feeling suddenly cold. "Who is that?"

"Jack Stratton-Porter, with the Talent Unlimited agency. A schmuck, as I mentioned earlier."

"It's him."

"I just said it was him."

"No, no. I mean that's the man on the phone." He started to get up out of his chair.

Max caught at his sleeve. "Sit. What are you babbling about?"

"The man Molly called that night."

"Unlikely."

"I know that voice, Max." He was on his feet. "I'll never forget that voice."

Max made a grab for him, but he got away clear.

Leonard, fists clenched, started working his way through the maze of tables.

Up on the dais the plump man was back at the mike. "We now come to the best mystery category," he said. "The candidates are *Death Takes A Cruise, Murder Won't Out,* and *The Body in the Gazebo.* And the winner turns out to be—oh, hey, this is great—*Murder Won't Out* by Leonard McGill and, God bless her, Molly Crane McGill."

People all around Leonard were standing up, applauding loudly.

Someone took hold of his arm, pointing him toward the platform. "You're a bit off course, old man."

He was still several tables away from Stratton-Porter, but there was nothing he could do now but trot up on the stage and accept the award.

He pushed ahead, climbed the rickety steps to the platform. He didn't say anything as the plump man handed him the Hobie.

The blonde in the glittering dress moved closer, obviously intending to kiss him.

He dodged her, moved to the edge of the dais, and scanned the audience. He saw the suntanned agent only a few tables away, grinning up at him.

"You son of a bitch!" Leonard tossed the statuette at him.

He missed.

Stratton-Porter kept on grinning.

Leonard jumped from the stage, shoved his way around the tables, and reached the one where the agent was sitting.

"It was because of you that she died," Leonard said.

He grabbed up a steak knife from the table.

He did better with that.

Ruby Nell's Ordeal

by Jan Grape

Nurse aide Vanita Gomez was tired when she walked into the employee lounge of the Adobe Creek Nursing Center at 10:25 P.M. on Friday night. She worked the graveyard shift four evenings a week, Thursdays through Sundays. She also worked Monday through Friday at the Adobe County Health Center from ten to four, which would explain her fatigue. As a single parent with two high schoolers, it took two jobs to stay afloat.

She only half listened to Sonja Walker, R.N., the outgoing charge nurse. All incoming personnel were required to hear a verbal report on the status of each patient for the previous eight hours. Usually there were only a few changes, ninety percent of the patients were just being warehoused until they died, and they did all die. Some quickly and some slowly, inch by inch. Whenever possible Vanita tried to be beside them when the end came.

Vanita thought it was sad for a person to live a vital productive life for seventy or eighty years, and end up this way. Pitiful little things, she thought, so helpless. Draining emotions and resources from their families. Why, she wondered, unable to stop herself from questioning, hadn't the Good Lord come up with a better plan for a human's departure? Something painless while the body was still mobile and the mind still alert.

In the meantime, she wiped their behinds, forced the pureed food down their throats, and turned their helpless bodies every two hours. She smoothed limp hair and lotioned dry withered limbs and sometimes cried silent tears as she worked. Some cursed her or reviled her for her efforts, but usually they were grateful for small comforts. Comforts like getting their teeth brushed or their fingernails cut. Their gratitude would show in their eyes even when their words were nonsense.

Vanita took care of the patients on Two-West, Rooms 200 through 210, half were private rooms and the remainder semiprivate. Full beds meant seventeen patients, but at night the patients mostly slept so it wasn't difficult. Besides Vanita, four other aides, an LVN charge nurse and one orderly made up the floor's night crew.

Sonja Walker, R.N., droned on—giving blood pressures, temperatures, pulse rates, medicine changes, orders from doctors, X rays, and lab tests scheduled and completed. From the nurse's notes she told of special problems, like who wasn't eating well and who had sluggish bodily functions, about visits from family or friends and the other myriad of details for each hour of the eight she had been on duty.

Vanita was half listening, half dozing, when she noticed a flash of movement out of the corner of her eye. She turned and saw a woman dressed in a black coat walking rapidly down the corridor toward room 202.

Vanita was poised to go after the woman to inquire about the nature of this late visit when she realized it was Ruby Nell Poteet visiting her mother. Mrs. Poteet's prognosis wasn't good. She had pneumonia and was fading fast.

Vanita felt sorry for Ruby Nell. Mrs. Poteet was often as cranky as a long-tailed cat in a roomful of rocking chairs. Ruby Nell, as the only child, had prac- tically given up her own life for her mother, but car- ried her burden without complaint.

Vanita settled back in her chair and noted Sonja Walker had finished the report. Sonja did have a final caution. "Keep an alert eye on Mr. Jenkins in room 206. He's got a wild hair about his wife, Maureen. Says she's been whoring around on him."

"But she's dead, isn't she?" asked Vanita.

"Two years now, but he doesn't remember. Twice today he got up all by himself and went stomping down the hall calling for Maureen at the top of his lungs. We had to get the orderlies from the first floor to help get him back in bed." Sonja closed the charts. "That's it, boys and girls," she said. "I'm out of this snake pit. Y'all have fun, now."

An hour later, Vanita Gomez walked to the nurse's station and informed Cynthia Washington, LVN, that Mrs. Poteet had expired. "Poor little soul can rest now," Vanita said.

When Sheriff Damon Dunlap came in for lunch, he was unusually quiet. His wife, Robbie, could tell he was worried, but she didn't ask what was on his mind. She figured Damon was mulling it over. After nearly thirty years of marriage, she knew he'd tell her, sooner or later, using her as a sounding board for whatever he was worrying about.

Robbie liked hearing about his cases. Damon said she had a morbid curiosity about things criminal. She placed bowls of homemade beef stew on the table and as they were sitting down, the front doorbell rang. It was Ruby Nell Poteet.

Ruby Nell was a twittery little woman approaching sixty. She had hair dyed an orangey-red color that some women her age thought was becoming, but wasn't. "I'm sorry to disturb you, Robbie," she said. "But I have to talk to Damon. It's important."

Damon led Ruby Nell Poteet into his study, and Robbie put her husband's lunch in the icebox. Why did they always come by at lunchtime? she wondered, shaking her head. The sheriff's office kept routine business hours, which were ignored about half the time. In small towns, people felt the sheriff was their own personal law keeper. They put him in office, and they could vote him out again.

Robbie Dunlap liked living in Frontier City, the county seat of Adobe County. She had grown up here and couldn't imagine living anywhere else. The town's population of a few thousand was nestled in the rugged limestone hill country, northwest of Austin. It was a pretty town, progressive, with a bunch of wonderful people and only a few troublemakers.

But because they lived six blocks from the courthouse square, Damon often received sheriffing visits at the most inopportune times. Robbie didn't begrudge them, but drop-ins upset her work schedule, and that aggravated her.

At fifty-five, and with their two children grown and fending for themselves, Robbie had decided to fulfill her dream of writing mysteries. She'd sold several short stories to the national magazines and recently submitted a partial manuscript; three chapters and a synopsis to the River City Mystery Association's First Novel Contest.

She'd already won the local and state contests in the P.I. sub-genre-category. The regionals were next, and her hopes of making it all the way to nationals were running high. The ultimate goal, winning the nationals, was an exciting challenge. The $15,000 first prize and publication of her book would help alleviate the guilt she had from giving up her job as an X-ray technician, and give her ego a tremendous boost.

Adobe County sheriff's pay wasn't the greatest, and that first-prize check would give their finances a tremendous boost, too.

To be eligible for the regionals, Robbie's manuscript had to be completed. The first draft was almost done, and the deadline was coming up fast. Being interrupted put her behind in her afternoon writing schedule. She hated being put behind.

"Robbie," Damon called out. "Can you come in here a minute?"

His request was unexpected. People usually wanted these talks with Damon to be confidential. Robbie was curious as she wiped her hands on a dish towel and walked to the study.

Ruby Nell Poteet, sitting in the big lounge chair was crying, while Damon stood near the window looking angry. "We've got ourselves a problem here," Damon said, in a terse voice.

"What's wrong?"

"Ruby Nell's mother passed away around midnight last night," he answered.

"Oh, Ruby Nell." Robbie knelt quickly by the chair and patted the woman's arm. "I'm sorry, I hadn't heard." Robbie looked at Damon and signaled an unspoken "what's up," but he shook his head.

She noticed his tightened lips and stiff shoulders. Something was definitely wrong.

"Ohhh, Rob-bbi-ee." Ruby Nell sobbed. "Damon thinks I-I, uh, killed Mama."

Her husband seldom jumped to conclusions, and she was surprised by his lack of sympathy. "Damon Dunlap," said Robbie, standing and turning to him with astonishment. "I don't . . . ?"

"Wait just a minute, Ruby Nell," Damon interrupted. "I didn't accuse you of any such thing." When he spoke in his official voice, he sounded as if all his six feet, four inches, two hundred thirty-eight pounds could smash you in a New York minute. And he could. But he never smashed women or even intimidated them. People usually relied on him when they were in pain or sorrow.

Ruby Nell began to caterwaul; she was on the edge of hysteria.

Robbie put her fists on her hips. "Damon, I don't care what the problem is. I won't have someone treated this way in my house. Go to the kitchen, please, and pour a glass of brandy for Ruby Nell." Robbie fought to control her temper.

Damon hesitated only a moment before he complied. He returned with the glass and handed it to Ruby Nell, who sputtered down half the contents.

Robbie walked down the hall to the bathroom, wet a washcloth in cool water, came back, and gave the cloth to the older woman.

In a few minutes, Ruby Nell seemed sufficiently calmed, and Damon's stance became that of a concerned friend again. "I'm sorry, Ruby Nell," he said. "I didn't mean to upset you."

"Tell me what's going on, Damon. I can't believe you suspect Ruby Nell of murder."

Damon sighed, and used "the sheriff" voice again. "This is an official investigation and since Miss Poteet is potentially a suspect, we shouldn't discuss it informally like this."

"Has she been charged with anything?" asked Robbie. "Are you arresting her?"

"No, of course not."

"Then I don't see any problem."

Ruby Nell spoke up. "Mr. Schmidt over at Schmidt-Weizer Funeral Home wouldn't let me see Mama's body yet. When I asked why, he wouldn't say. I persisted. Finally, he admitted there were some unexplained bruises on her neck, and that it looked like someone had smothered her to death. He said he'd reported his findings to the sheriff."

"I'm with you so far," said Robbie.

"I've been investigating all morning," said Damon. "I'm not at liberty to say what I've found. Naturally, I want to question Ruby Nell, but I think she should have a lawyer present when I do."

"Okay," said Robbie. "That's reasonable."

Ruby Nell said, "I came over to ask Damon what was going on about Mama, never dreaming he would think I killed her. Why would *anyone* kill Mama?"

"Ruby Nell," said Damon. "You'd better not say anything else without your lawyer present."

"This little problem is easy to solve," said Robbie. "You go on back to the office, Damon. Ruby Nell can call Fletcher." She turned to Ruby Nell. "Fletcher is your lawyer, isn't he?"

"Fletcher, Junior—Fletch," said Ruby Nell, and sipped some more brandy.

"After Fletch gets here, the two of them can come to your office so you can ask your questions."

Damon raised his voice slightly. "We're talking a murder investigation here, Robbie, and I'm not sure how it will look."

"How what will look?"

"A request for a lawyer coming from the sheriff's house."

"Oh, for heaven's sake, Damon. That doesn't make sense. People request lawyers from your office. What difference does it make?" Robbie took his arm, silently urging him to leave the room. "Besides, I don't care how it looks."

They walked out into the hallway.

"I meant how it might look legally," he said, in a low tone.

"I know what you meant. I'm telling you it won't

matter in the long run. Ruby Nell didn't kill her mother."

"And I suppose you're going to tell me how you know that."

"Not exactly. Damon, I've known Ruby Nell since I was six years old. She sacrificed her own happiness to take ..."

"Maybe she finally got a bellyfull. Maybe Mrs. Poteet wasn't the easiest person to get along with ..."

"Damon," Robbie said. "You'll just have to take my word for it. I have no doubts about my friend." Damon followed as she pulled him farther down the hallway.

"You're taking a strong stand here. I knew you and Ruby Nell were friends, but I didn't know you were close enough for you to go out on a limb for ..."

"We don't pal around together, if that's what you mean. We were very close when we were younger. In recent years, I've been taking care of you and the kids, and she's been taking care of her mother, but that doesn't change the ..."

"Honey, people *do* change. That's a fact of life."

"Yes, but there are things that happened a long time ago. Things I'm not at liberty to tell you, Damon. And because of what happened back then, I know she hasn't changed. And she would not kill her mother."

Damon started to speak, but Robbie put her hand over his lips. "You probably have evidence to the contrary, but there are some missing pieces that will tell you the truth. Go back to the office," Robbie said. "Do what you have to do."

"What about lunch?"

"Stop at Jack-in-the-Box and get a salad. Just go on—get out of here."

Damon smiled in defeat, walked to the kitchen and out the back door.

Robbie listened until his Ford Bronco pulled out of their driveway and went down the street. Only then did she go back to the study.

Ruby Nell was on the telephone to Fletcher Frankowski, Jr. "Okay, Fletch, I'll meet you at the sheriff's office in thirty minutes. Bye."

"You get things worked out, Ruby Nell?"

"I think so. Robbie, I'm sorry I got hysterical. That's not like me."

"Don't think a thing about it. You've just lost your mother and . . ."

"I still don't understand any of this. I mean last night the nursing home called and said Mother had died. I've been expecting it. With the pneumonia and her other health problems. Naturally I assumed she'd died from natural causes. But this morning at the funeral home . . ." She wiped her eyes again with a Kleenex.

"It's going to be okay, Ruby Nell. But maybe you shouldn't go into anymore details. What I don't know can't cause you any problems."

The women walked to the front of the house. "Are you going to be able to drive yourself?" Robbie asked.

"Oh yes. I'm fine now. Thanks, Robbie. Goodness, I must look a fright. I'd better run on over to the house and freshen up before I meet the sheriff and Fletch Frankowski."

Robbie gave Ruby Nell a quick hug. "I know you didn't have anything to do with your mother's death, and I'm sure everything will work out."

"I hope so. And thanks again, Robbie." Ruby Nell Poteet got into her car and left.

Robbie returned to her computer and her almost completed manuscript, but she couldn't keep her mind on her story. The real-life drama of her childhood friend was all she could think about.

She and Ruby Nell Poteet had grown up four houses from each other in a neighborhood filled with boys. Ruby Nell was older, but the two girls became close, almost as close as sisters. They told each other secrets, things they could never tell anyone else.

Robbie was a mature girl, probably because she was around adults most of her childhood and because her one close friend was older.

When Ruby Nell was thirteen and Robbie was nine, Ruby Nell had confided her most horrible secret. Robbie remembered that day in 1947 as clearly as if it had happened last week.

Robbie Jo Jamison was sitting on a low branch of the chinaberry tree in her own backyard waiting for Ruby Nell. Ever since Mrs. Poteet got sick, Ruby Nell didn't get to come outside often.

Robbie didn't really mind waiting, but she was anxious to tell her friend a secret. "My mother's giving me a Toni on Saturday," Robbie would say, "and I'm scared it's gonna frizz up like last time." Ruby Nell had naturally curly red-gold hair that never needed a permanent like Robbie's straight brown hair did.

Ruby Nell wasn't yet too old for telling secrets to, although she was beginning to look like a lady and, she was getting those big-lady-things on her chest.

"I'm getting a bustline," Ruby Nell had said.

Robbie knew they were called breasts, but nice young ladies didn't say those vulgar words.

Robbie heard someone running and the sound grew louder as Ruby Nell burst around the corner of the Jamison's house and climbed up on a tree branch next to Robbie.

Robbie hadn't known, at first, that Ruby Nell was crying.

"I hate him. I hate him," sobbed Ruby Nell.

"Who?"

"My, uh, my father."

"Oh, Ruby Nell, you don't really mean it. You're not supposed to hate your father. You love your father because ..."

"I can't love him."

"Why?"

"I try and try, but I'm not Mama."

"I know that silly," said Robbie.

"But he comes and gets in my bed with me and kisses me and stuff."

"What stuff?" Robbie wanted to know.

"Just stuff." Ruby Nell was still crying big drops and getting her blouse damp. "Oh, Robbie. He wants me to do nasty stuff, and I don't want to do it. He says he loves me and that if I love him, I'll let him kiss me and stuff."

Robbie didn't know what Ruby Nell was talking about. Fathers always love you, and her daddy gave her a good-night kiss every night before she went to sleep. "I like for my daddy to give me a good-night kiss."

"This is different. I can't explain it too good. You're just a little ..."

"Don't you say I'm just a little girl. I hear that all the time and I'm not. I'm almost as tall as you are."

"I don't mean ... oh, never mind."

The girls sat silently for a little while and suddenly Ruby Nell started talking. "Robbie, if I tell you a big secret, do you promise not to tell?"

Robbie started nodding her head.

"You've got to cross your heart and hope to die, stick a needle in your eye—if you ever tell."

"Okay," said Robbie, making a big X sign on her chest. "I cross my heart ..."

"You can't tell anyone."

"Not even my mother?"

"No one." Ruby Nell's voice got quiet. "Robbie? Have you ever seen your daddy in the bathtub?"

Robbie nodded her head.

"Well, boys and men have a thing ..."

"A penis. Mother told me it was a penis."

"Yes. And when grown-ups get married and they sleep together, sometimes the man puts it inside his wife."

"I know, Mother told me. To make babies, but how can he put it there?"

"It's kinda hard to do until you're a grown-up lady." Ruby Nell's voice lowered to a whisper. "My daddy puts his thing inside me at night, and he kisses ..."

"Every night?"

"Just about."

"He's not suppose to do that, he's your father."

"I know, but he says it's because he loves me. And he says if I tell Mama, it would kill her. I don't want my mama to die. I hate him, and I don't want to love him anymore."

"Me either. I mean, I don't like him anymore."

Nineteen forty-six was the year Ruby Nell's mother gave birth to a stillborn baby boy. Mrs. Poteet went into a deep depression afterward because she blamed herself for the loss of the baby. She became incapable of doing much more than getting out of bed once or twice a day to eat.

For the next year and a half, Ruby Nell took care of her mother, the meals, the laundry, the house, and her father. Mr. Poteet expected Ruby Nell to perform all the wifely duties his wife was incapable of doing, including meeting his sexual needs.

It had all happened years before anyone talked about sexual abuse. The girls had not known that what Mr. Poteet was doing was sexual abuse, but they did know it was wrong. Unfortunately, they didn't know how to stop it or what to do about it.

Eventually, Mrs. Poteet came out of her depression and slowly regained an interest in what was going on in her home. With her improvement, it didn't take long for her to discover what had occurred between her husband and her daughter. Mr. Poteet adamantly refused to stop having sex with Ruby Nell. He said his daughter was his property to do with as he pleased. He planned to divorce his wife and run away with his daughter. Mrs. Poteet took matters into her own hands, and Mr. Poteet died mysteriously.

The authorities were never able to prove anything, and no one ever knew the truth except Ruby Nell, her mother and Robbie.

Mrs. Poteet had killed her husband to save her daughter. Ruby Nell knew that her mother's love for her was powerful. For the rest of her life no matter what her mother asked of her or expected her to do, the daughter did, and did gladly.

Ruby Nell could never harm her mother because of the extraordinary bond between them. And because of the secret sworn between two little girls years ago, Robbie wouldn't tell Damon about it unless Ruby Nell gave her permission.

The late autumn sun was sinking behind a scrub cedar ridge as Sheriff Dunlap parked his Bronco in the parking lot at Adobe Creek Nursing Center and got out. He pulled his denim jacket tighter. They'd been having nice sunny days, but when evening came, things cooled off quickly.

He'd already questioned the late-night crew who had been on duty when Mrs. Poteet died. It hadn't been easy and took most of the day, since most of them slept during the day and those who weren't asleep held other jobs.

Damon took the elevator to the second-floor nursing station and introduced himself to Sonja Walker, R.N. Mrs. Walker was the nurse who'd given the report at shift change, and Damon wanted to know if she had seen Ruby Nell Poteet come by to see her mother. During his questioning of the graveyard crew, certain angles came up that he wanted to clarify.

One angle concerned Vanita Gomez, a nurse's aide who'd been on duty. Damon was determined to shed some light on what had really happened here last night.

Sonja Walker was about four-foot-ten and wouldn't weigh much over ninety pounds even when she was sopping wet, Damon thought. At his height he felt like a giant towering over her. He asked if they could talk in the employee lounge, that way he'd be able to sit down, and she wouldn't get a neck strain trying to look up at him.

Sonja, as she told him to call her, led the way. Her long brown hair was done up into a braid that his wife would know the name of, but he could only describe as an Indian girl braid. The braid swinging back and forth ahead of him came within his reach several times. He suppressed an urge to pull it and felt as foolish as a ten-year-old.

By the time they were seated and the nurse had poured coffee for them, Damon had put thoughts of childish pranks aside and was back into his sheriff role. "Sonja, I've questioned everyone on duty last night, and only one employee, Vanita Gomez, admits seeing Ruby Nell Poteet come in to visit her mother."

"So I've heard."

"Did you see Ruby Nell?"

"No, I was giving report, and all I was concerned with was finishing that and getting the hell outta here." Her face turned a light shade of pink with the frank admission. "I do have another life besides Adobe Creek Nursing."

"I would imagine so."

"But I don't doubt what Vanita said about seeing Ruby Nell here last night. Ruby Nell often came by around dinnertime in case we needed help in feeding Mrs. Poteet and, after her mother turned critical, she usually came back later in the evening, too."

"Then it wasn't unusual for her to come after nine or ten o'clock?"

"Not at all."

"But isn't it odd that no one saw her except Vanita?"

"Not with shift change. When you've added extra people for thirty to forty-five minutes and everyone is trying to get patients settled down for the night, it can be chaotic." Sonja suddenly looked at him wide-eyed. "Are you accusing Vanita of something?"

In an investigation a sheriff has to keep a poker face occasionally. He'd heard things about Vanita while questioning the others. The woman herself admitted how she liked to be around when a patient died. She was somehow pleased about it. "I just have to tie up some of the loose ends," he said.

"And Vanita is one of your loose ends?"

"More or less," he said.

"In a way, I'm not surprised. I hate to say it, but Vanita is a bit of an oddball."

"Oh. How so?"

"Her attitude about death. Sometimes I honestly think that if she could do it legally, she'd personally send them on their way to glory."

All right, Damon thought. He'd been hoping someone would come out and say it. "I understand. I got that same idea when I talked to her."

Sonja said, "Don't get me wrong. She cares for the patients. Actually, she probably cares too much. And she does have a valid point when she says we put our animals to sleep to put them out of their misery, and why don't we do the same for old people? I agree with her for the most part."

"Could she decide to help someone along in the death struggle? Or would she?"

"If you're asking hypothetically? Sure. Nurses working with terminal patients do have opportunities, but we don't take advantage. Or most of us don't. There have been cases right here in Texas where . . . but, you know all that. If you're asking if Vanita ever assisted a death, I couldn't swear one way or the other. I may have given a fleeting thought about her a time or two, but there was never anything I could prove. Never even anything I could report to a supervisor. It was just a gut instinct. Nothing more."

"How about the medical charts? Could someone look at those and discover a pattern or arrive at a conclusion?"

"I suppose, but I haven't done that." She got up and poured the last of her coffee into the sink and rinsed out her mug. "I'm like most people who work here. I try to do the best job I can when I'm on duty, but when I leave, I leave. I don't want to think about this place or talk about it or anything else. It's the only way I can keep my sanity."

"Sounds like a healthy attitude."

"Well, I need my job and I don't rock the boat, even if I have a question in my mind sometimes that Vanita is strange. I've never seen her harm anyone."

Damon knew he might be on shaky ground to get a court order to inspect the medical charts, but if he could come up with a reasonable way to get Sonja Walker to look, he might find enough for him to take to a judge.

"Sonja. I'm going to level with you. It will take a court order to go through those medical records. It's possible there is a pattern of actions about the woman. First thing Monday morning, I plan to ask Judge Smith to give me that court order."

He paused to see how she was taking it, and was mildly surprised to see the eagerness in Sonja's face. Somewhere down the line she's wondered about Vanita, but she's probably never expressed it out loud before. She wants to look at the records, too, he thought.

"Judge Smith has been known to delay a decision for two or three weeks on some whim or the other. In the meantime, if Vanita Gomez becomes suspicious about me checking her out, she might decide to leave town. I can't legally look at them, but you can. And maybe while you're there, I can look over your . . ."

"Let's go look then," Sonja said, interrupting him. "If Vanita is guilty of anything, I want to know about it. I want her stopped. The sooner, the better, before she gets us all into trouble."

Damon followed Sonja to the elevator. On the way she was interrupted by some commotion in a patient's room.

"Could you wait a moment?" Sonja asked.

Damon was prepared to cool his heels indefinitely, but the nurse didn't take more than two minutes.

"Mr. Jenkins," she said. "Keeps calling for his dead wife. He even tries to get up and go find her."

"He doesn't know?"

"Yes, but he doesn't remember."

Damon shuddered as they took the elevator downstairs to the basement. He hoped he'd never forget if something happened to Robbie.

Sonja guided him to row upon row of file cabinets. "This is going to take some time."

Damon thought that was an understatement.

It was 9:00 P.M. when Sheriff Dunlap returned home. As soon as Damon walked in, Robbie could tell he had good news. If it hadn't been written all over his jubilant face, she could have told by his jaunty step and attitude. "You've found evidence to clear Ruby Nell?" she asked.

He grabbed Robbie into his arms and swung her off her feet. "Better than that. I've got another suspect. A strong suspect." Damon set her back on her feet and kissed her.

"Great. I guess I can take your sleeping bag out of the doghouse now," she smiled up at him.

"Oh, ho. Is that where you were going to put me?"

"I was, unless you listened to the voice of reason." Robbie had worried all afternoon. Fletch Frankowski had called and admitted that after the talk at Damon's office, things looked bad for Ruby Nell. "I don't suppose you can discuss . . ."

"Not yet."

Damon looked in the oven to see what she had cooked for dinner. "Meat loaf. My favorite. Doesn't seem like you were too angry if you went to all that trouble."

"Even a condemned man deserves a favorite meal."

"You mean I was condemned already?"

"Being late almost ruined your dinner."

"Didn't Dispatch call? I asked them to call."

"They called, just in the nick of time, too. I was ready to put the meat loaf in the oven."

"So all is forgiven?"

"Don't push your luck." Robbie took a huge salad out of the icebox, and mashed some potatoes. "Damon, there are things about Ruby Nell and her mother that I wasn't at liberty to tell you earlier today. I've since talked to Ruby Nell, and she says it's okay." The women had agreed that with Mrs. Poteet dead, it wouldn't hurt if Robbie told Damon.

"Robbie, I was only doing my job." Damon helped

by setting the table. When the table was ready, he poured two glasses of iced tea and sat down.

"I know. That's why I wasn't really mad. I just got upset over Ruby Nell getting hysterical."

"So," he said. "Are you going to tell me what you couldn't tell me earlier?"

She put everything on the table and sat down, too. "Not right now. It's not very pleasant dinnertime conversation."

After dinner she told him.

Later, when they were in bed, Robbie said, "Damon? Will you hold me?"

He pulled her close. "What's wrong, babe?"

"I think I'm a little down in the dumps. Thinking about Ruby Nell and the past. What she went through messed up her whole life, didn't it? She has never been able to relate to men. She's never known the wonder and joy of loving someone. And she'll never have children. It's all so sad."

"I keep thinking about you. You were so young to learn about Ruby Nell's abuse. It's a wonder you weren't warped emotionally."

"I probably would have been, but my mother was always open with me and talked to me. When I was nine, she told me the facts of life and where babies came from. When I was twelve she talked about married love, and when I was thirteen she talked about how some men mistreat women. Looking back, I'm sure she suspected about the Poteets. I have to give my mom credit. She kept my head on straight."

"I've always thought your mom was special," he said. "Remind me to call and tell her that soon."

"Maybe now Ruby Nell can actually have a life. Find someone."

"Don't you think she's too old?"

"Damon. She's only four years older than I am, and we're not too old, are we?"

He laughed and patted her backside. "Not yet."

"Maybe she can find someone understanding."

"She'll probably have to go through counseling first."

"Well," Robbie said, "she needs to do that anyway. I'll encourage her along those lines. The rest will be up to the fates."

"Tonight, I only want to hold you close and comfort you, but does my fate include a little old-age excitement in the future?"

"Ask me again tomorrow morning."

On Sunday morning, Damon had an appointment to talk to the Adobe County DA. When he returned home, he and Robbie took a drive out to the lake. Central Texas weather in the fall can be a perfect time to be outdoors, and they decided on a picnic.

Adobe Creek wasn't really a creek at all, although the small portion that ran through town was what most people would call a creek. It actually was a fork of the Texas Colorado River. About two miles west of town, a dam had been built, and a small lake had formed. It was a huge part of the town's attraction.

Picnic tables, camping sites, and a small boat dock had been built on the side of the lake nearest the town. Robbie packed a lunch, and they ate and relaxed in lawn chairs under an oak tree watching the water and a sailboat nearby. They didn't often have a chance for good leisure time together.

Robbie knew something weighed heavily on Damon's mind, although he tried to hide it and not let it spoil their day. She wasn't too surprised when he finally spoke.

"I've got bad news and bad news. The DA says we don't have enough evidence against our suspect to make an arrest."

"Well, at least Ruby Nell is cleared."

"That's the rest of my bad news. We found out this

morning by an overnight fax, there was an insurance policy on Thelma Poteet, and her daughter is the beneficiary. Ruby Nell stands to inherit five hundred thousand dollars."

"But, that . . ."

"The DA says the odds of making a case against her just went sky-high. Of course, he doesn't know what you and I know and even if he did, an eyewitness puts her in her mother's room, less than an hour before Mrs. Poteet was found dead. And if getting out from under her mother's tyranny wasn't enough, the money gives her a strong motive. He's in favor of us making an arrest. I've managed to stall him for another twenty-four hours."

"What are you going to do?"

"I'm not sure. Try to come up with stronger evidence against my other suspect, but I don't know if there's anything else to find."

They got up and walked down to the shoreline. Usually Robbie enjoyed the lake and the huge limestone boulders that hugged the edge in places. If the sunlight hit the rocks just right, it was possible to see minute particles of calcite glinting. Damon's news about the possible arrest of Ruby Nell put a damper on everything.

When Damon was in the mood to explore more thoroughly, he would look for fossils imbedded in the boulders. Today Robbie noticed he walked over the rocks without seeing them.

They walked arm in arm, except where the going was too rough, and then he would steady her. They reached the water's edge and stopped, standing on a flat limestone boulder.

"Damon, I've racked my brain trying to figure out who could have killed Thelma Poteet. Who even would want her dead." Robbie stepped down, almost slipped—even with Damon supporting her—and was glad she'd worn her sneakers. "I know you don't like to say anything prematurely about your case, but even I can deduce a few things about the murderer."

"Let me hear your theory," he said. "It might help clarify my thinking."

"That insurance policy doesn't make any difference in my book; I still don't think Ruby Nell had enough motive to kill her mother. That means the only other people with access to Mrs. P., would be someone from the nursing home. But why would someone at Adobe Creek want to get rid of a sick old woman?"

"Good question. Do you have an answer?" He held out his hand to help her, and they sat down on the rock side by side.

"The only logical explanation is that Mrs. P. saw or heard something she wasn't supposed to."

"For instance?"

"How would I know?" She looked at him and saw his slight grin. "Oh, I see. You don't know either. What's wrong? Is it too difficult for you? You want me to try to solve your case?"

"I think I have it solved. I just want to hear your version."

"I don't have a version, I'm only thinking out loud," she said, and punched him in the shoulder. "I've helped you solve cases before. I'm not a novice. Besides, I read and write mysteries and . . ."

"Fiction isn't real life."

"I know, and truth is stranger than fiction." She paused for a moment. "Look, did you see that fish jump over there?"

"Sure did. Wish I'd brought my fishing pole."

"Anyway, back to Mrs. P.'s death. Let's start with the premise that the old woman heard or saw something. Since I worked twenty years in X ray, I know a little about what goes on in hospitals and nursing homes. I would make a guess that Mrs. P. saw someone stealing drugs or mistreating patients."

"You're getting warm there."

"The mistreatment part?"

"Along the right track, but a little different."

"Okay," Robbie said. "She saw someone doing something to a patient. That place is full of people who are terminal or will be before long. Did Mrs. P. see someone killing a patient to put them out of their misery?"

"Almost on the nose, old gal."

"Damon, if she saw a nurse or orderly kill a patient, she was in jeopardy. Maybe that explains why she got pneumonia in the first place."

Damon stood up and began pacing beside the boulder. "Whoa, I hadn't thought of that."

"What if a nurse or orderly injected her with a pneumococcal virus and when that didn't work fast enough, she was smothered."

"This raises some possibilities I need to check out." He strode off taking the shortest path, which happened to also be one of the roughest. "I've got to get back to town, Robbie."

"Wait a minute, you big lug. You better not go off and leave me." She stood and started after him.

"Okay," he said, and went back to help her. "But we need to hurry. I've got to check something out."

Later that evening, a friend of Robbie's named Iona Winston called to say she had fallen while visiting in Austin and had broken her hip. The doctors had fixed her up, and Iona said she was doing fine, although she still needed nursing care and some physical therapy treatments. Her daughter lived in Oklahoma City, worked as a teacher, and also had small children.

The only solution was for Iona to check into Adobe Creek Nursing Center until she was able to care for herself. She asked if Robbie would bring some fresh clothes and toilet items to her, and Robbie said she would.

Robbie was already asleep when Damon came in, well after midnight. She roused herself briefly when he got into bed.

"Tomorrow I'll grab breakfast out someplace and head back over to the nursing home," he said. "This case is driving me crazy. Everything I come up with falls apart. Nothing makes sense."

The next morning Robbie finished the final draft of her manuscript. At eleven, she went to visit Iona Winston at Adobe Creek Nursing Center, stopping by Iona's house first to pick up the necessary requested items.

Robbie parked in the visitor's lot at Adobe Creek and went inside. It had been awhile since she'd been to the home, and she was pleased to see some of the redecorating changes that had taken place since her last trip. New paint, wallpaper, and furniture had brightened everything. A noticeable difference was the center didn't have that odor of old age and illness anymore. The new administrator had improved the place tremendously. Robbie couldn't help wondering what the adverse publicity might do if an employee was arrested for the murder of Thelma Poteet.

At the second-floor nursing station, Robbie reported she was visiting Mrs. Winston, in room 202. When she reached the room, she realized it was the same one Thelma Poteet had occupied.

When Robbie walked into the room, Iona Winston had her eyes closed, but opened them at the sound of footsteps. Iona looked exhausted, and her eyes were bloodshot.

"Robbie, I've got to get out of this place. You've got to help me."

"What's wrong, Iona?"

"There's a crazy man in here. He came in my room last night. Yelling and calling me a whore, and he tried to smother me."

"For heaven's sake, Iona. How did you stop him?"

"I fought him off and finally got hold of the call bell and rang for the nurse. One of the aides came in and said for me not to get upset. That it was all a mistake.

"Don't get upset I said. That crazy man tried to kill me."

"Who was it? And why did he come in here?"

"Johnson, Jenkins. Something like that. He kept calling for Maureen. Calling her a whore and said he was going to kill me. He must have thought I was Maureen. Whoever she was. He had his hands around my neck for a moment. I managed to shove him away. He yanked the pillow out from under my head and tried to put it over my face."

"How horrible."

"Yes, it was and I shudder to think what might have happened if he had been able to mash just a little harder on that pillow. Or if I hadn't been able to reach that call bell. I would be laying here dead now instead of talking to you."

The implication of her words grabbed at Robbie. "So, that's how Mrs. Poteet was killed," she said.

Her friend looked puzzled. "What did you say?"

"Iona, I need to use your telephone to call Damon. Then I'm going to call your daughter and tell her to come down here to get you. I'll stay here with you until she comes."

"Oh, thank you, Robbie. Now, maybe I can get some sleep. I wasn't able to sleep a wink last night after all that." Iona closed her eyes.

"Thank *you*, Iona." Robbie patted her friend's arm, picked up the telephone, and dialed. When Damon answered, she said, "I've just solved the case for you ... What? ... Oh, I'm at Adobe Creek Nursing Center. I'm going to hang up now and call Ruby Nell. I've got to let her know her ordeal is over."

Of Tyrants and Sovereigns

by Billie Sue Mosiman

Marcilla, the mother of the crippled Galian, could hardly believe her ears when her young son came prattling frantically about his playmate, Tiberius Claudius Drusus Nero Germanicus.

"He might be killed," Galian said, trembling so hard that he could not keep his head still on the stem of his neck. Even his lips quivered and his hands danced like grain sheafs in a windy field.

"Not Claudius." Marcilla wished to waylay her son's fears. "He's of the royal house. No one would want to hurt poor Claudius, surely?"

"But it's true! When we played today near the fountain, we heard his tutor in conversation. He didn't know we were listening. He thought himself and his friend alone."

Marcilla thought long moments before she tried again to dissuade her child from believing what he must have truly heard with his own ears. "Did young Claudius hear it also?"

"Oh yes, Mother, and it hurt him so badly. He turned away his face and hid it in his robe so I could not see him weep quietly. Why would anyone hurt him, Mother? They all think him an idiot. They can't imagine him a threat."

"Who did his tutor say meant to do him harm, Galian?"

Here Galian paused, and he had to take a seat on

the floor at her knee. It was as if his strength had deserted him, the truth so terrible. "His grandmother, Livia."

Marcilla hardly blinked an eye. It had been rumored for decades that Livia, wife of the emperor Augustus, had a hand in family deaths—and even some outside her family, that she preferred slow-acting poisons. But, of course, no one near the court could possibly spread such tales in public for fear they might be true and Livia, catching wind of gossip, come for her revenge. Marcilla reached down and put two fingers against her child's lips. "You must never tell another soul what you have told me. On your life, you must swear it."

"I swear it, Mother. But what can we do? Could it be true? Will Claudius be murdered?"

"Not if I can help it," Marcilla said. "Now calm yourself. Go to the baths and soak so that your limbs won't swell tonight when you sleep. Put all thought of what you've heard from mind. No one will hurt our Claudius."

Though she made the promise, she was not certain she could save a person marked for death by Livia. The empress had, it was believed, dispatched her own sons and grandsons when they got in her way, she had caused Augustus to exile his own daughter to a dusty, barren island off the coast. She was made of metal and bitter root. Where her heart should have been, she preserved a rotten fruit in her chest, and her mind was a house overrun by worms.

Marcilla watched her son's slow tortuous assent up the steps leading from the garden. The reason he and Claudius had become friends was that they were both infirm, and it was thought, wrongly, that both were light in the head as well. Marcilla knew neither child lacked intelligence or spirit. Young Claudius was already studying the finest historians to learn their styles so that he might write a history of his departed father.

Galian had his mother to love him, though his father cared little for the boy with his defects, but it was said Claudius had no woman in his family who cared: not his mother or his grandmother. And his grandfather, Augustus, barely tolerated his presence.

The intrigues of Rome were so wearing. Now she might get herself involved in a plot that would be her undoing. But was she to ignore the righteous way and let things unfold as they would? Not to a child. An innocent who had caused no one the slightest injury. One who could not help that Nature had made him stutter like a fool when he was not, made his legs weak, and his face twitch oddly when he was excited. Livia might poison adults who should have seen her sly hand coming, but she had no call to send to death a boy who could pose no possible impediment to her power.

Marcilla went right away to Claudius in his mother's wing of the palace. She found him poring over a book lying open on top of a stack of histories. "Dear Claudius," she said quietly. "You work so hard for one so young."

Claudius raised his head and saw the mother of his friend enter the room. "I've nothing better to do," he said, smiling.

She came near and took a seat on a bench. She waited until he could get down from a high stool and come next to her. She waited until his smile dissipated.

"It's Galian, isn't it?" he asked. "He's told you of the secret."

"He's worried."

"As am I."

"Have you heard of the rumors concerning your grandmother?"

Claudius looked greatly saddened. He cast his gaze

to the floor and would not look her in the eye. "Do you ma-ma-mean the . . . poison?"

Marcilla took his hand in her own. "You must never eat anything she prepares for you. You must have a servant taste your food and drink, then wait at least six hours before partaking of it yourself. Do you understand? It is imperative you understand. If you can't use caution at any time, you must come to me and I will feed you."

"Livia won't have me at her table. She finds me too irritable. I make her na-na-nervous. She claims I ruin her digestion."

"I have heard that. But she might take a hand in sending your food to you. Will you be careful?"

"I most certainly shall try."

"Galian cares for you, Claudius. He loves you as a brother."

Claudius smiled again now, and his eyes shined. "And I love him, Marcilla. He is the best boy I have ever known. He's always ka-ka-kind to me and never cruel like the others."

"And you are kind to him."

Claudius waved that away as if it were nothing, not worth speaking of. "I could do no less for such a fine friend as Galian. Did he tell you he wants to be a poet? Like Homer? He writes poems on my tablets, but he won't let me show them to anyone."

"Poems!" Marcilla laughed happily. "Galian has kept a secret, after all. That little tadpole. I'll have to ask to see some."

Claudius grew somber. "I shouldn't have told. He won't be happy with me."

"Oh. Well, then, I won't say anything. I won't let on I know. How is that? I'll let my little tadpole tell me in his own good time."

As she left Claudius to his history books, she could not keep from grinning to herself. Her little son was

sincere of heart and as good as Livia was evil. She
should leave around some books of poems. He might
like Virgil. A poet, think of it! Just as they were unfair
to young Claudius, everyone thought Galian an imbe-
cile simply because his head shook uncontrollably, and
his muscle control was not as strong as it might have
been. The children taunted him for his bandy legs and
his large head, calling him a skinny chicken fit only
for the stew pot.

She called him, affectionately, her little tadpole. As
a babe he had squirmed always to be near her, to
suckle at her breast, to feel her arms around his thin
body at night when the wind blew cool through the
windows. He didn't much like the baby name these
days. But then he was nearly ten. Almost a man. She
must be careful not to keep him in childhood any
longer than he wished to remain.

Moving through the thronged streets, smelling the
open wine caskets and cooking meats, the sweat of
humanity, the stench of the sewer, she realized it was
nearly dark. Her husband would wonder where she
might be. She wanted nothing out of the ordinary to
come to his attention. It was Livia who was behind
his appointment to the knighthood not so long in the
past. He owed his loyalty to the emperor, and to his
empress. If he had to choose between his wife or his
son and his lord, he would naturally be obligated to
choose his lord.

Marcilla sat embroidering a muslin drawing of a
pheasant rising from a bamboo marsh while clandes-
tinely watching over the play of Galian and Claudius.
She was not getting many stitches complete, for it
thrilled her heart to see her son enjoy the day so
much. The boys had borrowed helmets and shields
from the guards stationed in the house down the way.
Claudius could have anything he liked to play with

merely by asking. Armed with willow sticks, the boys set out to make war on the pond frogs and crickets, they rushed at a brown bird unlucky enough to light in a bush in the garden, they swatted at butterflies, and cried like glorious soldiers defending the Rhine from German invaders. The willow branches bent without breaking so that their play went uninterrupted all afternoon. Just as Marcilla put in a half-dozen good stitches, she'd hear one or the other of the boys whoop out and, lifting her gaze, she'd see them stumble from hiding and fling themselves upon another hapless insect or pond inhabitant. Once Claudius fell headlong into the pool, and she rose from her chair, willing to rescue him, but up he came sputtering, stuttering, "I-I-I-am ... captain ... of the ba-ba-brave ship, and I wa-wa-won't be dunked without remedy!" He slogged out trailing epaulettes of water lilies over his small shoulders, brandishing his willow sword, the helmet sitting cockeyed on his head. Galian laughed wildly, escaping into a frothy hedge of bougainvillea, crying, "I'll dunk you again, if you're so brave! I'm a mutineer, and you're done for, Captain! Done for, I say."

That night when Galian begged off from his dinner and went to bed early, Marcilla checked his forehead for a fever. "It was too much play in the hot sun," she admonished.

"No, Mother, I just feel sleepy. I'm all right, really."

The next day when Claudius came after his classes to play, he found Galian sitting on the step next to where his mother worked on the embroidery. "I don't want to do anything today," he said. "Could we just sit and rest, Claudius? Would you be angry if we did?"

Claudius looked to Marcilla askance, but he did as his friend asked. He sat and waited. For an hour he waited, patiently, talking about the historian, Livy, and how much he was enjoying reading all his work. But when Galian showed little other than a courteous apathy, he finally took his leave.

"Here, let me check your head again," Marcilla said, alarmed. She put her lips against his cheek and then his forehead, and found them cool, too cool for her liking. "I think you're taking a chill."

"I want to go to bed. May I go to bed, Mother?"

"Of course you may if you don't feel well. I'll call for someone."

"Oh, you needn't do that. I'll feel better after I have some sleep."

But you sleep too much, little tadpole, she thought, already trying to think where she might find a physician at this time of evening. There were maladies that could carry away a small child as quickly as rain rinsing soil from a slope.

It took several hours, but Marcilla had the man who attended senators come to her son's bedside. Galian slept deeply, hardly waking a moment when his nightshirt was pulled high before falling deeply asleep again. The physician felt of his pulse and shook his head. He lay his hands on the child's body, feeling of his extremities, manipulating the flesh beneath his ribs. He opened his mouth and looked down his throat, pulled up the lids of his eyes, and peered there at the rolling whites. "It behaves like poison," he pronounced. "His color is bad, his pulse slow. Have you seen him eating berries or any wild thing? You must find the source."

Fear clutched its frosty fist around Marcilla's heart. Poison! Just what she had warned Claudius against. Who in her house might poison her child? How dare any of them slip something into his food or drink when she was not looking. Her cheeks flushed. "I'll try to ask him to find out," she said, careful not to mention her suspicions. But it could only be Livia, cruel, heartless Livia who was behind it. Had she heard that Claudius had been warned? Had she divined who told him to monitor his intake? Would she seek such low revenge as this, to take away another mother's innocent child if she could not rid herself of one underfoot in her own palace? Foul! Most foul and vile a woman had never walked the earth. Rome should have risen up long before and asked for the republic back again, and threaten to tear down the senate walls if they were not granted the wish of all free men not to be hampered and throttled by a monarchy.

It was her doing, all right. Augustus was but a puppet in her play, and one day he too might pay with his life for flirting so dangerously near such a corrupt entity that called herself his devoted wife.

Marcilla paid the man handsomely and sent him away. He had nothing to help her. He could not give an antidote for what he could not guess was working on the boy's innards.

Marcilla, frenzied, tried to wake Galian. She even took him to a cauldron of cold water and set him gently into it, trying to revive him to consciousness. Next she made a repulsive concoction for him to drink so that he might vomit whatever he might have left in his stomach. He gagged and swallowed and spit up but a small bit of matter. His eyes fluttered, and once he said, "Mother, let me sleep. I ache."

Her husband was worse than useless, he was like an old horse with a thrown shoe. He moped too long and spent precious time nursing his own fear of mortality. Finally he called another doctor who was just as helpless as the first had been. He questioned the servants about what his son had eaten previously, but all he could discover was that Galian had taken bananas from a dish the day before. Anything else he had eaten had been also devoured by his parents, who were, obviously, not ill from it.

Marcilla demanded the dish be brought to her. It was empty and as yet unwashed. Examining the bowl closely, she saw there was a residue on the bottom, as from bananas gone too soft, leaking their juices. It was this she scraped out and took with her as she left the house.

It was nearly dawn, and her throat kept closing from the urge to give in to her tears. She hurried along the street while vendors set up their stalls and shopkeepers opened their doors. She found the pharmacy she often used for poultices and plasters and salves. She showed the old man her scrapings and wasted no time explaining what she thought it was.

"It's something poisonous," she said, breathless from her hurried walk. "My son is dying of it. Please try to tell me what it is and how I might save him if you want a blessing of good fortune from all the gods that be."

He took it behind a curtain and was gone some time. When he returned, his head was bowed and she could not see his eyes. "What is it! You must tell me the antidote."

"I'm not sure, but it seems to be a poison from a fish, one that comes from far out in the sea. It is round and spiny."

"And a way to counteract its effects?" She had stopped breathing, her hope held fast and hard as a marble slab in her frightened mind.

He shook his head. She rushed to him and took him by the arms to shake him senseless. "If you tell me there is nothing I can do, I shall have my husband come and take off your head with his sword before the sun sets."

The old man, afraid for his life, but not foolish enough to lie, said softly, "Then send him quickly so that I won't wait through the heat and die of palpitations. There is nothing I know that can stop this deadly thing. A drop of it could paralyze an elephant from the far continent, it could kill a mighty horse. It will surely take your son before you are able to get back to him this day."

Marcilla cried out her anguish. She ran as swiftly as she could, her shawl flying from her shoulders and head to the street, her sandals breaking straps as she caught them on cobblestones. She rushed into the house screaming, "Galian! My little tadpole! My child!"

Her husband stood over the boy. He had already ordered the materials for the cremation and instructed the house staff to prepare the body. He already had the urn for the ashes waiting at the foot of the cot.

Marcilla threw herself across her son's body and let grief take her to that place where mothers beat their breasts and gnash their teeth and plead with the gods to take them now, in mercy, before they must live another minute without their beloved.

Marcilla sat in mourning in her garden, her hands in her lap. Claudius found her there, directed by one of the servants. He sat quietly at her feet until she felt she wished to speak.

"I miss him," she said simply.

"You saved my life, Marcilla. If I had known Galian would have to sacrifice his life for mine, I would have sent you away."

"You couldn't know."

Silence reigned again. Finally Claudius said, "I wa-wa-will remember him always. He was my only friend. When my grandmother is di-di-dying, I will go to her and remind her of this treachery. I will refuse to put the coins on her eyes."

"No, you won't. She is your flesh. If she asks, you'll place the coins."

"Or ma-ma-maybe she will do it for me. She's never

liked me. I will never be emperor, but she thinks I'm too clever and in her way."

"You must be clever enough to thwart her ruses. If she plots again, beware. Next time she will come in more stealth."

"I will run her through with my sword!"

This caused Marcilla to smile a small and delicate smile. It was what boys say. Prideful boast. And Claudius was a boy, however clever he might be. He was frail and sickly. Tics disfigured his face more often these days. The stutter was immeasurably worse. Livia probably realized she had no call to fear he might ever usurp any of the line she chose to put in place of power after Augustus. It was said she was grooming Tiberius, that lecherous wretch. What must she fear from a spindly cripple whose only ambition was to write his histories?

She might never have really wished to poison her grandson. It might have been a passing fancy. Something spoken in jest and taken to heart by a servant who spoke out of turn and was overheard by the tutor. But Livia meant to take Galian from Marcilla, warning that she not be meddled with, not ever.

"What will you da-da-do?" Claudius asked.

"I will grieve."

"And what will you do afterward?"

"Is there any afterward when the one you loved most is lost?"

Claudius held his counsel.

He was a good boy. And Marcilla hoped—she fervently prayed—he would refuse to place the coins on Livia's eyes when that old murderous woman's time came. Let the woman who slaughtered children face her fate with open eyes. Further, Marcilla asked the gods that be, if it so pleased them, that this little boy of royal lineage who lived in books and had played once a marauding soldier through the pond water, might one day take command of Rome. However unlikely that prospect appeared at the moment, she thought it only fitting that poor Galian should one day be remembered long and well by the emperor over all the Roman Empire.

It was little enough to ask in return for her great sorrow.

"I will ca-ca-come and see you again sometime if you like," Claudius said. "I can read to you from Livy."

"Will you read to me from Homer and Virgil instead?"

"If you wa-wa-wish."

She put an arm around his small shoulders and drew him close in embrace. "I do wish," she said. "I wish it most of all, dear, kind Claudius."

When a month of heartache had passed and nothing could vanquish it, Marcilla knew what she must do. She dressed in her best finery and went to the palace. She begged for an audience with the empress. Once in her chambers, she wasted no time. In a fearless voice she said, "You might have taken my son, but if you lay one hand on your little grandson, I will charge all my living heirs to extract any revenge they can manage against you and your house. This is my oath."

Livia, regal in a snow-white gown with gold braid, sat bemused, a smile on her face. "I have never desired to touch young Claudius Drusus, either alive or dead."

"Lies are beneath you, Livia. We know, you and I, your schemes to rule as only a woman can rule. You would take your own life if it furthered your malevolent goals. I have nothing more to say. I know you can have me brought before the senate for treason, you can have me beheaded or thrown upon the stairs to be picked apart by vultures. Nothing, however, not even my death, can stay my hand if Claudius is harmed."

Livia nodded her head in dismissal. The two women understood explicitly the terms.

It was not until the following week that Marcilla grew ill. True to her word she had taken aside all her sisters and brothers, all her nephews, nieces, aunts, and uncles, one by one. She had made clear her wishes. One of them must find a way to the empress if anything befell the child Claudius.

Marcilla's husband tore at his hair and went quite mad until she begged that he remember her oath and never forget it.

Claudius came to her on her deathbed. His eyes were red, and a storm shook his flesh with jerks and tics that rendered him incapable of speech. Marcilla reached out for his small body and drew him close. "I could not persist in this life without my little tadpole," she whispered. "I go to meet him where he frolics with the gods. You must not be stricken. You must not grieve at my pyre. I've made arrangements to protect you."

The boy began to cry great fat tears. He buried his head in her bosom.

Marcilla held him close and was reminded of her own child, doomed from infancy to ridicule. He had not had time for poetry or for dreams. He had been a pawn cruelly swept aside by the black queen.

"Who do you love, Claudius?" Her strength waned, and it was difficult to swallow.

"Germanicus, my brother. And you, Marcilla."

"Then love while you can before death ever calls for your good brother."

"I will run grandmother through with my sword!"

"No, no, little one. She will meet her destiny one day. You must write of her and tell the truth. Put it in a history so all the world will know her for what she is."

"I pra-pra-promise."

Marcilla felt her fingers go numb and then her arms. She took one last deep breath, and then she turned her head to the wall.

She had done all that she could do for Rome and for Galian. Now she was ready to leave the one and meet the other with nothing but a sigh between them.

Mrs. Talucci's Dinner

by Mark Richard Zubro

Paul Turner, Chicago police detective, took a deep breath of warm early May air, opened the door to his house, and strode in. He heard his sons, Jeff and Brian, squabbling in the kitchen about how to behave at tonight's dinner. They were expected next door at Rose Talucci's at her special invitation.

Mrs. Talucci's grandson, Angelo, and his best friends on his major league baseball team were coming to dinner at six. Mrs. Talucci had insisted that Paul and his boys get to come to dinner and meet some of the baseball stars. She knew how much Paul's boys loved sports and how they'd enjoy sitting down with real players at a meal.

Brian at sixteen pretended calm sophistication at meeting some of the heroes of baseball, but the eleven-year-old Jeff burbled happily and incessantly.

"Can I get their autographs, Dad?" he asked for the fourth time as he swung into his wheelchair for the trip next door. Jeff had spina bifida, a birth defect, and both Paul's house and Mrs. Talucci's had been made wheelchair accessible. Jeff had adjusted to the defect amazingly well even playing on a basketball team with other kids so affected and working out, as best he could, with a set of weights. The only time he'd gotten in a fight was last fall when one of the kids at school had called him a cripple. Before the offender could sprint away, Jeff caught him and began pummeling him.

Paul had been called to school, and he'd lectured Jeff about fighting, but he also let his son know there was a sense of all right about defending himself.

Mrs. Talucci often cared for Jeff especially because of the uncertain hours Paul worked. He was assigned to Area Ten, the highest crime rate section of the city.

The aromas of garlic, basil, oregano, and fresh-baked bread enveloped them as Paul watched Jeff maneuver his wheelchair through Mrs. Talucci's front door.

The players hadn't arrived from the game. Paul made his way to the kitchen to assist Mrs. Talucci in any last-minute preparations.

As Paul eased open the swinging door to the kitchen, he saw kettles steaming on every one of the burners on the stove, and through the glass in the oven, he could see two bubbling casseroles. He knew that in a stove in the basement other delectables roasted, steamed, or baked.

Mrs. Talucci stood next to the sink. The knife she was using thunked into a zucchini. Her chopping actions were abrupt and jerky, unlike her usual calm serenity when she created a meal. Normally Mrs. Talucci cooked with a sureness and tranquility that came from over seven decades of feeding substantial quantities of excellent food to hordes of assembled relatives and friends.

Paul knew Mrs. Talucci had been scheduled to attend a baseball game that afternoon to watch her grandson Angelo pitch. He had also gotten her a pass for the field before the game and a special box seat. This was Angelo's idea of a gift for his grandmother on Mother's Day.

Paul joined Mrs. Talucci at the sink. While they exchanged greetings, he picked up a knife, grabbed a cucumber, and started peeling. Paul asked, "How was the game?"

"Terrible," Mrs. Talucci said. "They're supposed to be grown men, but they wound up brawling like five-year-olds. They should have been embarrassed."

The internal bickering and tension on Angelo's team had made headlines more than once since the beginning of training camp. They had been expected to win their division, but they had lost more games than they'd won all spring training and had been in last place since the first day of the season.

"What happened?" Paul asked.

"On the field before the game, the manager Harvey Newton and one of Angelo's friends began shouting at each other. I was five feet from them. The words they used were disgraceful. Pay them millions of dollars, and they talk like that?"

She shook her head, then continued her story. "In seconds they were throwing punches, rolling on the ground. They knocked into me. One of the players caught me at the last second, or I could have been hurt."

"Are you all right?" Paul asked.

"Nothing broken or damaged, except my pride."

"Any of the players get injured?" Paul asked.

"Two of the players who tried to separate them had to go into the clubhouse," she said. "One held his arm funny, and the other had a lot of blood by a cut on his eye."

"How about the two men in the fight?"

"Men! Ha! Boys is more like it. They stared at each other like angry beasts in a forest." She grabbed another vegetable to peel. "I don't know much about sports teams," she said, "but I think Angelo's team is in big trouble. The players hate their manager."

"That's in all the sports pages," Paul said.

"I don't read the sports," Mrs. Talucci said, "and I

don't mean just the ones in the fight. They all do. Something terrible is going to happen."

Paul reached for another cucumber. He didn't contradict what she said. He'd learned to respect Mrs. Talucci's insights over the years. Her shrewd brown eyes saw everything.

They peeled vegetables in silence for a moment, then Mrs. Talucci said, "What was worse was the way the office people treated me. As if I was an old lady, too feeble to take care of myself."

"They probably thought they were being helpful," Paul said reasonably.

"That I can forgive," she said. "What I cannot forgive is rudeness."

With little encouragement she gave him the details.

"The snotty young woman, Rita Wilford, who met me in the reception area didn't introduce herself. She just started telling me rules. Where I could go. Who I could talk to. She didn't even say hello."

Paul knew that the basics on courtesy were vital to Mrs. Talucci. He agreed with her.

"Then the security man. He nearly shoved me through doors. He couldn't get rid of me quick enough."

"Where was Angelo?" Paul asked.

"Who knew?" she responded. "I asked the young woman to tell him I was there. I don't think she ever did."

Paul didn't ask why none of her other relatives had gone with Mrs. Talucci, to watch out for her or smooth her way. At ninety-two years she still insisted on doing things herself, staying as independent as possible and not relying on friends or relatives to chauffeur her around.

In the last five years, Mrs. Talucci had slowed down some. She rarely cooked the holiday dinners for the family anymore and on occasions such as today, ac-

cepted help. Brian had spent several hours after school
Thursday and Friday helping with scrubbing and
cleaning. He also toted the turkey and other dishes
up and down stairs so Mrs. Talucci could set them to
cooking in the stove in the basement.

She ruled her extended family of four generations
with an iron will. Because of all the internal family
bickering about which sets of relatives various generations of the family would spend Mother's Day with,
Mrs. Talucci had decreed that this year their family
would celebrate on Saturday. Hordes of in-laws would
be pacified, and Angelo would get a long promised
"real" Italian feast for his friends.

"When did Angelo show up?" Paul asked.

"Half an hour later with his teammates. They had
a meeting he couldn't get out of. He wanted me to
meet his friends. I was a joke to them, and Angelo
was embarrassed. I could tell. I love Angelo," she said.
"I'm proud of his success. I've promised this dinner
for him for a long time, but it is a strange world he
lives in. Not what I'd choose for my grandson. Supposedly he's rich. Gave his parents a new house. Tried to
get me to move. Wanted to give me a new condomin-
ium in the suburbs."

Paul knew Mrs. Talucci would never leave the Tay-
lor Street neighborhood. She'd grown up in Chicago
and would never leave.

"I came home after I saw Angelo pitch one inning,"
she said. "He gave up two home runs." She shook
her head.

Minutes later the members of the team arrived. Paul
met Danny Helton, Michael Schneider, Cyril Meeks,
Kurt Horstman, and Enrico Lopez. Danny had won
eighteen games last year and was the one who saved
Mrs. Talucci when she almost fell. He wore honey-
colored jeans and a pure white short sleeve flannel
shirt. Michael and Cyril were the third baseman and

catcher, and Kurt and Enrico were starting outfielders. Michael wore gold leather jeans, a navy blazer, and white T-shirt. Cyril had a large bandage over a puffy left eye. He wore a flax-colored blazer over a plaid shirt and chocolate-colored, generously cut, linen trousers. Kurt, who had fought with the manager, wore a loose linen trench over a boxy vest, linen shirt, pleated tie, and pleated knee-length shorts. Enrico wore a striped Trader Bay rugby shirt and black Levi's. His left arm was in a sling from the fight, but he assured everyone that it was only a strained shoulder muscle.

Angelo in gray suit and black tie fluttered around his buddies, constantly emphasizing the fabulous meal they were about to have, almost to the point of confirming his grandmother's observation that he was embarrassed.

Paul knew Angelo from the neighborhood. He remembered him as a kid being tremendously egotistical. The attention from the major league teams early in his teens had sent his self-concept into orbit. He tended to return to the neighborhood and lord it over those less gifted.

Their talk before dinner was filled with the details of the fight that afternoon. When the game was over, the team had been besieged by the press until all the reporters had been tossed out of the locker room.

Paul only caught snatches of their conversation because he spent a great deal of time in the kitchen helping Mrs. Talucci with last-minute preparations. Finally in the dining room, he and Brian helped Mrs. Talucci carry steaming platters to the assembled guests. The table laden with the openings of a feast, the meal began. Mrs. Talucci sat at one end and observed the players eating. She smiled. She took great pleasure when people obviously enjoyed her cooking.

The ballplayers chowed down enthusiastically on salad and pasta. Paul watched them with amusement.

They put away Mrs. Talucci's homemade bread, salad made with lettuce and other vegetables fresh from the garden, followed by bowls of *paste fagiole,* then pounds of a cold *rotini* salad, and two types of homemade ravioli. Then Mrs. Talucci, Paul, and Brian brought out the main course. A roast done rare, a golden turkey, Mrs. Talucci's homemade sausage in a special sauce, bowls of green beans and carrots with slabs of butter melting in the middle, and breaded zucchini that even Jeff, the fussiest eater, liked.

Danny Helton said, "Is there more after this?"

Angelo said, "I warned you guys."

"Only dessert is left," Jeff said.

From his first bite, Jeff had asked questions of his two neighbors Cyril Meeks and Enrico Lopez.

Jeff sat close enough for Paul to hear the questions, but his father didn't stop him from asking anything he liked. Paul figured if the players didn't want to answer, they were adult enough to handle an eleven-year-old.

Just after Mrs. Talucci finished dishing out the turkey, Jeff asked, "Why do you guys dislike Mr. Newton so much?"

"Haven't you been listening?" Enrico asked. "We haven't talked about anything else since we've been here."

"But I don't understand why you had a fight," Jeff said. "I've read everything about your team that I could. My dad even bought me some of the sports weeklies and news magazines, but nobody explains why, how it got started. When we fight at school, my teacher always asks who started it?"

"Hey you guys," Cyril said, "here's a kid who reads all about us. Probably the only one in the country. He wants to know why we don't like old Harvey."

"You shouldn't ask things like that, twerp." Brian as older brother felt compelled to intervene.

Danny Helton said, "Kid asked a question. There's

no reporters around. I'll answer." He took a bite of sausage, chewed a moment, then said, "I won eighteen games last year in spite of Harvey Newton. I could have won way more than twenty, but he always yanked me too fast in the games. He started the same thing this year. Our bull pen is average at best. Half the games I lost, I could have stayed in and won plenty more."

He pierced a piece of turkey from the platter in front of him and hoisted it to his plate. "All the other guys here," he said, "if they were honest, would have the same type of story."

With little coaxing the others told their stories.

Michael Schneider, the third baseman said, "He sent me down to the minors three seasons in a row without giving me a real chance."

"You were batting less than .150 each of those times," Kurt said.

"And this year I'm batting .321," Schneider said. "And I could have been all along, if he'd had patience. The only reason I stayed this time was because we got a new general manager."

Cyril Meeks said, "He's been platooning me for two years with a guy who barely has as much talent as I have in my little finger. I'm a free agent at the end of the season. If he'd played me, I'd be worth more on the open market."

Kurt Horstman said, "I've got nothing to say."

"Come on," Danny said, "we all know he thinks you're flirting with his wife."

"I'm not," Horstman said. "I went to dinner with her once. It was innocent. We were the only two in a bar in New York, and nobody was around, and it was time for dinner, so we went out. It's not my fault he married a woman twenty years younger than he is."

"How was she in the sack?" Angelo asked.

"Angelo!" Mrs. Talucci said.

The effect of that one word on Angelo was instantaneous. His light olive skin turned bright red. "I'm sorry, Grandma," he muttered.

His teammates looked amused at Angelo's chagrin, but they forbore to comment, Paul assumed in deference to Mrs. Talucci. They'd razz him about it later.

Enrico Lopez said, "He doesn't like me because I came from a poor Mexican family."

"What does he do that shows he doesn't like you?" Jeff asked.

"He slights me. He doesn't treat me with respect. I talk good English."

They spent most of the meal elaborating further on their problems. It was obvious to Paul that they had discussed these before with great relish. One odd thing he did notice about the ballplayers' conversations: While the fight was a major topic, and Jeff had asked only baseball questions, since the players had entered the house not a one of them had expressed the slightest interest in Mrs. Talucci, Paul or his work, or his sons. Not a word was spoken unconnected to baseball.

Plates began to look empty after second and third helpings, when they heard a loud knocking at the door. Paul motioned for Brian to answer it.

His son returned with a woman Paul had never met.

The players began greeting her, but she held up her hand for silence.

"Harvey is dead," she announced.

Stunned silence filled the room.

Finally Enrico Lopez asked, "What happened?"

"Danny told me earlier where you were eating," she said. "I drove over as soon as I could. The cops said they'd come here to question you, and we've got to have a story together. It's awful enough to have this murder, but I've talked with the team owners. They want to minimize this as much as possible."

Jeff and Brian helped Mrs. Turner called Area Ten headq mander repeated what Wilfo what little he knew, and said of the case would arrive as so the crime scene, and that Tur

"I'm a detective with the Chicago Police Department," Paul said. "I didn't catch your name."

She glared at him. "I'm Rita Wilford," she said.

Paul recognized the name as that of the person who had been rude to Mrs. Talucci that afternoon.

"I'll have to insist you leave," Wilford continued. "I have to talk to the players." She wore a pastel yellow suit with a long jacket with three brass buttons down the front and a flippy skirt.

Mrs. Talucci spoke from the other end of the table. "No one insists someone in my home leaves." Her voice was soft and unassuming, but no one could miss the underlying authority and control.

"You the old lady that was at the ballpark today? I guess I recognize you. I don't care who any of you are. I've got a right to talk to these guys, and I've got to do it now."

Mrs. Talucci rose and drew herself up to her full five-foot-two. Total silence enveloped the room. When Mrs. Talucci spoke, her gentle words dropped like crystals of arctic ice. All she said was, "I beg your pardon." She held Wilford's stare until the younger woman's face turned red. Rita dropped her eyes and looked away.

The detective said, "Ms. Wilford, no one is going anywhere until the police arrive. I need to check in with the station. After that, while we're waiting for them, why don't you tell us what happened, and why you needed to rush here?"

M.. Talucci clear the table.

group with cups of coffee supplied by Jeff, Brian, and Mrs. Talucci. A few players picked idly at their dishes of *tarami su*.

Jeff finished his dessert and wheeled himself to the entryway between the living and dining room. Brian pulled up a chair next to him. They sat quietly in the background. Mrs. Talucci returned to her place at the head of the table.

Turner wanted to see the reactions of the players to Wilford's story. Maybe one of them was the killer and something that was said might cause a slip. He announced officially that they would all have to stay.

"You mean we're stuck in this dump?" Mike Schneider asked.

"This isn't a dump," Angelo said.

"I don't care what you call it," Danny said, "you can't make us stay here."

"Headquarters said there was an excellent reason for doing exactly that," Turner said.

"What?" Kurt Horstman asked.

"One of you was the last to see Harvey Newton alive," Turner said.

This announcement provoked a general uproar.

When some semblance of order was restored, Horstman asked the obvious question, "Who claimed one of us was the last to see him alive?"

"I don't know," Turner said. "Maybe Ms. Wilford can fill us in on the details."

Wilford said, "I talked to Charlie P̶o̶r̶l̶

takes his whirlpool last thing, after the reporters leave, and most everybody is gone."

"Sometimes they make the bus wait over half an hour," Meeks said. "Just so the old man can take his leisurely time."

"Everybody knew this?" Turner asked.

"Yes," Wilford said. The men around the table nodded

"How do they know Charlie didn't do it?" Schneider asked.

"Charlie did his regular routine cleaning around the mess everybody made," Wilford said. "He said he saw all of you. Then he left the locker room for ten minutes to deliver the dirty clothes for the day so they could be washed and make it to New York, the next stop on the road trip. He found the body when he came back."

"Maybe someone came in while he was gone," Meeks said.

"There was a security guard on the door at all times," Wilford said.

"It was Lopez's fault we were so late," Horstman said. "He primps in front of a mirror for forty-five minutes. We all had to wait for him because we were coming here. Angelo insisted we all arrive together."

"Were you in each other's sight all the time?" Turner asked.

For half an hour they tried to reconstruct everyone's movements. The only sure conclusion they came to was that each of them had left the main area of the locker room at various times: some to go to the wash-room, or make calls, others to meet with reporters, or friends. All of them at some point had enough time to step into the training room unseen by anyone else. ... one there.

Back in the dining room, he found the assembled

"Everybody knows we all disliked him," Cyril said. "It could have been any one of us."

Turner watched them begin to eye each other suspiciously as they realized one of themselves could be a murderer.

"I still think Charlie could have done it," Lopez said.

"Or how come they don't think somebody from management or a reporter or anybody from outside just walked in and killed him?" Cyril asked.

"Security was tough after the game," Wilford said.

"How so?" Turner asked.

She said, "We had a security man at the door because of all the reporters. You guys were the only ones around after he shagged them out. Before you six left, he saw Harvey Newton alive. When he got rid of everybody, he stayed at the door to prevent reentry. After you six left, the only person who went in or out was Charlie. He claims the training room is always the last place he cleans."

Lopez said, "That's true. He told me all about how he always waits to do the training room last. I sat next to him once on a long plane trip cross-country. I thought he'd never shut up."

"Far as I know, him and Harvey never had the slightest problem," Cyril Meeks said. They all nodded in agreement.

"Charlie was nice to everybody," Horstman said, "but he sucked up to Harvey. Always did everything the manager said right away."

"Guy was a saint," Angelo said.

But as much as they liked him, and thought he was a good guy, after another half an hour they'd come up with him as the murder suspect. A lull followed the realization that they'd come to this conclusion.

Then Angelo snapped his fingers. "Why couldn't the security guard have done it?" he asked.

"He claims someone was always in the corridor talking to him," Wilford said. "When I left, they were asking his buddies if this was true. They backed him up."

"Why did you hurry here to have them get their stories straight?" Paul asked Wilford.

"I'm the publicity person for the team," Wilford said. "It's my job to minimize bad press. I knew this was horrible. I came here after I heard these were the last ones to see him alive."

Silence fell, and Turner let it develop and linger. He wanted them uncomfortable and off-kilter. If one of them was the murderer, he might make a slip.

Finally Horstman said, "Why can't we go? I mean we all like Charlie, but if he's a killer, there's no reason to keep us."

"You'll have to stay until the detectives get here," Turner said.

"I'm going to call my agent," Helton said, "and my lawyer. They can't do this to us."

Schneider pointed at Turner, "He can't do this. He's bluffing. We make more money in one week than he does in a year. He's just trying to show how tough he is."

Turner stood up. "Leaving would be a poor decision at this point," he said. "I realize this is an inconvenience, but if you are gone when the detectives on the case get here, they will simply go find you, or more likely, have some uniformed cops hunt you up and bring you to the station. Everybody gets inconvenienced, and maybe it will look suspicious to them if one of you tries to leave."

They grumbled but remained compliant. Paul knew it could be hours before the detectives arrived. With a high-profile murder, half the police brass in the city would be sticking their noses into the investigation, keeping annoyed detectives from their real work of squeezing the crime scene for any shred of evidence.

He left the players scattered around the dining and living rooms. He entered the kitchen. Brian, Mrs. Talucci, and Paul started in on washing the mound of dirty dishes. Paul wasn't worried about the players concocting a story together. He doubted they were all in on a conspiracy to murder the manager, although it was possible. If they were, they'd set up their story long before this. He did think it was curious that none of the players had expressed sorrow at the manager's death. The hatred expressed in their stories earlier must run very deep.

The three of them scrubbed, washed, dried, and put away. While working they traded theories on which one could be a killer, but none of the three could come up with a likely suspect.

Forty-five minutes later, Jeff and his wheelchair plowed their way into the kitchen. Paul began a reprimand, but Jeff burst out, "I know who killed Harvey Newton."

"Ha," Brian said. "You're just a kid. How would you know?"

"Don't come bursting through the door like that," his father said.

"Dad, I know who did it. You taught me."

Paul put down the kettle he was drying, and the towel he was using, and walked to his son.

Brian said, "You can't just look at them and tell who did it. You've got to have clues and everything. Don't be a little kid. Let the cops handle it."

"I know who did it," Jeff insisted.

"How do you know?" Paul placed a hand on his younger son's shoulder.

"Brian thinks he's so smart, let him go in there and figure it out." Usually the boys got along fairly well, but their spats could become drawn-

tions. The younger brother desperate to have his intelligence recognized even though his body couldn't match the feats of his athletic brother. Despite all Paul's coaxing, Jeff wouldn't tell what he thought he knew. The boy insisted his older brother go into the living room, come back with an answer, and then they would compare. "We'll see who's right," Jeff said.

"That's stupid," Brian said.

But Jeff got stubborn and to avoid a full crisis among the boys, Paul insisted that Brian go see for himself.

Brian did his best teenage mutter under his breath and marched to the door of the living room and slapped it open. The sound of soft jazz music from the CD player filled the kitchen for a moment.

Ten seconds later, Brian burst back into the kitchen. "I know who did it," he gasped.

"Does one of them have a big sign on his forehead?" Paul asked, "or is the killer foaming at the mouth?"

"Just go look, Dad," Brian said. "You'll see."

Mrs. Talucci returned with the three of them to the living room.

Helton leaned against the wall near the front door in earnest conversation with Wilford.

Lopez paced the floor.

Horstman and Schneider argued in low voices about who they had seen and when in the locker room.

Angelo sat on an ottoman and wrung his hands. Paul heard him muttering to himself. He caught snatches of, "They're going to accuse me. This is awful. I'm going to be blamed."

Cyril Meeks sat in the cloth lounge chair fast asleep.

Paul heard Mrs. Talucci sigh. He looked down at her. Their eyes met. They too knew who had committed the murder.

"It's Cyril Meeks isn't it, Dad?" Jeff whispered.

Turner looked at the sleeping man. The tension from the other players was palpable.

In one of the training courses for detectives an old dragon of a cop had come to talk to them. A lot of the prospective detectives laughed at the old guy behind his back, and a few asked sneering questions, but Paul had found the sergeant's stories fascinating. One of the most startling bits of information he remembered was the man's tale about putting a group of suspects together in a room.

The cop had said, "You put them together, and you can always tell who did it. You leave them alone for a good solid length of time. When you come back, it's the one who's asleep who's the killer, because all the others are going nuts being under suspicion. They don't know what happened. The killer does and so isn't under the same kind of tension."

The old cop had claimed this method, when usable, had never failed him. Paul had long ago told this story to his sons and Mrs. Talucci. In his eight years of being a detective, he'd never had an occasion for this to happen. Now it had, and he wasn't certain what to do with the knowledge. An old cop's stories, no matter how true, weren't evidence.

Before Paul could stop him, Jeff wheeled over to Meeks's chair. He poked the ballplayer. Meeks opened one eye.

"How come you killed him?" Jeff asked.

Meeks came wide-awake. Everyone stared at the youngster looking with sad brown eyes at a baseball hero.

"What's with the kid?" Meeks asked.

Through the living room window, Paul saw an unmarked police car pull up. He met them at the front door. He briefed them on what had happened so far and asked for their cooperation in dealing with Meeks.

When he brought the detectives into the living

room, Meeks was saying, "Why are you all looking at me? You're all just as likely suspects as me."

A couple players asked what was going on, but none of the detectives answered. Paul glared at Jeff before the youngster could speak. Nobody broke the silence for what seemed like five minutes. Jeff looked like he was ready to burst.

Finally Meeks himself broke the silence. "Look," he said. "You can all stare at me all night in silence. That's not going to make me a murderer. Maybe nobody killed him. It could have been an accident. Maybe he slipped and hit his head."

"Someone belted him in the head with a blunt instrument," one of the detectives said. "Newton was alive but unconscious when he went into the whirlpool. We got a preliminary finding from the medical examiner. We could see the wound ourselves. Nobody here knew about him being hit except the killer."

"I said it as a 'maybe,' " Meeks said. "I didn't say I knew that's what happened. It could have happened. That's all I meant."

"Let's reconstruct your movements, Mr. Meeks," Turner said. "We've got all your buddies here. Let's try and figure it out."

Meeks licked his lips and stared at the group. Most of the baseball players looked away. The cops stared with bland expressions. Mrs. Talucci and Brian frowned. Jeff poked at Meeks again and said, "You're supposed to be a hero, but you're a bad man. I know you killed him."

"Get this kid out of here," Meeks said. "I can't stand little kids anyway. Who cares what a crippled kid thinks?"

Jeff launched himself at the adult, coming half out of his wheelchair. His fists pummeled at the man almost twice as big as him.

Paul and Brian dragged Jeff away from Meeks. The

eleven-year-old swore and cried. His son used language Paul didn't know he knew.

Meeks leapt to his feet. He seemed about ready to advance on Turner and his family. Two players grabbed him on either side. He shook them off.

Mrs. Talucci drew up to the standing Meeks. Paul left a slightly calmer Jeff in Brian's hands. The two detectives glanced at Turner. They were still following his lead.

"You are an evil man," Mrs. Talucci said. "Making a cruel comment about a child, and you're a murderer."

Meeks snapped. He began to bellow and raised his hand to strike Mrs. Talucci. Everybody surged toward him. Mrs. Talucci stood rock still. Angelo and Paul got there first. They held Meeks back, but red-faced and spit flying from his mouth, he continued to rant. Mrs. Talucci still hadn't moved.

"Yes, I killed him, you old bat!" Meeks shouted. "I'd take a swing at all of you, so proud of how nice you've got it! Old Cyril has to take everybody's leavings! Newton couldn't manage to let me have the career I deserved or make the money I wanted. He's sorry, and you will be, too!"

It took several hours before the police sorted everything out. They took statements from everyone in the house. Paul had insisted Brian and Jeff be talked to early and then sent home. He spent tedious time with the police brass that filtered into Mrs. Talucci's house. Eventually a minicam from one of the television stations and a few reporters started clustering around the front yard.

Paul learned details from Horstman about Cyril Meeks's dislike for the manager. Horstman finished, "He wasn't all that much different from the rest of us. He just had too much and then snapped."

Paul knew this described the vast majority of those who committed murders.

Finally the detectives led Meeks away. The other baseball people left. Paul stayed behind. He found Mrs. Talucci sipping a cup of tea in the kitchen. She seemed to have been the calmest of them all throughout the evening. She told him she was fine.

At home Paul found his sons in the kitchen talking quietly over bowls of ice cream.

"How can you guys eat after a meal like that?" Paul asked.

"That was hours ago," Brian said. "We were hungry."

Paul didn't bother to marvel at the eating capacity of his eldest son.

"We did it, didn't we, Dad?" Jeff asked.

Paul hugged his younger son. "Are you okay?" he asked.

Jeff assured him he was fine. Paul decided to save his paternal warnings about temper and fighting until tomorrow.

A Matter of the Heart

by Bill Crider

The telephone woke me from a pretty good dream, one in which my knee had never been damaged and in which I was just being handed the football by the head lineman after going over a thousand yards for the third straight year as a Dallas Cowboy. I was reaching for the ball as the cheers of the sell-out crowd turned into the shrilling of the phone.

I turned on a light and looked at the black plastic Casio on my left wrist. Then I picked up the phone. "It's four fifty-six," I said into the mouthpiece.

"I didn't call for a time check," Dino said. "I got a job for you."

"Somebody wants a house painted at four fifty-six in the morning?"

"It's not that kinda job. Are you gonna come over here or not?"

I wanted to say no and get back to the dream, but Dino was an old friend, if friend was the right word for the guy who'd ruined my knee when we were in college and nearly gotten me killed a few months back when his daughter was kidnapped. But it was his house I was living in.

"Right now?" I asked.

"What, you think I meant next week? Of course, right now."

"I have to get dressed."

"Fine. Get dressed. Then get your butt over here."

He hung up. Sometimes I think he takes me for granted.

I rolled out of the bed and looked around for my jeans and short-sleeved sweatshirt. They were lying on a chair with the book I'd been reading the night before—Fitzgerald's *The Beautiful and Damned*. I was trying to improve my mind.

After I dressed, I opened the back door to look for Nameless. I didn't have to look far. He came charging through the opening, skidded to a stop by his food bowl, and looked back over his shoulder at me.

I ripped open a pack of Tender Vittles and dumped it into the bowl. "Sorry I'm so slow," I told him. He didn't answer. He just started eating.

I had to wait for him to finish because I knew he'd want to go back outside as soon as he was done. Dino would just have to wait, too, but nowhere on Galveston Island is very far from anywhere else. I'd be at Dino's soon enough.

"I don't see how you can drink that stuff, much less at this hour of the morning," Dino said.

I tipped up the Big Red and took the final swallow. "It's not so bad when you get used to it," I said when I lowered the bottle.

He shook his head. "Liquid bubble gum."

I set the empty bottle on his coffee table. "You didn't ask me over here to talk about my drinking habits. What about that job you mentioned?"

"It's not house painting."

"You said that."

"And it's not alligators."

I'd looked into the matter of a dead alligator for an old friend not too long ago. "How about kidnapping?"

"It's not that, either."

"Well," I said, leaning back in the chair, "now we know what it's not. So what is it?"

"I think it's a murder."

"Oh, boy," I said. "You got another Big Red?"

I'd come back to Galveston after a few years as a private detective. My sister had disappeared, and I was going to find her. I supported myself by painting houses, but Dino involved me in looking for his daughter, who had been born of one of the prostitutes who worked for Dino's uncles back in the days when the island was as wide-open as it was possible to be in Texas. The woman's name was Evelyn; she had long since given up her trade, but she and Dino had never lived together, though the kidnapping had brought them closer.

I took a drink of the fresh Big Red. "Who do you think's been murdered?"

"A woman named Sue Traylor."

The name didn't mean anything to me, and I said so.

"She worked for my uncles."

"Same job as Evelyn?"

"Right. She got out of the business just as Evelyn was getting started, but she was Evelyn's what-do-you-call-it?" He looked at me. "One of the big buzzwords these days."

"Mentor?" I asked. Considering the profession we were talking about, it didn't seem like exactly the right word.

"Mentor, yeah. Anyway, a few months after Evelyn got started, Sue moved to some little town up close to Dallas. Corsicana. Got a job, married a lawyer. He'd been married once before and had a kid. The lawyer died a couple of years ago, but she and the son lived happily ever after, until yesterday."

"She got murdered in Corsicana? I'm not going to Corsicana."

"She didn't get murdered there. She got murdered here."

"Oh," I said. "Maybe you better tell me about it."

It seemed that Sue Traylor had been wanting to come back to Galveston for a nostalgic visit for a number of years. The lawyer and the son thought she'd grown up there, but they didn't know anything about her profession. She talked all the time about missing the Gulf breezes and the sound of the waves, so the son had bought her a ticket on the train as a Mother's Day present. She'd arrived in Houston on the Amtrak and then taken the excursion train to Galveston. She checked into the Galvez Hotel, one of the oldest and best on the island.

"She and Evelyn had been in touch for years, like they were sorority sisters or something," Dino told me. "Maybe she'd been in touch with some other people, too. Anyway, they arranged to meet for lunch, and they had a fine time talking over old times. They went back to the room and talked a little longer, and that was that. Evelyn went home. The maid found Sue the next morning, dead in the bed."

"How did she die?"

"It looked like natural causes at first," Dino said. "Heart attack."

That explained why I hadn't read anything about it in the newspaper. It wouldn't have been exactly front-page news; it wouldn't have been in the paper at all if the hotel could keep it out. People aren't fond of renting rooms that other people have recently died in.

"But it wasn't a heart attack," I said.

"Right. Turns out she was poisoned."

All that was interesting, but I didn't see what it had to do with Dino.

"Did you know her?" I asked. "Back when she was working for the uncles, I mean."

"I saw her around, yeah. I don't remember her very well. I was pretty young then. And I wasn't one of the people she stayed in touch with, if that's what you're asking."

"So why are you so interested? And what's the job you've got for me?"

"I want you to find out who killed her."

"Why?"

"Because the cops think it might've been Evelyn."

I suppose it was only natural. Evelyn had been seen in the hotel dining room with Sue Traylor at lunch. She'd gone back to the room with her and talked. As far as anyone could determine, no one else had been to the room since that time, and Sue Traylor hadn't left it. Therefore Evelyn must have been the killer. She hadn't been arrested yet, but Dino was sure it was just a matter of time.

"That's why I called you," he said. "They're starting to get rough with her. They picked her up about midnight and took her down to the station. Questioned her for a few hours, then took her home. You know the drill."

"And she called you when she got home."

"Right. And then I called you. What do you think?"

"I think I'd better talk to Evelyn and then find out who else went to that room," I said.

I went by McDonald's and ate an Egg McMuffin before driving by Evelyn's. She lived on a street named for a fish, like all the streets in the neighborhood, and she wasn't happy with the way she'd been treated.

"I'm a respectable citizen," she said. "They didn't have any right to get me out of bed like that."

"Who were they?"

"One of them was Gerald Barnes. The other was—"

"Never mind. I know Barnes. He might talk to me."

"Good. I didn't like him much."

"He doesn't like me, either, but that doesn't mean he won't talk to me."

"I hope he will," she said.

She was wearing a purple robe and drinking coffee. She was also smoking a cigarette, though I'd thought she was trying to quit. I didn't blame her. She probably needed something to calm her down.

"Tell me what happened when you met Sue Traylor," I said.

We were sitting at her kitchen table. I didn't drink coffee, and she didn't keep Big Red in the refrigerator for me like Dino did, so I just leaned back in the chair and laced my fingers behind my neck.

She took a puff of the cigarette. "There's not much to tell. I visited with Sue, we talked about how our lives had been since the old days, and I left."

"Did she seem unhappy? Depressed? Was she satisfied with the way her life had worked out?"

"She seemed perfectly happy to me. I don't think she killed herself, if that's what you're getting at. Besides, there was no note." She paused. "At least that's what the police said."

"What about her husband? Didn't Dino say he'd died recently?"

She shook her head. "Not recently. Five years ago. She's gotten over that, and he left her very well off, financially. He was a lawyer, but his family had oil money. She was probably a millionaire."

"What about her son?"

Evelyn gave me a look. "What do you mean by that?"

She thought I was making a crack about her and Dino's daughter, who'd had a pretty tough time when she found out that her mother had once been a whore.

But that wasn't what I had in mind. "I mean, do

they get along? How about the father's money? Did the son get any?"

"They get along fine. She told me that she was always talking about coming down here again, but she just never had the nerve to do it. He's the one who had the idea of buying her a ticket for Mother's Day. That was just the little push she needed, and she really loved seeing the island again." Evelyn crushed out her cigarette in the saucer that held her coffee cup. "But it didn't work out very well in the end, did it?"

"No," I said. She hadn't answered my question about the inheritance, but I let that go. I'd find out later. "So why did you get the blame for what happened?"

"As far as I know, there was no one else Sue was going to get in touch with here. She mentioned that I was the only one she was interested in seeing; she hardly remembered Dino. She was just going to spend some time alone relaxing in the hotel. And when she got tired of that, she was going to walk across the street to the beach, and sit and look at the waves. Alone."

"You told the cops that?"

She laughed. "Stupid of me, wasn't it? And no one else seems to have gone to her room. The glasses we drank out of were still on the table when the maid found her."

"What about a lawyer?"

"I haven't been arrested yet. I don't think I will be. For one thing, I didn't kill her."

"I know that," I said. "But that doesn't mean a thing."

"I didn't have a motive," she said, reaching into the pocket of her robe for another cigarette. "And there's certainly no evidence against me."

"That's another point in your favor. The question is, who did have a motive?"

She lit the cigarette with a Bic lighter and blew out a plume of smoke. "That's what you're supposed to find out."

I stood up. "I'll try," I said.

Gerald Barnes had thinning hair and wore glasses. He looked more like a math teacher than a cop. All he needed was a plastic pocket protector.

"What do you want, Smith?" he asked when I walked up to his desk.

"I just wanted to ask a few questions about Sue Traylor."

He picked up a chewed yellow pencil from the top of the desk and pointed it at me. "You've been talking to Dino."

"Let's just say that I'm curious."

He dropped the pencil. "So am I."

"Maybe I can answer a question or two for you, then," I said. "If you'll answer a few for me."

Barnes looked at me over the tops of his glasses, as if he were trying to decide whether I was worth the trouble. After a few seconds, he pointed to the straight-backed wooden chair beside his desk.

"Have a seat," he said.

I sat down and leaned back. "You first."

He thought about what he wanted to know. "What's Dino's interest in this?" he asked finally.

"He's interested in seeing that a friend of his is treated right. She didn't have anything to do with Sue Traylor's death, and Dino doesn't want her arrested."

"He probably doesn't have anything to worry about on that point," Barnes said. "But what about himself? Was it possible that he was worried about something that the Traylor woman might have told us?"

So that was what Barnes thought. I laughed quietly. "Everybody on the island knows all there is to know

about Dino and his uncles. He doesn't have anything
to hide."

Barnes nodded. "Yeah. That's what I thought."

"Then why the hassle with Dino's friend? What
have you got, anyway?"

"Not much." He ran a hand through his thinning
hair. "All we know is that Sue Traylor didn't have a
heart attack."

"How do you know that?"

"The autopsy. She was poisoned, all right."

"With what?"

"Hard to say exactly. But it was some kind of heart
medicine, one of the glycosides. Digoxin, maybe."

I didn't know much about heart medicines, but
Barnes explained that glycosides strengthened heart
contractions.

"And if you don't have a weak heart to begin with,
you can be in trouble," he said.

"I take it Sue Traylor didn't have a weak heart."

"She had heart disease, but it was the wrong kind
to take digoxin for. She had high blood pressure. So
the digoxin—or whatever it was—was fatal."

"And Dino's friend was the only person to go into
the room."

"As far as we know. The door wasn't bolted on the
inside, though, so someone else could have been in
there. We didn't find any fingerprints."

"What about the glasses that she and Evelyn used?
Was there any evidence of digoxin in them?"

"None," Barnes said.

"And you checked the rest of the room?"

Barnes looked at me over the tops of his glasses
again. "You're kidding me, right?"

"Maybe," I said. "What did you find?"

"I don't really like you very much, Smith. You
know that?"

I nodded.

"But I'm going to tell you anyway, because this has got me puzzled. There was no sign of any digoxin in that room. There was a suitcase, but all it had in it were the normal things a woman would bring on a trip to Galveston. Beach clothes and a bathing suit, but that's all. In the bathroom she had the usual stuff, toothpaste, makeup, her blood pressure medicine. But that's all."

"You've had the blood pressure medicine analyzed?"

"You really think we're idiots, right? But you don't want to hurt my feelings by telling me so." He picked up the pencil and rolled it between his fingers. "Of course we had it analyzed. Every single capsule. It's Procardia. Standard medication for high blood pressure."

"What was the date on the bottle?"

"It was two days ago. She must've picked it up just before she came down here."

I stood up. "Well, it looks like you've covered the ground pretty thoroughly. I guess you checked out the maid."

He sighed. "We checked out the maid. She's been in the country two years, barely speaks English, and didn't have any idea who the dead woman was. It wasn't the maid."

"All right," I said. "You don't have to get defensive. I was just asking. What about the other hotel personnel? The desk clerk, the—"

"The desk clerk's not more than thirty. He probably doesn't even remember the old days. Hardly anybody there in the hotel remembers."

"Well, at least you checked."

"Right. You can find your way out, can't you."

I could, and I started toward the exit.

"Don't forget to give us a call when you get it figured out, Sherlock."

"Don't worry," I said.

*   *   *

Thanks to the uncles, Dino still had some influential contacts in a lot of places, even a small town like Corsicana. I drove by his house and asked him to make a few calls. I sat in his living room and drank a Big Red while I waited for him to get the answers to some of the questions that were bothering me. The phone rang a couple of times as he got replies to his calls, but I didn't bother to get up and try to listen in.

"The son didn't inherit," he said when he came back into the room. "Not much, anyway. Seems like he wasn't his father's favorite person. He was always getting into scrapes with the cops, nothing big, but enough to be aggravating. Went to college, but never graduated. Has quite a way with the women, and he's been in a few scrapes because of that, too. Never held onto a job more than a week or so at a time. Maybe he was sucking up to Sue by giving her the trip and treating her to a Mother's Day present. Anyway, he just got ten thousand a year; not a whole lot. Not enough to live on, even in Corsicana."

"Gives him a motive if he was named in Sue Traylor's will," I said.

"That's something else I found out. He's in the will. Sue didn't have any other relatives. Her parents died about the time she came here to work for my uncles. But anyway, according to a guy I talked to, the pharmacist says that Sue's the one who picked up the medicine on her way to the station. So it was just Procardia, like Barnes told you. Nobody else touched the bottle."

"So much for that idea, then. There has to be another answer. Someone who knew her from the old days, who didn't want the past to come out."

"Maybe," Dino said. "But who?"

"That's what I'm supposed to find out," I said.

*   *   *

But I didn't. I talked to the maid, I talked to the desk clerk, I talked to the house detective, I talked to the waiters, I talked to Evelyn. None of them came up with a thing to help me.

By then nearly a week had gone by, and Dino wasn't very worried about it anymore.

"They haven't been bothering Evelyn," he said when I stopped by his house. "You must've put a scare into 'em."

"Sure I did. Cops are scared to death of me. You know that."

"Okay, so maybe I was exaggerating. But they've dropped it."

They hadn't, of course. Barnes wasn't the type to let something like murder drop that easily. But if Dino wanted to think so, it was all right with me.

"You want me to forget about it then?" I asked.

"Hell, no. I'd like to know who did it. Wouldn't you?"

"I guess so," I told him, though I wasn't really sure I cared.

Another week went by, a week in which I didn't find out any more than I already knew, mainly because I didn't really try. I talked to Evelyn again, and as far as I could discover, Sue Traylor didn't have any deep dark secrets to reveal. There was simply no reason anyone would want to kill her.

The house-painting business wasn't booming, so I sat around the house and finished reading *The Beautiful and Damned* and started on *The Great Gatsby*. Then one day while I was sitting in a lawn chair out front, enjoying the Gulf breeze and thinking about the difference between life in East Egg and in West Egg, Barnes drove up and parked on the oyster-shell driveway.

"Well, Sherlock," he said as he got out of the car, "have you got any answers for me?"

I pulled my book mark out of the back pages and stuck it in to mark my place. Laying the book down by the chair, I said, "Not yet. Do you have any for me?"

Barnes leaned back against his car. "Not really. I did a little searching into Sue Traylor's history. I heard that she had a thing going with one of Dino's uncles for a while. Did you know about that?"

"Dino didn't mention it. I imagine a lot of the girls had a thing going with one or another of the uncles from time to time."

"You don't suppose that Sue Traylor could've taken digoxin instead of Procardia by mistake, do you?"

Barnes walked away from the car over to where I was sitting. I was in the shade of the house, and he must've been getting pretty warm leaning on the car in the sun.

"There's no way she could've made that mistake. Digoxin comes in very small pills. Procardia comes in very large capsules. I'm just glad I don't have to swallow one."

And that's when it came to me. Maybe Barnes's calling me Sherlock had something to do with it. Anyway, we'd eliminated every other possible answer, so the one I'd just thought of had to be the right one.

"What was the pharmacist's name?" I asked. "The one who filled the prescription for the Procardia."

"The pharmacist's name? What difference does that make?"

I told him.

Barnes was back the next day. I had finished *Gatsby,* but I wasn't ready to start another book. I was thumbing through an old issue of *Texas Monthly.*

"You were right," Barnes said, walking over to my chair. "I don't know why we didn't think of it before."

"You don't think of pharmacists as murderers," I said. "That's why."

"Her name was Yeager, by the way. Jane Yeager. And she wasn't much of a murderer. She broke down and confessed before they'd questioned her fifteen minutes."

"How'd he get to her?"

"Just like you thought. Told her he loved her but that he couldn't marry her until the old girl was dead. He worked on her for months. He'd really put the pressure on lately. Told her they could travel around the world and live in the South Pacific on coconuts and pineapple."

"And she believed that?"

"Looks that way."

"Well, Dino said he was supposed to be pretty handy with the women." Nameless came out of the foliage and looked at Barnes. He wasn't impressed. He twitched his tail and went back to lie in the shade. "How'd she do it?"

"Crushed the digoxin tablets and put them in one of the Procardia capsules. It held more than enough to do the job."

"And just one capsule, of course," I said. "It didn't really matter when she took it, I guess, but it worked better that she took it here."

"Not really," Barnes said. "I don't think there would've been an autopsy if she'd died at home. It was just bad luck that she died in Galveston. Otherwise, he might've gotten away with it."

"Why did he get her to do it? The money? Couldn't he have just married Jane Yeager? I thought pharmacists pulled down pretty good salaries."

"They do, but not when you're thinking in terms of millions. He did it for the money, all right."

"Some Mother's Day present," I said.

"He wasn't really her son," Barnes said. "He was her husband's son."

"Does that make a difference?"

Barnes stood there silently, as if he might be thinking of the dead woman as a real person instead of just another bothersome corpse.

"Not to her," he said.

Empty Arms

by Mary Wings

Christopher Robin breaks the egg, an omelette for Babar! Soon, it will happen—soon! I will call him Christopher Robin. I know it's a boy. Don't ask me how. I just know these things. I am very good at planning. I plan everything in advance.

Oh, how my arms ache! Never mind. The crib must have adjustable rails, an adjustable mattress, to raise and lower, the easier to pick him up, put him down, keep him safe. Safe. Absolutely safe.

To hold him! To watch him grow! Those perfect little hands! I will wake up every morning—and probably several times during the night—and I will count his little fingers, his little toes, and make sure that there are ten. And I will never stop counting.

I'll have one of those low to the ground rockers, perfect for mothers. White, with a rush seat. Some kind of painted decoration—I haven't decided about that yet. Which childhood motif? Common memories of all those delightful characters. Beatrix Potter? Winnie-the-Pooh? Pooh! Everything will be white in this nursery. That's it. With a few attendant blue notes of course. But I want some toddler furniture. Something really beautiful and fun that we can look forward to when he's old enough.

My God, I'd better get his layette ready! I want everything in sixes. The tiny undershirts with the little satin bows, diaper covers, stretch sleepers. I'll have a little dresser, white wicker, the drawers sliding on smooth runners. I will fold the tiny items and put them in. Then I will take them out and fold them again and put them back. Glorious repetition! Horrible waiting! How empty my arms feel. I want the nursery to be perfect. It has to have a theme. Mary Poppins? That bitch? Pat the Bunny. Better.

The christening robe, the fabulous outfits for showing him off, if only to myself. Italian organdy! White lawn! All to be hung on miniature satin-padded hangers. I can do a bit of embroidery myself, handy with a needle, I am. The beginning of a mother's skill. My arms positively tingle in longing. Every piece shall have his initial, to show he's mine, mine alone. And with each stitch, a moment of my love before he comes. I'll do up a perfect pillow, velvet embroidered chenille studded with pearls, spelling out the arrival date, his name. All will be trimmed in frothy lace, fairy fine.

Knit, pearl, the tiny cuffs for those perfect little hands. Soft booties, soft for a baby's feet. Hard to cover up those tiny toes! Must be done! Every day! My arms ache so, as if he's here already, as if, as if I've been holding him for hours. For years. What will be that nursery motif?

Silver! Silver for my baby boy. Porringers, cups, even a silver rattle, with tiny little silver beads decorating the bells at either end. Silver knives and forks, baby bowls. Handles shaped like bunnies . . . bunnies! That's it! That's the theme park for Christopher Robin. I want bunnies and rabbits for my boy. They'll hop away with him into realms of fantasy.

What will he remember of this room when he's older? Will it be the smiling faces of rabbits, the curling initial, a stitch of a mother's love. Because, of course, that's all there will be. A mother's love. Bye-

bye baby bunting. **Daddy** hasn't gone hunting. He's left us in the lurch that bastard.

And soon the aching in my arms will stop.

Mrs. Harriet Fant, Salesperson,
Tot Trifles, East 97th Street, New York City
Sure I checked out her credit card limit, what do you think I am, stupid? I do that sort of thing with every purchase. But especially with these kind of custom orders. We're talking custom designs from Milan, you don't want to screw up or have any misunderstandings about anything that gets shipped over the ocean. Believe me.

She went for the most expensive Italian hand-painted designs. We have a whole catalog right here, look. Raggedy Ann chairs, hearts on her cheeks, a trademarked design, I want you to know. We have elephants, moon and star, (very popular with the baby boomers right now, sort of psychedelic) Puss N' Boots, but no, she didn't want any of that. Flipped through page after page, getting more and more frustrated. Couldn't find what she wanted. I thought she was going to tear the perforated holes in one of the plastic display sheets, in such a hurry, she was. These sample books aren't easy to get you know, all the way from Milan!

Irritating customer, I tell you, but just like every customer, always right. There she was flipping through the Mother Goose section, and she gets the idea. Rabbits! Bunnies. That's what's going to do it for this lady.

Okay, fine. She wanted the backs of the chairs painted like rabbits. Mr. Tollini, I'm telling you, he can do anything, I assured the lady. I showed her the Alice and Wonderland Tea Ensemble just in case she might have missed that page, but she would have none of it. I told her I would fax Mr. Tollini and have the preliminary sketches made up for her approval. I warned her it would be costly, but she just waved that credit card and told me it had better be express. She didn't like to wait. She was the kind who planned everything well in advance.

So three weeks later the initial sketches for the custom-made tea service arrived.

The back of each chair painted just like a fully dressed rabbit, waiting politely for tea to be served. Huge long ears grew out of the back of the chairs. Some of them were flopped over. Cute rabbit faces, little pink triangular noses, softly brushed fur. Realistic touches, like pink eyes with little tear ducts in the corner. You know the Italians. So good at these things. The sketch itself was suitable for framing.

And the table! A checkerboard with faux teacups, tea cakes, petits fours, even little sugar cubes with rosebuds painted on! That's standard, actually, with the Granny Goose Ensemble you get that, too. She came into the store and loved it. Do it up, she said, have Tollini build it and paint it and put it on a plane.

And then she set out to order the rest of the furniture. She ordered the white muslin curtains with the ribbon-threaded eyelet trim at the bottom. Also custom. And she even had a valance embroidered with small rabbit faces, ordered through Pickering Company of Somerset. I'm telling you, this lady went all out, price apparently being no object for *her*.

She didn't go for plated either. Her silver had to be solid. We don't ask questions here. But how can the kid tell the difference? Half the time it's going to be full of egg yolks. And you can't put solid in the dishwasher. Whatever.

The rest was all going to be Victorian wicker. White. She ordered a cane-woven suspension cradle. With wheels. That way the mother can take the infant into whichever room she wants. Over the basket where the baby lays—you understand we use German hardware, everything is stainless steel ball bearings—there is a crown of white *broderie anglaise,* a curtain of lace to protect the infant's skin from you know, any harsh rays. The mother can add extra layers to the crown immediately after the birth, if she so desires. The nursery should be kept dim anyway the first few weeks. Not that this mother was going to miss a trick. We do special hand weaving, should the client prefer, and of course she did. The handwoven fibers come in beautiful lily patterns. This particular cradle is called the "Victoria Regia." It's a copy from an 1851 piece. Woven into shapes reminiscent of the Queen Victoria's own lily, the largest waterlily in the world discovered by Mr. Livingston, I presume, in Africa. This stuff has history!

People love the Victorian look. So romantic. That's when lace baby clothes really came into popularity. Among the upper classes of course. Of course, it was quite an indulgence in those sentimental times—a lot of laundry. So many infants died, you know. Mothers too, in childbirth. Not anymore, thank God.

*   *   *

My God, all the furniture came today. In one load!

I was up late, scrubbing the floor (they called and said delivery would be this morning—but I didn't expect it to be so early). It's almost ready now, the nursery.

The little rabbit faces, they look like rabbits sitting in chairs, on either side of the table, painted with its tea service already brewing and steaming. The light long layers of white curtains, shot with the blue ribbon. Rows of bunting, Daddy's gone a hunting—

Fuck, there's the doorbell. Shit.

I cannot tear myself away from this room.

Stop ringing!

Oh, they know I'm home. I have to give up. Close the door on this lovely land here.

Goddamn! Stop that ringing! I'm coming, I'm coming.

Worse than the movers.

Probably that Rosalind and her girl Angelica. I like Rosalind, as much as I like anybody these days. But I wish she'd shut up about Angelica. A thoroughly unremarkable child!

Bye-bye Christopher Robin Room. I'll come back and see you soon.

Coming!

Mrs. Rosalind Churry, neighbor

If you ask me, she didn't like children. Why the way she went after Angelica, when all the child wanted to do was take a peek into the room! What did she expect, the hallway all piled up outside her door with cartons. And packing materials of all kinds still on the carpet. Don't tell me kids don't notice that stuff. Angelica notices *everything*. Excelsior, Styrofoam popcorn, bits of it were floating all over the floor when we stopped by to see her.

She was an interesting enough woman, very educated. I felt a little sorry for her. Children seemed to make her nervous. Her husband, I think, left her some time ago. She never mentioned it. Kept to herself. It was hard to get close. I kept on coming by. A habit. Stay in touch with neighbors in times of trouble. That's the way I was brought up.

Probably too smart for her own good. Degree in anthropology, lots of books everywhere. Except in the room where Angelica peeked. That's how it started.

You know, I try to get to know people in the building. She kept more to herself after her husband disappeared. I understand, people have tragedies and tragedies can rip the union of marriage asunder. People lose jobs, parents, children. Some couples just never get past the troubled times.

But that was no reason for her to go after Angelica like that.

We'd just sat down to tea when my daughter toddled over to the door and reached for the shiny knob. Why, there was a noise hardly human! Our neighbor screamed—no—she *roared!* for Angelica to stop.

I never want to hear her raise her voice again to my daughter. I'm never going back, I don't care how tragic the whole thing has been.

*   *   *

Thank God she's gone. It's time to get ready. Of course I'm nervous. It's just like before. I have the overnight bag packed. Everything is white, this time, I made sure. I have the soft-soled shoes, starched and pressed linen. I am going to do this right this time!

I'll call a taxi. No, wait, I think I'll walk. That's it. The exercise will do me good. Allow me to prepare. I'll start the breathing exercises now.

Nurse Annette Tropi, St. Luke's Hospital

Motherhood. I have seen it all here. And it isn't just roses and mottos embroidered on pillowcases.

Yes, there is the wonder of birth, of new life, but babies emerge coated with placenta, and they have to be spanked to get their lungs in gear. I know, there's women giving birth in hot tubs and in darkened rooms. But don't put me there. I want to assist in a sterile environment.

And mother is something you suddenly are. Not everybody takes it so well, believe me. All this stuff about the natural mother, I'm sorry. I don't care what the anthropologists say. Mothers are made and not born. It's a hell of a lot of work from the first contraction. Worth it? yeah, sure. Been going on for centuries. Hey, did I say it wasn't worth it? I wouldn't be working on this ward if I didn't enjoy the assisting in birth. The baby's job is easy.

The women have to *become* mothers. I've mostly seen people happy to be bringing new life into the world. But there are those mothers who are afraid of their babies. Are they going to make a mistake? What does the baby want? Why doesn't she eat?

And there are the mothers who have postpartum depression.

I've seen mothers reject their babies altogether. I have seen it!

No, enough of the natural mother. They all learn it eventually. What's natural for them.

*   *   *

St. Luke's Hospital! Birthplace of Christopher Robin.

I'm nervous, even though I've been there twice before. Once was purely research. Getting used to the layout. Breathe deeply.

Inside the doors I see a friendly elderly gentleman at the information counter. A volunteer no doubt. He's busy and overwhelmed as he can't figure out the telephone system. Now, where are those elevators again? I was too sedated last time. This time I'm going to keep my wits about me.

Elevator bank—a quiet, uneventful ride to the top where the nurseries are. I'm tense, shaking even. It doesn't matter. So is everybody else. Is that an expectant father there? Why isn't he by her side? They let men into the delivery room now. I should know.

Bing! Ninth floor. We all step out, me with my little overnight bag and my wide-brimmed hat. I make for the bathroom.

Damn these nurses uniforms have a lot of buttons. Right now I want nothing more than a good stiff drink. Have to wait.

White stockings, shit, I got them twisted. It would be disaster to have a run. There, completed. The thick-soled shoes. The jaunty nurses cap placed just so. I

even have a little name tag. Copied it off one I saw
a nurse wearing on my research expedition.

A look in the mirror. Perfect for the part.

Nurse Annette Tropi
I can't believe it happened on my shift. I just can't
believe it. That mother is so distraught. Out of her
mind. My God. Oh, my fucking God.

*   *   *

It was easy. I glided down the hall quietly in the
heavily treaded shoes issued to nurses. I kept my eyes
to the ground. Everyone was so busy, with something
in hand, a test tube, a cart, an infant.

An infant. Jesus. Here's the viewing room. Keep
back.

There they are inside that window. All those new
little lives, just beginning. Beautiful. But which one?

Who knows. They are all there. One of them is him.

A nurse, talking to someone, in a corner.

The room is dark, dim.

The nurse, she's stopped talking. She knits her eyebrows. There's a problem. She gets up as if to leave
the nursery.

I'm praying. She's walking now, toward the door,
with her colleague who's making gestures. She shrugs
her shoulders and walks through the door—through
the door! She's out!

There's a backward glance at the nursery, I'm flattened in a doorway now. She can't see me and then
she's around the corner. Christ, I'm going to make it.

The nursery! I run in. Babies! There are so many,
in so many colors! I hadn't thought about that.

He must be here. He knew I was coming.

The babies have started crying now. One has set off
another, like howling dogs.

But it didn't keep me from hearing the noise. The

tiny suckling sounds of Christopher Robin. Or who will grow up to be Christopher Robin.

"Thank you for waiting for me, darling!" I say, picking him up and carrying him quickly back down the hallway to the bathroom, where my overcoat waits in one of the stalls.

Epilogue
Police Officer, Laura DeLeuse

We had the profile, of course. Everybody knows it. That wasn't the surprise.

We were looking for a woman in her mid-twenties to late thirties who had recently lost a child. That's standard.

Of course, we check the hospital records for all the women that have lost children at that hospital. It's a pretty exhaustive search, and not likely to get results.

The best thing going for us in this situation is the media. "Baby Carrie," "Baby Eddie," the parents giving heart-wrenching interviews, that kind of thing. Networks eat it up. And everybody gets to play a bit part. There is no more public outcry than around the situation of a baby stolen from its mother.

Basically, we almost always solve the case on a tip from a neighbor. Women who suddenly have babies in their households tend to act very secretive, but do you know how hard it is to hide a baby? Think about it. The crying alone is one big baby alarm. And a baby's crying knows no clock. Not to mention the disposable diaper boxes, or a diaper service, or what have you. Babies are really hard to hide. Especially in a city like New York.

So we found her. Neighbor's tip. Mrs. Rosalind Churry noticed the baby crying. Pamper boxes. Quite a little nursery, too. Said she didn't want to call the police. Felt sorry for the woman.

She didn't put up a fuss. It'll be a psychiatric defense. Good lawyer, too.

Parents united with baby. End of story. Almost.

Then the mail started coming in. No, not the congratulations to the mother or the lynch-mob hate mail for the perpetrator of the crime.

Oddly enough, we received mail only sympathetic to the kidnapper. We forwarded a lot of envelopes to the jail. The writers were all women who had something in common. They had lost children. Although not moved to crime, they all recounted the same phenomenon that had set our kidnapper off. They all felt that their arms were suddenly empty. And ached. They all had it, they wrote. Empty arms, they said, the feeling that never went away.

There's Something Wrong Out There

by J. Madison Davis

The denizens of my city celebrated Mother's Day by killing five people. Two of the dead were actually mothers. The rest were the usual muthahs. But the fifth vic left me with no choice but to call back Al Prentice, who was on his way home after a twenty-hour shift. "What am I gonna do?" I said into the phone. "I'll give you the easy one, a gang banger Nfbamed T-Square at Seventh and Brace. No shit: T-Square. A Korean ventilated him and called us."

"Listen, Cap," said Al, "I'm tired of this affirmative action shit. Send one of the white boys: Fenelli, Cszytovski . . ."

"You're all I got," I said sharply. "That's an order!"

There was a moment of silence on the line. My tone of voice had been harsher than I'd intended. None of my white detectives ever threw affirmative action in my face, though I could see that look sometimes: Chief Detective of Homicide, colorization at its finest, whether he earned it or not. "You're all I got," I said more quietly. "Al?" I thought for a second he'd fallen asleep in the phone booth.

"The address," he sighed.

I repeated it, mentally daring him to make another crack. He'd called me the "Black Massa" in the past, not always friendly like, but today he had no fight left.

How little he had left, I had no idea at that point. He simply hung up.

For a long time we've all been worn as thin as toilet paper. Homicides have more than doubled in this city since I left the beat. Homicide detectives have increased by a grand total of three—two brothers and a woman. We've tried everything we can think of to deal with the slaughter. We hardly ever work with a partner anymore. We draft guys from Larceny and Fraud, but they always need them back in a couple days. We don't close as many cases as we used to. Only one of my detectives has managed to stay married more than five years. Four of them go into alcohol rehab every so many years just to get themselves a rest. When it comes down to it, the people in the state capital look on the problem as niggers killing niggers: never much of a problem, certainly a less horrible thing than raising taxes.

I'm not complaining, exactly. This is my life. Tote that barge! Lift that bale! I'm just thinking that maybe if I'd've taken the T-Square thing myself, it would've saved a few lives. But I was in the middle of another memo justifying overtime. I don't mean that as an excuse. It's just a fact.

I was still writing the memo at about eight-thirty that night when Al Prentice leaned in my door without knocking. His eyes were wide, as if forcing them open had frozen them that way. His café au lait skin seemed even paler in the fluorescent lights, but the bags under his eyes were very dark, as if the pigment in his skin had all drained there.

"What are you doing here?" I said. "The Korean's already been ROR'ed and gone home, why not you?"

"I couldn't sleep," said Al.

"You're back on shift tomorrow at six. You'd better get your ass home."

He glanced back at Cszytovski, who was manning

the phone and typing a report. "I've got to speak to you."

"The case was a hole in one, right?"

"Yeah, but—"

I expelled a long stream of air and snapped off the Selectric. "Come on in," I waved.

"I think I should close the door." He glanced out again.

"So close it." I took a sip of my warm diet Coke: one calorie and enough caffeine to keep me limping.

He twisted the knob and eased the door shut, as if afraid someone might hear it close. He pulled a chair up close and leaned forward, speaking almost in a whisper.

"Have you noticed there's something wrong out there?"

"In the squad room?"

"No, in the city. On the streets."

I blinked. His face gave me no clue as to how I was to react. I chuckled. "You shittin' me?"

"There's something wrong."

I held back nothing this time. My laugh ricocheted off the cracked ceiling. "Who put you up to this?" I asked.

Al stood, his eyes smoldering.

I sobered up, reached out, and gave his necktie a yank. "Sit down," I said. "Everything's wrong. What have you got in mind? Go on, sit down."

Al glanced back over his shoulder through the pebbled glass, then quickly scanned my office, as if it was a crime scene. What was he looking for? When his eyes settled on me, he seemed to be boring into my head, trying to read my mind. It was about as comfortable as a root canal. He finally made a decision, pulled his chair up close to the desk, and leaned forward. He whispered, "It's serial."

"Did you say 'serial?' "

He glanced over his shoulder again and nodded. "We're dealing with serial killers."

"Killers?"

"Yes!" His face was eager now. It was the same expression you get on somebody who's been living with a terrible secret and is relieved to finally be able to confess. "You've got these murders every day, every night."

"Tell me about it."

"And we think people are killing each other like they never killed before. But what's different? People were poor in the past. People had drugs in the past. People had guns. There were gangs."

I hardly moved.

"And the increase was so sudden. There wasn't time enough for people to become this different. They just want us to believe all this because they think we're inferior."

I raised my finger. "Excuse me, brother, but you said something about serial killers?"

"Yes! That's what I'm explaining. I was looking at the Yolanda Burton case file—"

"That was a drive by."

"That's what it looked like."

"The juvie's admitted to it. Are you saying he's your serial killer?"

"No, let me explain. There was something about it that bugged me, and then there was the shoot-out in the crack house: Ramon Garcia and his brothers."

"They're related to the Burton killing? She was hit by accident."

"That's what I'm saying. I had the feeling. You know my radar was tingling, and when I went out on Jenkin Brown—"

"Jenkin Brown? What the fuck you talking about? His wife stuck him. What are you telling me?"

"That the same persons are behind all this."

If he was putting me on, he deserved an Academy Award. "Al, what *are* you saying? Two of these cases are closed. None of these was related at all. The weapons were a MAC-10, a serrated knife, and an assortment of sawed-offs and automatic pistols."

His eyes widened with pleasure. "But that's exactly it, don't you see? They know how we work. They make the M.O.'s different each time."

"They?"

"The people behind it!" He said it as if I was stupid. Normally that would have rubbed me wrong, but my head was swimming, like my Coke had been spiked. "How many murders we got this year?" he continued. "One a night, at least, and it's picking up. We're going to hit a new record this year, easy. Next year, they'll average more than two a night. You figure it out. If you double every year, how long will it take? It's the genocide, man."

"Al," I said loudly, "the juvie confessed, Mrs. Brown confessed, a witness ID'ed the Ice-Rockers leaving the crack house. What are you saying to me?"

"Genocide," he hissed. "You believe everybody out there's so bad they would kill each other like they are? It don't happen out in Hamilton Park."

"In Hamilton Park they have fifty-inch TVs and swimming pools and a couple of rooms for each kid. Sometimes they kill each other anyway, but most of the time they whack a golf ball instead of each other."

"So?"

"Is that your answer? 'So?' " I took a deep breath and spoke slowly, as if to a child. "Al, you're a smart dude, right? You went to Fisk while I was up here dragging my sorry ass through the city college. You've had some night-school law, right?" He twisted in the chair, and I remembered hearing he'd flunked a couple of courses. "Well, use that brain of yours. Listen to yourself. You need a good night's sleep, and everything will look different."

A wall had come down between us, the steel shutter in front of a closed pawnshop. "It's cop syndrome, brother," I said, "that's all. You see everything ugly in the world, and it hurts, right? But if you try to make sense of it, you'll lose it. It's just ugly out there. Do the job, get laid, and forget it. A guy like you could be mayor someday, but not if you go around making up fairy tales. Are you listening to me?"

"I know what I know."

I rocked back in my desk chair. "I'm giving you a week's leave effective immediately. You've got a bad case of flu—no, lower-back pain. Sleep all day. Take your wife to the beach. Go for a drive in the country. I don't care. I'll cover for you."

"In a week," he said dully, "there'll be at least another dozen dead."

"But you are ordered—*ordered*—to forget about it. Am I clear?"

He nodded, rose shaking his leg as if it had gone to sleep, and left without a word. When I finished my memo, I stopped in the squad room. Cszytovski was opening a thick corned-beef sandwich that Fenelli had just brought in. He must have noticed my inhaling the fragrance of that big pickle. "Take a half," said Cszytovski.

"Corned beef jacks my blood pressure," I said.

"Nothin's good for yuh anymore," said Fenelli.

I tried to sound casual. "Prentice seem okay?"

"Tired," said Fenelli. "Showing the strain."

"Who ain't?" said Cszytovski. There was a cynical narrowing of his eyes, as if he was thinking, since when do you care?

"His back's messed. A lot of pain. I'm giving him a sick week, or it might get serious."

"His back?" said Fenelli. "I guess that's why his wife dumped him. No motion like the ocean."

"His wife ran off?"

"With a lawyer," said Cszytovski. "A *lawyer*! Insult to injury. Whatta slut!"

The phone interrupted us, and I walked out fighting my knee-jerk impulse to see what the call was about.

For two days I gave no thought to Al. A couple of days of vegging out in front of the tube, taking a drive in the country, whatever gets you out of the slaughter-house and into life, all of us need it, just to be re-minded what it's all about. I know that there are a few buzzards in Internal Affairs who are going to raise the question of whether I was showing favoritism to Al Prentice. They won't say it, but the hint will be that it was because he's a brother. If I'd've suspended him, on the other hand, the uniformed brothers would accuse me of playing Uncle Tom. Damned if you do and damned if you don't. I did what I did because I thought it was the right thing. I said I'd seen the doc-tor's note and put it in my file. Evidence gets lost, that's not news. IA will be looking for a scapegoat, and maybe I deserve a little blame, mistaking Al's problem for combat fatigue, but I'm not taking more blame than they can prove. If Al had needed just that week off, I could've ruined his career by leaving a record he had a screw loose. My only real mistake was not recognizing how loose that screw was.

Even when I next heard of Al, I didn't think any-thing of it. I was putting on my raincoat to go down-town for one of those goddamned budget meetings, when Eamon O'Brien, our oldest detective, came in from a body in a dumpster. "Hey, Cap," he said, "Al's back, looked pretty good to me."

"What?"

"I seen Al. He parked in front of a juice joint on Fourteenth and went inside."

"So maybe he needed a bottle of gin."

"Before my back operation, driving was the worst thing."

"That so?" I said. "Nobody said he needed surgery."

The one thing that gets you in deep with the men is malingering. It was something O'Brien liked to lay on anybody new, but especially anybody not Irish, which was just about everybody now. That was harmless enough. What made me wonder on my way to city hall was why Al would be in that neighborhood. Fourteenth was the border between the Ice-Rockers and the Bloods, the heart of the murder district. Al's apartment was five miles uptown. It bothered me, but I thought maybe he was tying up a loose end or maybe hunting for some warm consolation for his wife's leaving. A cop has no trouble finding the right hooker if he wants.

But the next morning, Fenelli mentioned that Al had shown up at the shooting on Carner. He'd hung around, asked questions, then left without a word at about 4:30 A.M. Sandra Rodriguez then said he'd shown up at the double overdose discovered in the Kessler projects around 2:00 P.M. He helped secure the area and bagged some evidence. "Sandy," I asked, "did he say why he was there?"

She shook her head. "He was a big help, though. He left before I could thank him."

"Did he say anything? How'd he look?"

She shrugged. "Preoccupied, but happy. He didn't say much of anything. When we first enter the premises, he looks down at the bodies and says, 'This just about nails the sucker.' "

"Did you ask him what he meant?"

"No. I was getting the heavers from the smell."

I went back to my paperwork, but couldn't get it out of my mind. I tried his home number. I tried his beeper. I left a little early and drove by his house. If he was in, he wasn't answering. An officer eating his gun may be a cliché in cop movies, but it's no cliché to cops. I got the manager to let me in. He wasn't home. The milk in the refrigerator was sour. There was a spiral notebook next to a stale can of beer on the dinette table. The front of it was filled with notes from a class on torts. In the back of it was a neat list of the homicides over the last two weeks and a sketchy map with red circles for the locations and black lines connecting them. There were mathematical problems being worked in the margins: square roots and algebra-like stuff. I felt a prickle on my neck and had the feeling Al was dead somewhere. I don't know why.

I got to my son's basketball game late, but it was safely in hand, so Casey got to play most of the fourth quarter. My mind wasn't on the game, however, and I kind of went through the motions of asking him about his mother. I gave him a few bucks to treat his friends to sodas, then went to my car. I looked at the high school and the tree-lined streets surrounding it. I was glad his momma had remarried and moved out here. It would be awhile—maybe not long, but awhile—before the killing spread out here. Something *was* wrong, as Al had said, and everybody was getting used to it.

I woke at dawn in my recliner. A chirpy white woman was giving out hints on wallpapering. I couldn't remember what I had set out to watch the night before. My milk had gone to cheese, too, so I skipped the instant coffee and headed for a diner. It was a slow day until mid-afternoon. It started as usual, it continued as usual. Life was setting me up to be blindsided.

"Is this Chief Detective Emerson?"

"Speaking."

"Captain Fielder. I need you at the Hamilton Park

Country Club, right away. The subject wants to talk to you."

Fielder ran the SWAT team, hostage situations, talking down jumpers. I felt that prickle and already knew who the "subject" was. I can't say particularly why. I just knew. "Twenty minutes," I said, and I believe I broke about every regulation we have on driving in getting there.

The country club sat atop a round hill facing away from the city and the middle-class suburbs. The long driveway was jammed with police cars, TV and fire trucks, and ambulances. A stunned man in a crisp tennis outfit sat on one curb getting a nasty flesh wound bandaged by the paramedic. I heard that three people had been killed and twelve wounded. Then I heard five and eleven. Al was holed up in the walk-in freezer in the back of the narrow kitchen, I was told. Fielder could try a frontal assault, but not only the subject, but some of his men would become casualties, as he put it. Even positioning a man to lob tear gas into the freezer was very dangerous. If the gas didn't land inside the freezer, the subject could close the door and the canister might set fire to the building. "Maybe," said Fielder, "the subject wants to make peace with you over something before he offs himself."

"That 'subject,' " I barked, "is one of my men."

"Not anymore," said Fielder.

I crossed the elegant dining room. Crystal goblets lay in puddles of red wine, ice, and orange juice. The linen tablecloths, a delicate white, were spattered with blood. The wounded had been evacuated, but two faceless corpses lay near the door. Sawed-off was my guess, but the neat holes in some of the booths and in the mural of Venice looked more like a MAC-10. Al had learned a lot working homicide.

I thought of my son Casey and swallowed hard. The SWAT men on each side of the kitchen door nodded.

One of them extended his arm and eased open the swinging door.

"Al!" I called. "It's me. Captain Emerson."

There was a moment of silence, then something rattled. "Cap?"

"Yeah, it's me. Are you okay?"

"I solved it, Cap! I'm sure to be mayor now." He laughed. "I'll make you chief. You'll have three men on a case from now on. The killing's over. Kids can grow up safe."

I stepped a little closer to the door. The SWAT men moved to warn me. One of them had a swollen lip, as if he'd just had dental work. You notice funny things in situations like that. "Can you come out and talk about it, brother? You don't need those weapons anymore."

"I want to explain it to you, first. They'll want revenge. If they get me, you can tell my story."

"They won't hurt you if I'm here. I'll have their badges for it." I listened for several seconds. "Al?"

"You come in."

The SWAT men shook their heads. I walked straight in, anyway. One of them grabbed the tail of my raincoat, but I let it slip off my shoulders and left him with a handful of vinyl. "Al? It's me. Al?" I was halfway down the kitchen when I knew that he was just as likely to want to kill me. Maybe I was too tired to worry about it anymore. All I know is I didn't hesitate. I eased the heavy door wider. He was sitting in the back on a crate marked "Alaskan King Crab Legs." A jolly, crown-wearing crab was visible between Al's skinny shins. Al lowered his sawed-off and smiled. The MAC-10 lay on the shelf beside him. He rushed forward and hugged me, like a woman in an airport meeting her long-lost sister. He pulled away and raised his hand for a high five. I slapped it weakly.

"I solved it, Cap! It was a tough one, but I put the ball in the hole." There were tears in his eyes.

"You hurt a lot of people out there."

"They were the ones!"

"The ones?"

"You got it."

"You were supposed to rest up, my man."

"I was too close. Too close." He looked down as if reliving the pleasure of the "case." When he raised his eyes again, he turned and went back to his crate. "Pull up a seat," he said.

"Kind of cold in here, isn't it?"

"It feels good! Chill out!" He laughed. "I should be dead on my feet, but I feel so alive, so good."

"Fill me in," I said, like it was routine and he'd just collared the prime suspect.

"I knew it was a serial. A conspiracy. Why would our people be killing each other like that."

"People that kill aren't my people," I said.

"Exactly. That's when I figured out it was like the South American thing, like Brazil. Death squads."

"Death squads?"

"Sure. You ever notice when we get people confessing that their eyes aren't right?"

"How do you mean?"

"They're glassy, like they're high. They say why they did it, and it don't make sense: he was dissing me, I liked his jacket ..."

"Some of them *are* high."

"But not from what we think."

"No?"

He leaned forward. "A mind-altering drug! The death squads tell the brother or sister that they did it, and the drug makes them believe."

I blinked.

"That's it, Cap. I don't know how they get it in

their systems, you know, but I think it's with the asthma thing."

"What asthma thing?"

"That Helmick carried."

I cleared my throat. "You're losing me, Al. Could we go out where it's a little warmer?"

"I saw Helmick cruising down there in his Jag. He was down there, sometimes three times a week. He wanted to look like your typical blow-head. He'd pick up a hooker, too, and drive her out to the Shangri-La motel off the interstate. This was just his way of setting up the hits. If you ask the girls that been with him, most of them don't remember him at all."

"Hookers are paid to forget. Maybe he was a good customer. Maybe they turned so many tricks they don't remember. Maybe they thought it was all a crack dream. For God's sake, Al! You killed a bunch of people!" I stood and grabbed a shelf. I shook it, and frozen chops clattered on the concrete floor. When I looked back, Al was smiling.

"I got the brains behind it, Cap. They would play tennis each Thursday and do lunch. Helmick and Chamberlain and Roth and Carstairs. All the other members knew about it, but they weren't behind it. I couldn't help it a few of them got hit, too."

"Is that it?" I said quietly.

"I think so. You look into it. You'll see I'm right."

"Well, brother," I sighed, shaking my head, "you'll be sitting on top of the world now. You're going to be a celebrity now."

He stared straight ahead. "I'm a better man than any lawyer. Louise will come begging back for sure."

I almost asked him who Louise was, and then I remembered. She had run off with a lawyer. Whatta slut, Cszytovski had said. She would become the explanation for what made no sense. I reached down and gently took his arm. "Come on," I said. "It's time to meet the press."

"You understand?"

"Yes, I understand." I patted him on the shoulder and let him out.

The SWAT team closed in and absorbed Al Prentice like an amoeba at feeding time. The blob, bristling with raised M-16s, swept out of the dining room toward a similar mass of reporters.

I was left alone in the dining room. A salmon entrée sat undisturbed with white sauce and a curled sprig of dill on top. At the next setting, there was blood in the pasta salad and a burn in the tablecloth where a cigarette had been dropped. I should've taken my momma out to eat last Sunday, I thought. I'd even forgotten to send a card. She'd probably never eaten a chunk of salmon that didn't come out of a can. There were a lot of people who only saw meals like this in magazines or on their TVs. For a moment, just a moment, though it was totally crazy, I knew Al Prentice was right. I felt no horror over what he'd done, only numbness. There were death squads. Some of them met in this room. Maybe they lied to themselves and didn't know they were death squads, and they didn't have to operate like Al had fantasized, but they killed people every day. Every black man feels it, even if the killers don't. This is a knowledge, not a thing you can prove. What Al in his confusion had failed to see, was that killing off one, two, a hundred of them wouldn't slow things down. They had fueled the train up and opened the throttle, but, hell, it was a runaway now, crashing down the mountain on its own momentum.

What could I do about it? I took a melba toast from a basket and ate it slowly. I rubbed my eyes with both hands and felt very old. I straightened my tie and toughened myself to push through the press. No com-

ment. Time to go home. A hot tub. A few beers. Tomorrow I go back to trying to slow the big machine
by stacking little piles of memos and reports in its
murderous path.

Unkindest Cut

by Larry Segriff

Her sudden lunge caught me by surprise. I rocked back on my heels, but I couldn't get out of range, and her blade *thunked* solidly against my mask.

"Nice shot, Sue," I said.

She grinned. "Not really. If you'd quit looking at my legs so much, you wouldn't be such an easy target."

I shrugged. "Wear knickers, then."

"What, and miss all these easy shots? Are you crazy?"

I had to admit, she had great legs, and as long as she was going to wear those high-cut running shorts, I was going to look. At practice, anyway.

She sketched a brief salute and came at me again.

I couldn't help myself. I grinned, and dropped my gaze to her legs once more.

I was between cases at the moment, a situation I was all too familiar with these days with my little one-man detective agency. I fenced for the enjoyment and the exercise, and for the occasional paycheck I picked up directing at the bigger meets. Once in a great while, I'd help put on a demo somewhere, too, but mostly I fenced for the fun.

We were a university club, and on this Friday evening, the last regular practice of the year, turnout was light. It was the end of finals week, Mother's Day just two days away, and most of the students were gone. Of those who were still in town, most of them were down at the bars, celebrating, instead of sweating on the strip.

I couldn't say I blamed them, of course. My own college days weren't so long ago that I couldn't remember what it was like. Still, I was glad for those few—either too young to drink or too old to get excited about it—who'd shown up to fence.

Sue was in that latter category, maybe twenty-five or so. She was a grad student in paleontology, but I hadn't yet been able to interest her in my old bones. We'd gone out a time or two for beers after fencing, as I'd done with almost everyone in the club, but it had never progressed beyond the friendship stage.

She was short, maybe five-three on her tiptoes, well below my nearly six-foot frame. Her hair was dark, as was mine, but hers was more nearly black while mine was a flat brown. She had gray eyes; mine were green, but changed according to the light.

Sue fenced foil, mostly. She was using a saber tonight because it was my birthday, and she wanted to be kind to me. Maybe that was why she wasn't wearing her knickers, too.

She lunged again, and I parried, and she parried. I picked up the remise of her initial attack with a *prise de fer* counterattack, a strong taking of her blade, but she was ready for that. Maintaining pressure on my blade so I couldn't release, she turned her lunge into a flèche and ran by me.

No point either way, but it was a nice phrase, and I said so. She smiled, came back on guard, and lunged again.

Happy birthday.

"So, we going out afterward?" she asked.

I shrugged. "That's up to the rest of you. I'd like to, of course. Maybe out to the East Ender." That was our favorite watering hole, an English-style pub—or as close as you were likely to find here in the heartlands—that served sandwiches and wonderful onion rings until nearly midnight on Fridays and Saturdays.

"Sounds good," she said. "I'll ask around."

Then the fencing got serious, and we had no breath for talking.

As it turned out, there were only eight of us at practice, and half of us went out. Sue and I were joined by Linda and Jeff. They were no more a couple than Sue and I were, though Jeff gave clear signals that he'd like them to be.

Linda was young, just finishing up her first year of classes at the university. I hadn't really tried to get to know her yet, but I thought I'd heard her say she was from Nebraska. Tall and blond, with surprisingly warm brown eyes, she made quite a contrast with Sue when the two of them fenced.

Jeff was a bit older, maybe twenty-one or -two. An engineering student, he was in his junior year and doing quite well from what he said. He was sandy-haired and stocky, and worked out a lot.

We found a table in one of the corners and ordered a pitcher. Linda was underage, but the waitress knew us and brought her a glass anyway. She also brought a pitcher of ice water and a plate of garlic bread, without our having to order them.

We were pretty good customers, even if most of us couldn't afford much of a tip.

"You fencing in the meet next weekend?" Jeff asked me. He was on his third glass of beer already. I was still drinking water.

"Thinking about it," I said. We always liked to kick off the summer with a fun meet. Those of us who lived in town—and there were a surprising number of us, for a university club—got together and fenced and grilled burgers and drank beer. The last couple of years we'd opened it up to other regional clubs, and some of the hotshots, like Jeff, were pressing to make it even bigger. Like me, Jeff was a saber fencer. Unlike me, that was just about all he fenced. If he kept with it, he had a shot at being very good in a few more years. "I might just direct instead."

He nodded. "Be a good thing if you fenced. Might help draw some folks from out of state."

I frowned. I've never liked pressure, even from friends. "Like I said, I'm thinking about it."

He nodded again and took the hint. Helping himself to more beer, he turned toward Linda and asked her the same question.

Sue leaned over to me, and I didn't get to hear Linda's response. Not that I really needed to. She was just learning to fence, still practicing her footwork. I'd be surprised if she felt ready to compete.

"I hate to see him drink so much." Sue spoke in a low voice directly into my ear. "He has a tendency to get mean."

I nodded, remembering a few incidents. Jeff was a stocky guy. He worked out a lot, mostly to keep the beer off his gut, I thought, and there had been several times in the last couple of years when I'd pulled him out of a bar where things were starting to get nasty.

A real nice guy, even on the strip—which was surprising for a saber fencer—but he didn't mix well with booze. Following Sue's eyes, I saw that he had his hand on Linda's arm and was leaning in close to her. She seemed to be handling it all right, though, so I decided not to say anything.

Instead, I flagged the waitress so we could order some food. Most of us didn't eat before practice, and I hoped that putting some food in Jeff's belly would slow him down.

It didn't work. He muttered something about being low on cash and simply ordered more beer. I didn't bother offering a loan. If he could afford to drink, he could afford to eat. Clearly, it wasn't his wallet that was stopping him, it was his priorities, and I couldn't loan him any of mine.

All in all, we had a pretty nice time. Sue and Linda chipped in to buy my beers, but I wouldn't let them pay for my meal, too. My income was small and irregular, it was true, but I could still afford to eat. I couldn't always say the same for them.

We walked out to the parking lot as a group and headed over to Sue's car, a battered old Ford in even worse shape than my Toyota.

Jeff, huddled against the chill of the wind, caught at Linda's arm. "Give you a ride?" He gestured toward his motorcycle, but the leer on his face and the emphasis he'd placed on the last word indicated a different meaning altogether.

My heart went out to Linda. She had to be used to such advances, I knew, but still I felt sorry for her. There was an air of innocence about her that I hated to see sullied.

She handled it well, though. "Thank you, Jeff," she said, answering only his words, "but not tonight. It's too cold, and I'm still sweaty from practice."

"I'll keep you warm," he said with that same disgusting leer.

"No, thanks," she said again, and this time there was an unmistakable edge in her voice. Turning away, she got in the passenger's side of Sue's ancient Ford.

Jeff glowered and stomped off.

"Do you think he should drive?" Sue asked me.

I didn't answer her. I was already walking off after him.

"Jeff!" I called. "Wait up!"

He didn't slow, but he didn't speed up, either, and I caught up with him as he was mounting his bike.

"She's right; it is too cold for that. Why don't you catch a ride with me?"

He put the key in the ignition before raising his gaze to meet mine. "Jax," he said. "Fuck off," and kicked down hard. The engine fired and caught, and he roared off without another word.

I sighed and stared off after him. That kid was getting hard to be around. Zipping up my coat a little higher, I turned and went back to Sue.

"I saw," she said. "God, he was really disgusting, wasn't he?"

"Yeah. Be sure and talk to Linda about it, will you? I'd rather she didn't hate him because of it."

She gave me a hard look. "I don't understand you, Jax. How can you defend him so much?"

I shrugged. "Hell, he's just a kid, Sue. I don't want to see his mistakes follow him for the rest of his life." I looked away, reluctant to add anything further, but after a moment I brought my gaze back to her. "Hell, Sue, I've done some pretty stupid things myself. I'm only glad that most of them are safely in the past."

She frowned, but didn't respond.

"Speaking of stupid things," I went on, "I was going to ask you for a birthday kiss, but he kind of put me out of the mood."

She took an involuntary step backward. "Don't," she said, then stopped. I hadn't moved. "Oh, Jax, I wish—"

She didn't say anything more. Just turned and opened her door and got in. A moment later she was gone, as abruptly, as inexplicably, as Jeff.

Shaking my head, I went to my old Toyota and took myself home. Some birthday.

I spent the next day at my small office, riding the desk and hoping the phone would ring. It didn't. No belated cards came either, which was exactly the same amount that had arrived on time. Oh, well.

Sunday turned out no better. Mother's Day: just

another square on the calendar, right? Only this one always carried a load of grief and guilt for me. Not that Father's Day was much better.

Sue showed up a little late, looking like she'd been crying. I wasn't fencing at the time. Two novices—young, local kids—were the only ones there, and I didn't feel much like giving a lesson. She didn't say anything. Just slipped her mask on and grabbed a foil. I didn't feel I could ask her what was wrong. I merely nodded and pulled out my own blade and didn't even kid her about leaving her sweatpants on.

On Sundays, practice usually ran from one to about three. Now that we had started our summer schedule, we fenced until nearly five. When Linda hadn't shown up by the end, Sue started asking about her.

"She said she was coming today, didn't she?"

I shrugged, toweling off. I knew she was staying in town for the summer, but I didn't know about this weekend. "I don't know. She talked to Jeff more than to me." Which didn't help much. Jeff hadn't come to practice, either. "You don't think they're together, do you?"

She snorted and shook her head. "Not after what she had to say about him Friday."

I frowned, unable to find anything to say to that. She obviously hadn't tried to stick up for Jeff, but I couldn't really blame her for that.

"So what do you think?" I asked.

"I think I'll drop by Linda's on my way home. Want to come?"

"Sure," I said with no hesitation. I wasn't particularly worried about Linda, but I thought spending some time with Sue might shed a little light on her own behavior.

We drove over separately, Sue in the lead. I knew which dorm Linda lived in, but I'd never been to her room.

It was a large, brick building with almost no on-street parking. The U liked to funnel all cars to very large, and very faraway parking lots. Being Sunday, with lots of moms and pops picking up their bright, young progeny, we were unable to find spots together. Finally, pulling over into a quasi-legal space, Sue rolled down her window and yelled, "Eighteen-oh-seven. Come when you can."

The car behind me honked, and I waved and drove off. It took me ten minutes to find an empty spot of my own, and ten more to walk back to Linda's dorm.

The door to 1807 was closed, and no one answered my knock. After a moment, I tried the knob, found it unlocked, and went on in.

A glorified shoe box, like most dormitories, this one was maybe fifteen feet square. There were two beds in it, hardly more than cots, with twin dresser-desk combinations built into one wall. Next to the door, a large, double closet stood, with accordion-fold doors to offer a modicum of privacy.

I saw all that in a glance, filling in details from when I'd lived in a similar room, almost fifteen years before. Then I saw the two women and the blood, and had no more time for sightseeing.

The nearest of the two beds was unmade. Glancing at it, I could see a smear of blood and other stains. I felt immediately I knew what had happened, and a quick look at Linda confirmed it.

She sat in a chair near the window, as far from the door and that bed as she could get. Her knees were pulled up to her chin, her face bore a tortured expression, and she wasn't moving. Sue was kneeling at her side, trying to offer some comfort, but Linda was not responding. She just kept staring at that bed.

I took one look at her face and then looked away, unable to bear the sight any longer. There was some puffiness to her lips, and a darkening ring around her left eye, but it was the suffering in those eyes that made me turn away.

She'd showered—obsessively, I'd have guessed—and was dressed, but that was as far back to normal as she'd come. Her long, blond hair was a tangled mess, and she'd made no attempt to cover any of the marks with makeup.

I took one step into the room, Linda's name on my lips, but Sue stopped me before I could say anything. "Go home, Jax," she said. "I'll call you later."

I didn't want to leave, but it was clear I could do no good there at the moment. Feeling woefully inadequate, I nodded once and left.

Perhaps I should have gone straight home. Instead, I went downstairs to a university phone, opened up the directory, and got Jeff's address. Then I took myself there.

He didn't live far away. In fact, his frat house was just up the street. It was a glorious spring day, showing none of the chill we'd had on Friday, but I hardly noticed as I strode down the cracked sidewalk.

Delta Rho was the fourth house from the end, and I went in without knocking. Some pledge looked up from where he was doing scut work in the kitchen and asked if he could help me.

"Jeff Carlton," I said. "He live here?"

"Sure," the dweeb said. "Should I call him for you?"

"I'll go up. Where's his room?"

"You're not allowed—" he began. I cut him off with a look.

"Where's his room?" I repeated.

I don't normally think of myself as a dangerous man, but something of my rage must have shown through because the kid told me. "Upstairs, second floor, last room on the left."

I headed up the stairs without another word. Behind

me, I could see him diving for a phone, but I didn't care. I didn't think I'd be there long.

At the first landing I headed left, watching for signs of Jeff. The kid could have lied to me, of course, but I didn't think so. I'd seen his face, and I believed him.

The last door was closed. I kicked it open. Jeff was inside, in a room slightly smaller than Linda's. It had only one bed, but his wasn't bloody and he was sitting on it.

"Jax," he said, looking up at my entrance. "What the hell?"

That was as far as he got. In two strides I was right next to him. Without a word, I swung my fist as hard as I could.

He made no move to protect himself, and my blow landed high on his cheekbone. He cried out and fell back, and then I felt strong hands grip me from behind.

"No!" Jeff cried, struggling to get back up. "Jaws, Ape, it's all right. Really."

At his words the grip on me fell away. I could hear a small crowd gathered behind me, but I didn't turn to look at them. I kept my eyes on Jeff.

"You son of a bitch," I said when his gaze came up to meet mine.

"Jax—"

"I just left her. She's a mess, literally a mess. Friday night she was a nice, pretty, young girl, with her whole life ahead of her. Now she's a broken woman with nothing to look forward to but nightmares and terror for years to come. Are you proud of yourself, Jeff? Just tell me that. Are you proud of yourself?"

"Jax," he said, and this time I let him talk. I had nothing more to say, and I didn't feel like hitting him again just yet. "What in the hell are you talking about?"

I almost did hit him again, then. He must have seen

that on my face because he lifted his hands defensively. I chose to batter him with words, instead.

"Linda," I said, spitting the name at him. "I just left her, like I said. I saw what you did to her."

He lowered his hands, and I saw confusion blooming on his face behind them. "What I did to Linda? Jax, I'm going to ask you again: what are you talking about?"

"Jesus, Jeff, do I have to spell it out for you? Sue got worried about her, so we went over to check on her. And we found her, just as you left her Friday night."

He was shaking his head. "Jax, I left her at the same time I left you: in the parking lot at the East Ender. I swear, I have no idea what you're talking about."

"Christ, Jeff. You raped her. What do I have to do, search your room for her panties to make you admit it?"

He had gone pale at my words. "Rape? God, Jax, no. I didn't."

My hands formed themselves into fists again, but this time he didn't move. "Come on, Jeff. You weren't surprised to see me, and you weren't surprised to see me furious."

His face grew even grimmer at that. "Yeah, Jax, you're right. I wasn't surprised when you burst in here, but not for that reason." He rose to his feet, and I let him. It would just be that much more satisfying to knock him down again, if I decided to.

Unconsciously, his right hand came up and massaged the beginnings of the bruise I'd given him. "Did she say I did it, Jax?"

I shook my head. "She wasn't talking at all when I was there. But," I added, unwilling to grant him anything, "she didn't have to. It was obvious. My God, man, you were all over her Friday night. Sue and I both saw it."

He nodded. "Yeah, and I'm sorry for that—"

"Sorry!" I broke in. "Jeff, I've stood up for you a lot of times, but this is one situation where an apology just isn't enough."

"Jax," his eyes were boring into mine with a seriousness I'd never seen from him before, "I was picked up Friday night, not more than ten minutes after I left the pub. Drunk driving. I know you're in tight with the cops, so I figured you'd have heard all about it. It was after midnight when they arrested me, so they were able to hold me until today. I got home only a few hours ago." His look was, if anything, even bleaker. "You've got to know how sorry I am about what happened to Linda, but it wasn't me, Jax. It wasn't me."

I felt as if my punch had rebounded and landed in my gut. "Jeff, I—"

He waved it away. "Don't worry about it, Jax. You're right, you've gone to bat for me a lot. I had it coming. Let's just forget about it, okay?"

I shook my head. It was fine if he wanted to forgive and forget. I wasn't going to let me off that easy.

"I've got to go," I said and, without another word, spun on my heel and left.

I don't remember much about the walk to my car. It must have calmed me somewhat, however, because I made it home without any further problems. At least, I didn't have any accidents, and no cops stopped me.

I tried to drink a beer after I got home, but I didn't really want it. I just kept replaying that scene with Jeff. Part of it, of course, was that I was furious—and more than a little disillusioned—with myself for losing control like that, and at the wrong person. Mostly, though, I kept asking myself, *If not Jeff, who?*

There was no answer to that, and the day finally wound down to a dark and cheerless close.

Monday evening, I returned home from work to find Sue sitting out on my porch. The warmth of yesterday was but a memory, and the bite in the air had turned her cheeks and nose red. Still, she sat quietly, an unopened six-pack on the swing beside her, seeming not to notice the chill.

She moved the cans as I came up the steps, and I took the spot next to her.

"She's going home." Sue handed me a beer and opened one for herself.

I nodded. "How's she doing?" Stupid question, I knew, but there didn't seem much else to say.

"She's shattered, Jax. Absolutely shattered." Sue tipped back her can and took a long, long drink. "I got her to the hospital and called the Crisis Center for her, but it didn't do much good. I only hope she can get some help back home."

I opened my beer and drank some of it. "Call the police?"

She shook her head. "She didn't want me to. Said she just wanted to forget about it." She gave me a dark look. "That was more than an hour after you left. It took me that long just to get her to start talking."

I had to look away. It made no sense, but at that moment I felt partly guilty, as if being a man was enough to incriminate. From what I saw in Sue's eyes, maybe it was. "Did she say who did it?"

That earned me a scornful look. "She didn't have to."

"No, Sue," I shook my head. "That's what I thought, too, but I was wrong." I told her about my visit to Jeff. At first she was unwilling to believe me, but after I showed her the box in the newspaper she had no choice.

"Damn," she said.

"Yeah. It was bad enough when we had someone to blame. Now . . ."

We both drank some more beer.

"Jax?" she said after a while.

"Yeah?"

"I've never told this to anyone."

"Sue," I didn't know what I was going to say. The pain in her voice pulled the word out of me, but she didn't let me go on.

"I was raped once. Back in high school. I'd gone out with this guy, a friend of a friend, and we had a good time. Up until I said no, anyway. We'd been drinking a little, not much, and he decided I didn't really mean it. I did. I pressed charges, but he walked. The jury found it a case of implied consent. Said I'd agreed to go out with him, I'd agreed to go back to his place, even knowing his parents were out of town. Like that meant I agreed to everything else. Bastard. That's why I fence, and why I study martial arts." She trained in Tae Kwon Do, I knew, and Shotokan karate. "That's also why I've never let you . . ."

Her voice trailed off, and there was nothing I could do. I wanted very much to hold her right then, but I didn't think she'd be receptive to the idea.

"I just can't," she finished.

I thought back to yesterday, and how she'd looked when she first walked into the fencing room. Had she gotten pregnant, I had wondered? If so, I had the feeling Mother's Day was even worse for her than it was for me.

My hands had closed around the beer can I held until I was almost crushing it. I looked down at them, surprised, and forced them to relax.

"What happened to him?" I asked, my voice low and rough.

She gave a bitter little laugh. "He went on to college—not this one—and then into business with his father. Last I heard, he had a wife and a couple of kids. Sometimes, I dream about going back and finding some way to make him pay, but I can't, Jax. Anything I do to him would affect those others in his life, the innocent ones. I can't hurt them like he hurt me, Jax."

She finished her beer, tossed the can in one corner of the porch—standard procedure for my place—and stood up.

"Leaving so soon?"

"Yeah. I need to talk to Linda. If she'll talk. You say Jeff didn't do it; I'm going to find out who did."

I rose, too. I didn't offer to help her investigate, and she didn't ask me to. Hell, this wasn't a case. It was a vendetta.

"Call me," I said.

She nodded and was gone, leaving four full beers behind. I looked at them briefly, then took them inside and put them in the fridge.

I made myself a minor dinner, something from the freezer, and was picking at it when the phone rang. It was Sue.

"She's still not saying much. Said her roomy is gone for the summer. She left Thursday, after her last test. No help there. As for who the guy was, Linda wouldn't say. Flat out refused to name him, or even say whether she knew him. She says she's trying to forget about it, and doesn't really want to talk about it. I told her that won't help, but believe me, I understand what she's feeling."

"Okay, Sue. Thanks for letting me know."

"No problem. I'm going to talk to some of the people in adjoining rooms, see if anyone saw or heard anything. It was pretty late on Friday, though. Won't have been many students still around. It's worth a shot, though."

"Yeah," I agreed. "And listen, anytime you want to talk, you know where I am."

Silence for a moment, then she said, "Right. Thanks, Jax. I might take you up on that sometime." And then she hung up.

Something was nagging at me. Something she'd said, maybe, or something I'd seen, but I couldn't put my finger on it. I worked at it for a while, then shrugged and gave up. Tossing the remains of my supper, I helped myself to one of Sue's beers and went looking for a book to read.

The next day was Tuesday, a practice day. We usually met over at the Field House around seven. I still had nothing in the works so I showed up a little early, skipping dinner as was my wont.

Sue was already there when I arrived, and we had a chance to talk, but it turned out there wasn't all that much to say. She'd asked around, but had learned as little as she'd expected. Most of the people on that floor had been gone; the few that were there hadn't heard or seen a thing.

I asked her to fence, but she shook her head. "No, Jax. The mood I'm in, it'd probably be a painful experience. I'll inflict it on somebody else."

It was one of the worst practices I could ever remember. Through it all, I kept thinking about what had been done to Linda. My mind kept replaying the scene in her room, showing me visions of her hunched over in that chair, bloodstained and broken. I raised a few welts that night myself, and spent most of the evening apologizing. Sue and I had decided not to say anything about what had happened, so explaining was out of the question. Like her, I simply had to pick my targets with care.

Jeff didn't show up until 8:45, barely fifteen minutes before we normally knocked off. He had his gear, though, and since I had run out of people to beat on, I offered to fence him. He agreed, and the swelling on his left cheekbone was a strong reminder to me to take it easy.

"How's it going, Jeff?" I asked as he got into his gear.

He shrugged. "I'm not drinking anymore, if that's what you mean."

Well, no, that wasn't what I meant, but I didn't blame him for being a little edgy. "How about some épée tonight? Gear up for the meet."

He nodded, and we grabbed our blades. We didn't speak again until we were out on the strip.

"How's Linda?" he asked.

I stiffened partway through my salute. "She's back home," I said. "And, Jeff, Sue and I agreed that no one needs to know what happened. She deserves that much at least, so let's not talk about it here, okay?"

He nodded, and we started to fence.

Anyone watching would have wondered what the hell was wrong with us. We were both stiff and tentative, a far cry from our normal styles. Fortunately, no one was watching us.

I had just landed a solid shot on his chest, bending my blade. There was a pause in the action while I attempted to straighten it. The time honored but not-recommended method was to run it under a foot, putting weight on it the entire time. As I was doing that, I brought up something that had been bothering me.

"Listen, Jeff, I want to apologize again about poking you on Sunday."

"Forget it, Jax," he began, but I cut him off.

"No. Hear me out. It's not just the poke. Like you said, maybe you had it coming. I still feel bad about it, but I can live with it. The part that's really bugging me is that I was so convinced that you had done it. If you hadn't had that alibi ..."

My voice trailed off, but he didn't seem to notice anything amiss. "Like I said, Jax, forget it. I was way out of line that night. Anyone would have thought the same thing. Jax?"

I had frozen while he spoke, the tip of my épée still trapped beneath my left foot.

"Jeff," I said, and even I could hear the difference in my voice. "That alibi." At those words I could see him stiffen.

"Yeah?"

"What time did you say the cops picked you up?"

"After midnight, Jax."

"Right. Ten minutes after we left the parking lot?"

"Something like that."

I tensed, and felt the tip of my épée break off beneath my foot. "Nice try, Jeff. You know I don't wear a watch to practice. It would have worked, too, on a different night. Friday was my birthday, though, as you may recall, and I was keyed up when I got home, too keyed up to sleep. I turned on the tube for a while, just long enough to see that Jay Leno was still on. It wasn't midnight yet, Jeff, not by at least an hour, and the paper said you were picked up at 1:25 A.M."

"You did it, Jeff. You raped her."

His shoulders fell and so did the point of his weapon. "So what are you going to do, Jax? Hit me again? Or are you going to turn me in to the police, Mr. Private Investigator?" There was a note of defiance in his voice, an almost childish taunt.

"No, Jeff," I said. "I'm going to fence you. Come to guard."

"It wasn't really rape," he said. "I mean, she never said no or anything."

I stiffened at that, fury filling my limbs with the desire to throttle him. "Did she say yes, Jeff? Did you give her a chance to say anything at all?"

He didn't answer.

"Come to guard, you son of a bitch," I said.

Reluctantly, he did so.

In a few years, he probably would have been a good fencer. On that night, however, he was not good enough. As he came to guard, I brought my own blade up, revealing the jagged end for the first time. I thought I heard him gasp, but by then I was already moving.

I beat once and felt his point slip aside, and then I lunged, full out, putting all my fury, all my pain, and all my sorrow into it. I could have gone for his throat; I could have tried for a weak spot in his mask. I didn't. I aimed much lower than that.

I hit him in the groin, and I felt my blade sink into him a long ways. He cried out, once, and collapsed, my épée still buried in him.

What the hell, I thought as I removed my mask and watched the sudden commotion. What I'd just done could cost me my license, I knew, but at the moment I didn't really care. Besides, I suspected the whole thing would be written off as an unfortunate accident. He'd live, and he had to know that if he tried to bring charges against me, I'd tell the cops what I knew. I only hoped my aim had been good enough to make sure he never raped anyone again.

I wondered if I would ever feel bad about what I'd just done, but I decided I probably wouldn't. After all, I realized, it wasn't really an attack. I mean, he never said no, did he?

Iron Frog

by Rick Hautala

"Frogs at the bottom of the well see only a small
part of the sky."
—A Chinese proverb

"I think I . . . I might've seen Pop last night."

Mark Stover was sitting across from his mother at
the kitchen table. Overhead, a single lightbulb cast a
dull yellow patina, like a coating of dust, over the
well-worn linoleum floor, the faded and chipped
countertop, and the frayed, red and white checkered
tablecloth. Ellen Stover, Mark's mother, sat silently
with her hands folded on the table in front of her.
Between her forearms was a steaming cup of tea,
which she hadn't yet sipped. The light made the skin
on the back of her hands look as pale and worn-out
as the old white teacup, almost translucent. Pencil-thin
tendons and twisting blue veins stood out in sharp
relief beneath her skin as she twisted and twined her
fingers together.

"Wha—what do you mean?" Ellen said in a low,
tremulous voice that was almost a whisper.

Mark heaved a deep sigh as he leaned his chair back
on two legs and took a long pull from his beer bottle.
When he swallowed, his throat made a loud gulping
sound that almost would have been funny except for
the sensation he had that someone with ice-cold hands
had grabbed him by the throat and was slowly
squeezing.

"Well, I . . . you must realize how . . . how tough it's been for me even to come back here after . . . after all this time," he said.

His grip around the beer bottle tightened as he absentmindedly flicked the edge of the bottle's label with his thumbnail. His vision went unfocused as he dredged up the memory of the nightmare he'd had last night. It had been his first night sleeping in his boyhood home in almost ten years, and he certainly hadn't slept very well.

"No, it wasn't Pop . . . I mean, not exactly, but I was thinking about him and trying to—you know, to . . ."

He ended lamely, letting his voice drift away to nothing.

His mother sighed as she shifted her gaze away from him, blinking her eyes rapidly.

"Well, you know that it . . . that's just not possible. Your father's been dead more'n eight years now."

"Umm, yeah. I know," Mark said in a low, raspy voice. "I still feel bad about not making it to his funeral."

"Well, what's done is done," his mother said with a shrug. "But let me ask you, where were you when you *thought* you saw him?"

A numbing chill gripped Mark as he allowed the memory of his nightmare to intensify. For a moment, he couldn't find the breath to speak, but he finally managed to croak out the words, "Up in my . . . bedroom."

"Uh-huh."

The expression that crossed his mother's face for only a fleeting instant made his stomach tighten. His heart went suddenly cold in the center of his chest.

I know exactly what it is! Mark thought, fighting back the violent shiver that skittered up and down his back. *The bastard's still here! No matter how long he's been dead . . . no matter how deeply we bury him . . .*

he still casts his shadow over this house and over both of our lives.

He wanted to say this—or something like it—to his mother, but the sensation of cold hands tightening around his throat got even stronger. To relieve it, he let his eyes go unfocused as he looked up at the ceiling and took another swallow of beer.

After a lengthening moment of awkward silence, he cleared his throat and said, "Do you have any idea how much I hate this island?"

His mother sighed and, looking straight at him, nodded her head but said nothing.

"I mean, how much I *really* hate this place! ... The whole thing! Glooscap Island and the goddamned ocean that surrounds it! Everything about it! You know—" He sniffed with suppressed laughter as he narrowed his eyes for a moment and shook his head. "I think it's really funny how, every summer, this place is overrun with tourists and summer people—"

"And every year, it seems to get nothing but worse," his mother added, sounding wistful, almost sad.

"Yeah, and what do they come here for? Tell me that."

His mother shrugged. "Why, they come here to get away from it all, I suppose," she said. "Away from the crime in the cities, the hustle and bustle. They want to be surrounded by the ocean so they can relax and forget all about their problems back at home. They want to breathe in the fresh, clean ocean air and—"

"Yeah, exactly," Mark said sharply, "but do you know what this island smells like to me?"

He paused a moment, but when his mother didn't answer, he continued.

"All it's ever smelled like to me is the choking stench of dead, rotting fish!"

His mother seemed to consider his words for a moment, then she nodded, staring at him silently. Mark sniffed the air, flaring his nostrils as though testing the wind.

"I can even smell it right now, can't you?" he said. His voice rose with an edge of tension. "God, ever since I can remember, that's all this house, this town, this whole island has ever smelled like—a barrel full of dead, rotting, putrid fish." His voice trailed away as he shook his head slowly and finished, "It smells just like Pop's bait barrel."

He took another swallow of beer, draining it, then carefully placed the bottle on the table in front of him.

"That always was Pop's smell, wasn't it?" he said, almost chuckling. "It was like his . . . his own, personal cologne or something—a mixture of—what? Dead fish, gasoline fumes, cigar smoke." He swallowed again, noisily, and added, "—And cheap whiskey."

"Well, what do you expect? Your father was a lobsterman."

"Yeah, but do you realize how . . . how embarrassing it was? Good God, all through high school, I never even dared to invite any of my friends into the house because of that smell. I was so embarrassed by the way the *stink* of him seemed to permeate *everything*. I remember I used to shower once, sometimes two or three times a day just so that god-awful smell wouldn't cling to me the way it did to Pop."

Ellen tilted her head slightly to one side and shrugged.

"Well, your father wasn't the only man on Glooscap Island who smelled like that, I can assure you."

"Yeah, but . . ."

Mark took a deep breath before continuing.

"There's something I never told you, and over the past few years, going through therapy like I've been doing, I finally remembered something that happened back when I was nine years old. Do you remember that summer when Dad broke his foot, and I went out with him to help him haul his lobster pots?"

Ellen nodded. "Who can forget? In fact, I think that's when his drinking started getting worse because he was so ... so depressed about that. It really set him back, you know."

"Yeah, but I never told you about what he did to me one day out there, did I?"

His mother shook her head, silently encouraging him to continue. Mark leaned back in his chair and heaved a deep sigh.

"You see, up to that point in my life, I always figured, when I grew up, I'd be a lobsterman, just like Pop. There didn't seem to be any other choice, really. He was a lobsterman, and I was a lobsterman's son. There was never any question that, eventually, I'd take over his job, setting my traps in the same areas where he set his."

Mark winced and picked up the empty beer bottle, rolling it back and forth in his hands as the memory of that day sharpened in his mind.

"Well, you see, one of the first days we went out together, it was right after a storm, and one of his pot lines had gotten fouled up with someone else's. There was a real danger that the rope would get tangled up in our propeller. While I was hauling in the line, because of the way the rough sea was tossing the boat around, I had to lean over the side of the boat. I was trying my best to unfoul the ropes while Pop held the boat steady into the swelling sea, but I was scared as hell that with each rising wave, I would pitch over the side of the boat and into the icy cold water."

"Well, lobstering can be dangerous at times, no doubt about that," Ellen said. "In fact, I had more than a few arguments with your father about how I thought you might be a little too young to be out there with him, working as hard as that."

"Umm—yeah. But you see, by mistake I cut Pop's pot line, and his trap sank to the ocean floor, and the other guy's buoy stayed afloat. Pop totally lost his temper. He was so mad about losing that trap, he started shouting and swearing at me, calling me all kinds of things I'd never even heard before. He slapped me around a few times, and then he took me by the scruff of the neck and shoved my head right down into the bait barrel. He held me there so long I thought I was going to die."

Mark ran his hand over his throat as though to relieve some pressure that was still strangling him.

"God, that stench of raw, rotting fish just about killed me! I think that was the first day I ever had— you know, that really scary feeling, knowing that— someday—you're gonna die."

Mark paused a moment and looked at his mother, trying to read her reaction, but her face seemed almost totally blank of expression. It looked as though she wasn't the least bit surprised by this revelation, as if her thirty-plus years of living with Ernie Stover had made her immune to any surprises about his violence and abuse.

"Well, then," Mark said after clearing his throat, "you can see why that smell still bothers me ... how after all these years, I still can't get it out of my memory. It's like it's still clinging there in the back of my throat, and I'll *never* be able to get rid of it. I was so ... so scared. I was absolutely convinced that I was going to choke to death on those dead fish. I thought Pop was trying to kill me right then and there, and that he would simply toss my body over the side of the boat and let it sink. All for losing one lousy lobster trap! I mean, how many did he lose every year due to storms or whatever? It was crazy for him to react like that! And that's why, after all these years, I can truly say that I ... I think I feared and hated Pop more than anyone else in the world."

Mark took a deep, shuddering breath.

"And I ... I *hate* him for dying before I could tell him that!"

Mark looked at his mother, shocked and a little bit embarrassed to see the single tear that was running down from the corner of her left eye, shimmering like glycerin on the puffy, deeply pored skin of her face. His stomach twisted up, and his eyes started stinging as though he were about to start crying, too, but after so many years of bottling up all of the rage and hurt inside himself, it seemed almost too easy to say these things out loud ... at least to his mother. If only his father were still alive so he could tell *him*!

"And you know," he said after taking a moment to compose himself, "I don't think it could possibly have been a conscious decision at that age, but from then on, I knew that I could *never* become a lobsterman, that I would have to do absolutely everything within my power to get away from this island ... to get away from *him*! That's why I studied as hard as I did in school. I was sure that a college education was my ticket off Glooscap and away from a life that smelled like ... like dead fish."

"Do you really think I didn't know that?" his mother said softly.

She stopped twisting her fingers together, and then slid both of her hands across the table. He was surprised by how small and delicate her hands felt as she twined her fingers around his and squeezed. She had always seemed so big, so strong to him, but now it was a shock to realize how small and fragile she really was.

A sudden, blinding surge of anger filled him. He thought how easy it would be to squeeze his mother's hands together and grind her knuckles to powder. But after three years of therapy, he knew that none of his anger was directed at her. Although she had never spoken to him about it, he knew that she had suffered horribly at the hands of her husband, as much if not more than he had. Shortly after his father died, his mother had been hospitalized—for nervous exhaustion, the doctor had informed Mark at the time, but he had recognized the truth—she'd had a nervous breakdown.

"You know what?" Mark said, fighting hard to maintain control of his emotions. "There's really only one thing I really wish for. I wish that Pop was still alive so I could ... could tell him just how much he's hurt me, and how, over the years, I've worked so hard to ... to forgive him for it."

"I know that," his mother said, giving his hands a tighter squeeze. Her hands felt unnaturally dry and rough.

"I try to do it, too ... in my heart," Mark continued. "Try like hell. Last night, as I lay awake in bed, staring up at the ceiling and listening to the ticktock of my old alarm clock, I tried so hard to imagine that he was there in the room so I could talk to him ... so I could tell him that. But every time I tried to visualize him, I couldn't get a clear mental image of what he looked like. Instead, all I could see was this ... this—"

The strong, cold clutching sensation gripping his throat spread a tingling panic through his body. Sweat broke out over his forehead, and deep inside his chest, he could feel a scream building up, threatening to burst loose at any second.

"You know you don't have to talk about it if you don't want to," his mother said mildly. "I know there's been a lot of pain in your life, and I ... I feel absolutely miserable that I was so powerless to help, that I wasn't able to protect you."

"Hey, Mom, you did the best you could at the time. I realize that," Mark said in a shattered voice. "It's just that last night—"

Again, Mark shivered with the memory of his nightmare. Squeezing his eyes tightly shut for a moment, he tried to bring the mental image more clearly into focus. He knew that he had to do it so he could start to deal with it, put it behind him. Shivers wracked his body as he tried to imagine himself as he had been last night, lying there in his darkened bedroom, trying to conjure up the image of his dead father's face.

"Do you—?" he started to say, but tears were welling up in his eyes, and his voice cut off abruptly. Gripped with a swell of emotion, he squeezed his mother's hands all the tighter, as if hoping to find in her clasp even a small measure of the strength and reassurance he needed right now.

"Whenever I . . . I try to remember what he looked like," Mark said in a high, halting voice, "all I ever get is this . . . this . . ."

He sighed heavily, closed his eyes for a moment, and shook his head, wishing the image that was burned into his brain would dissolve, but he knew that it never would.

"I know how weird this must sound," he said at last, forcing a chuckle, "but all I ever see is a big iron frog."

Ever since he had first mentioned this image to his therapist, two years ago, he had hoped that just saying the words to his mother would make him feel some sense of relief, but now that the words were out, all they did was make the mental image of the frog resolve all the sharper in his mind, and with it came a bolt of blinding, white terror.

Last night!

He wasn't even sure if he had been asleep or awake. There was no way of knowing if the image was inside his mind or really out there in the room, hovering in a blue, ghostly glow in the darkness beside his bed—the wide, grinning face of a huge frog. It's round, bulging eyes were slitted with golden, catlike pupils that stared at him from out of the darkness. The wide face was split by the thick, dark line of a grin, but there was no life, no animation in the features. The frog's face seemed starkly immobile, as though it had been cast in metal that was marked with black and rust-red splotches of corrosion. Once or twice, the frog's mouth seemed almost to twitch as though the creature were trying to make a sound ... or about to speak.

"An iron frog," Mark said, his voice sounding as flat and broken as a distant echo. "I think it's, like, an image I made up for Pop, you know? Maybe I always thought, even while I was growing up so scared of him because he hurt me so many times, that underneath it all, he still loved me somehow. He was probably quite vulnerable, too, you know? Like he was this soft squishy thing—a frog—inside a hard, protective shell that he had to put on to protect himself."

"Maybe," his mother said, nodding, "but I remember that we used to have an iron frog."

"What?"

Mark shoved himself away from the table so violently his chair fell over backward. His foot kicked against one of the table legs, knocking his empty beer bottle onto the floor where it broke.

"Sure," his mother said in a light, detached sounding voice as if she hadn't even noticed his reaction. "Don't you remember it? You gave it to me as a gift, many years ago, for Mother's Day. Come on, you *must* remember it. It was the cutest little thing. Actually, it was quite large. A big, cast-iron bullfrog about—yea big." She held her hands about two feet apart. "You said you got it for me to put out in my flower garden."

"Oh, my God! *Oh, my God!*" Mark said, reeling

backward, his hands clawing through his hair. "Oh, Jesus! No ... *No!*"

Whimpering softly, he began to pace back and forth across the kitchen floor, all the while slapping his fist into the flat of his hand, making wet, smacking sounds. His breath came in burning gulps. Even before his mother had finished speaking, something he hadn't remembered in years had come rushing back to him all at once, crashing on top of him with the irresistible surge of a tidal wave.

"Yes," he whispered in a raw, gasping voice. "Yes, by Jesus, I *do* remember it!"

His mother looked at him and laughed lightly.

"I thought it was so nice of you to pick out something like that for me. I mean, Good Lord, you were only—what, maybe ten or eleven years old when you bought it for me? I couldn't imagine how you could have afforded something like that."

"I couldn't," Mark said flatly, shaking his head. "I didn't *buy* it ... I stole it."

The memories were sweeping over him, swirling inside his brain like a whirlpool of oily, black water. His face and hands had gone ice-cold. With every step as he paced back and forth, he felt as though his legs were going to fold up under him.

"You didn't? Why, Mark! I'm surprised that you would ever steal anything!"

"Oh yes, I did. I stole it off Old Lady Burns's lawn, but you want to know what? The funny thing is, I ... I never even planned to give it to you."

Squinting as she looked up at him, his mother shook her head as though thoroughly confused.

"What do you mean?"

"I mean I wanted to *kill* him!" Mark suddenly shouted as the long buried emotions exploded out of him. "I wanted to kill that miserable son of a bitch!"

He took a deep breath in an effort to calm himself,

but it did no good; he was swept up in a maelstrom of emotion.

"I was on my way home from school when I stole that iron frog. It was a Friday afternoon, I remember. Sometime in May. I knew—as usual—that Pop would be lying on the couch in the living room, either watching TV or else passed out. I was . . . was planning to sneak up on him while he was asleep on the couch and smash his goddamned head in!"

Hot, burning panic raged inside Mark. For a moment, he wasn't exactly sure what his mother's reaction was. She had her face in her hands, and her shoulders were shaking.

Oh, God! he thought. *She's losing it. She's freaking out that I could even think or say something like that! Christ, she's so upset, she's sobbing hysterically.*

But when she looked up at him, and he saw the sparkling glint of genuine amusement in her eyes, he realized that she was laughing. Low, sniffing chuckles were gradually building up into a gale of rippling laughter. Mark stopped his pacing and stared at her, dumbfounded.

"What the—" he muttered, his voice no more than an airy gasp. "What the hell's so damned funny?"

"What's so damned funny?" his mother echoed. She pressed both of her hands to her temples and, cupping her face, shook her head from side to side. Her body was rocking back and forth with uncontained merriment.

"What's so damned funny?" she said again. "Why— why because that's *exactly* what I did!"

"What?"

"Your iron frog . . . Eight years ago, that's what I used to kill your father," she said, now shaking with uncontrollable laughter. Tears filled her eyes and were streaming down her cheeks. She sniffed and wiped them away with the palms of her hands, but still, more came along with her rising peals of laughter. She sounded hysterical.

"I'd finally had enough of his abuse, too, you know," she said between vain attempts to catch her breath. "After all those years—I finally couldn't take it anymore—so one day I . . . I smacked him a good one on the side of the head with that iron frog. Killed him on the spot. Once he was dead, I dragged his body over to the stairway, and then I called the ambulance."

She took a deep, sputtering breath and managed to gain a measure of control.

"I told them that I'd been out shopping—and he must've been drunk and fallen down the stairs and banged his head on the steps or something. No one ever questioned me about it. Then, late that night, way past midnight, after I'd been to the funeral home and all, I went outside and threw your iron frog into the well. The mouth was all stained with blood, like it had this big, bloody grin, and there was some skin and hair still stuck to it."

"I don't believe this," Mark whispered, finding it difficult—no, *impossible* to process any of what she had said.

"It must still be down there at the bottom of the well," his mother said, shrugging her shoulders as though easily dismissing the thought.

Mark righted his chair and sat back down heavily. He felt as though his whole body had been drained of strength. He pressed his fingers hard against his closed eyes until bright spirals of lights exploded across his vision. From somewhere far way, he heard a high, sniffing sound.

Was that his mother still laughing?

Or was she crying now?

He wanted to say or do something to help her, but he was paralyzed with fear. The mental image of the iron frog was growing steadily sharper in his mind, and after a heart-stopping moment, it started to blend gradually into a human face. Stunned speechless, Mark saw—and recognized—his father's face staring back at him with a cold, dead light in his wide, frog-like eyes.

You son of a bitch! Mark thought, sobbing so hard it hurt his chest. *You lousy, rotten bastard! You hurt me, and you hurt her, and you didn't even give a shit, but—goddamn you!—you finally got what was coming to you!*

The image of his father's face twitched into a grimace of pain as it began to vibrate with bright, shimmering colors. Then it began to fade, dissolving gradually into the pulsating darkness inside Mark's mind. Mark realized that his mother was speaking to him, but her voice was muffled and distant. At first he couldn't understand what she was saying, but finally, something she said drifted into his awareness like the soft, sad hiss of the sea breeze blowing over the beach.

"I've been wanting to tell you or *someone* this for a long time," she said. "But do you want to know something else, Mark?"

Mark opened his eyes and stared blankly at her. His throat was dry, and when he opened his mouth to say something, all he could manage was a strangled groan.

"That iron frog," his mother said, leaning toward him and smiling with deep satisfaction. "I'd have to say that was the *best* damned Mother's Day present you ever gave me."

The Business

by Jack Ketchum

The cockroach was not too big but it was coming right at him, moving in that drunken way they have, a little to the left, a little to the right, appropriate in this place, moving past Mama's beer spill on a trajectory that would take it directly yet indirectly to his Scotch.

"Hey Billy," he said to the barman, "pass me another napkin, will ya?"

Billy didn't like him. Howard knew that. He couldn't have cared less. He got service because he left a decent tip, and that was that. Billy handed him the cocktail napkin.

Howard squished the bug. If you had a potato chip stuffed with onion dip, that was what it felt like.

Mama didn't notice. First, she was busy talking to his brother Norman and his bimbo soon-to-be-wife girlfriend Sonya, and second, Mama was going blind as a stump, bless her.

He balled up the napkin and set it on the lip of the bar for Billy to throw away, one less bug in the Apple, and sipped his Scotch and listened.

They were talking about the building over on 71st between Columbus and Central Park West. There was a major problem with the plumbing there. One of the tenants had been watching television two nights ago when the wall behind the television started to balloon out at him like some huge sudden off-white zit, and then it started to trickle. It had been necessary for

Gonzales to turn off all the water in the building while they knocked in the bedroom wall and then the bathroom wall behind it in order to get at the pipes. All this at eight o'clock at night no less. People wanting to cook, wanting to shower, wanting to do the dishes. Tenants were screaming.

They'd have screamed a lot louder if they'd gotten a look at the poor guy's pipes.

And at their own.

So now his mother and Norman were talking plumbing contractors, and, personally speaking, Howard was bored to tears. Because the decision on who to hire, finally, was not going to be Norman's in any case. Not this time. Not anymore. There was no point discussing it.

Sorry, big brother.

Sure I am.

"Hey, Mama," he said. "Enough with the business. It's Mother's Day. It's a party. We came here to enjoy ourselves, right?"

She turned to him and smiled and patted his hand. He thought Mama had a real nice smile.

When her teeth were in.

"You're right, sonny," she said.

He hated it when she called him sonny, but she did it all the time. It was ridiculous. He was pushing fifty for God's sake, practically bald, he had problems with his cholesterol and his blood pressure. He had weathered two divorces. And now the big guy down at the end of the bar, the Texan or Southerner or whatever the hell he was who always wore the same baseball cap and fishing vest like he was about to go pull some pike out of the Raritan or some damn place was looking at him and snickering. Because Mama had called him sonny. He hated *sonny.*

But it was Mama.

And you had to love Mama.

It was impossible, in fact, for him to even stay mad at her very long. Even when she was treating him like some idiot who would never have half a head for business while his brother Norman got treated almost like the second coming of Nate, their father—with that much respect. It happened sometimes.

Even then he couldn't stay mad at her. Because unlike Norman, and unlike their dear dead pain-in-the-butt father, Mama always encouraged him in what he *did* do.

Which, granted, wasn't much.

What Howard did was he invested in shows. Off-Broadway shows mostly, especially the cabaret type that were big these days in the supper clubs. Like *Forbidden Broadway* and *Forever Plaid,* though he didn't have a piece of either of these—God knows he wished he had. No, the shows he backed had names like *Spike's Stiletto-Heel Review* and *Recession Drag.* Some made money and some didn't. *Most* didn't. But they kept him busy. And Mama had encouraged him.

So you had to love Mama.

His brother Norman was a whole other matter.

Look at him, he thought. The cheapskate. Standing at the bar drinking well-whiskey in the cheapest joint on Columbus Avenue.

The guy was worth over thirty million dollars.

He'd checked.

"We haven't even ordered yet," said Mama. "Come on. Let's order."

The bartender handed them each a menu.

Silence as they studied the cuisine. Buffalo wings and onion rings and fries. Chicken fingers. Burgers and clubs and reubens. Oh yeah. And the Mother's Day Special Brunch Menu at eight ninety-five, all the Frexinet you could guzzle straight up or mimosa included.

Damn cheapskate.

It was Mother's Day for God's sake!

And Mr. Big Spender says last night at dinner that he's taking them all out for brunch, his treat, how about that! And Mama's delighted of course—and then they wind up here.

Mama didn't seem to mind.

She seemed quite happy in fact.

He minded.

He'd been minding for a long time, and now, finally, he was doing something about it. The wheels were in motion. He'd greased the skids.

Norman was going to fall.

Outside the big plate-glass window the girl of his dreams cruised by on rollerskates, a moment's suggestion of what for Howard was the promise of eternal grace, and was gone.

You could keep your Sonyas, your blond big-breasted short-waisted Little-Annie-Fannies of this world—Howard's tastes were more refined. His notion of a thing of true beauty was five feet, ten inches tall or taller—though he himself was only five-six—long in the leg and in the neck, delicate of wrist and hand, small-breasted, slim-hipped, and young. Especially young. Your basic fashion-model infanta.

And he would have her. He'd have her soon.

He got flushed just thinking about it.

Nobody noticed.

He glanced at Sonya. Her eyes all squinty, puzzling over the one-page menu.

Sonya was pushing thirty. And not his type. Still it galled him that Norman was older and fatter and even more bald than he was and yet he had this younger woman, this *considerably* younger woman, this slightly aging bunny in fact—who was willing to marry him. While Howard remained womanless.

Except, of course, for Mama.

It was all about money. He knew that. Norman had

the woman because Norman had the money, the buildings and the business all controlled by him, his father's will had set it up that way—with Howard granted a certain amplitude of hard cash but no sure way of turning it into more. While Norman had ten brownstones and four high-rise apartments up his sleeve at all times.

No fair.

"I'll have the Special," said Mama. "Two eggs over easy, the bacon, the toast, and the home fries. Oh, and a mimosa, please."

Billy scribbled it down.

"The Special," said Sonya. "Western omelette, ham, toast, fries, and a glass of just the regular . . . you know . . . the champagne. I mean, no OJ. You know?"

"Make mine the same," said Norman. He hugged her, smiling. She wrapped her tanned, firm naked arm around his waist, hugged him back, and giggled.

They were bonding over a western omelette.

My God.

"Steak and eggs," he said. Billy looked at him. "I know it's not on the menu. But you must have some kind of steak back there. Tell the cook to broil it medium and give me two eggs over easy and some fries. Green salad on the side. With Roquefort dressing. And forget the champagne. Just keep the Dewar's coming."

Mama elbowed him lightly in the ribs, smiling at him conspiratorially. "Spendthrift," she said.

"Only when it's on Norman's tab."

She laughed and leaned over and kissed his cheek. "He *is* a little tight, isn't he, sonny," she said. She sighed. "But that's all to the good now, isn't it."

He presumed she meant *now that he was marrying Sonya.* Though it was hard to see how even a shop-till-you-drop clothes-horse like Sonya was going to break Norman. If she got the opportunity.

Which she wasn't.

It had actually been very easy to arrange. Even easier to conceive. As a matter of fact it had come to mind right away when Norman announced last month that he and Sonya were going on vacation together, a sort of pre-honeymoon honeymoon. To Mexico.

Mexico, he'd thought immediately. *Where life is cheap.*

Wasn't that an ad for some movie or something?

They'd be gone a week, said Norman. Or longer.

Howard was already focusing on the *or longer* part.

There was a tenant in their 45th Street building in Hell's Kitchen. His name was Castanza. By trade a painter and a carpenter. *Supposedly.* He and Mama and Norman had talked about Castanza many times because on two occasions now, police had been over to the office to question Norman about the man's activities. Had they had any complaints about him? Was he paid up on his rent? What did they know about how he made a living? Had they noticed any significant spending? On the apartment perhaps?

When pressed, one of the investigators suggested— only suggested, mind you, and completely off the record—that they would probably do well to be careful in their dealings with Castanza, that any irregularities in his behavior toward them or any of their tenants should probably be reported immediately to the authorities, that he had been linked—not conclusively linked, but *linked*—to a number of disappearances in various places throughout the city. He and the battered old Ford truck he drove, which the meter maids kept ticketing constantly outside the building.

They'd noticed nothing and heard nothing but the suggestion stuck, distressing and sort of thrilling.

Castanza was possibly dangerous.

Possibly even a killer.

Castanza was from Mexico City.

A wholly conscienceless killer, Howard found, who worked for hire and actually worked pretty modestly. He was already down there. Waiting for Norman's flight, the red-eye out of Kennedy this evening.

So that what Norman and Sonya would find down there was not the Mexico City of green expansive parks, monuments and plazas, of cappuccino in chic cafés and romantic moonlight strolls. What they would find down there was death.

He did not know where or how. He did not care to know. That was up to Castanza. The man had assured him that in Mexico it would not be difficult to make it appear drug related or perhaps *brujo* related—a touch of Santeria. Did he have a preference?

He did not.

The man knew Norman well and had no love for his landlord. Maybe that was why Howard was getting the price he was getting. Sonya he didn't know at all—but Sonya was just window dressing anyway, she was *nada*, just some woman who'd be traveling with Norman.

By next week, the business would belong to him.

A begrudging provision of Nate's will.

Nate would be turning over in his grave right about now. Mentally, Howard gave him the finger. The men in his family had always been prize bastards, and his dad was no exception.

Howard was looking at his brother for the very last time.

As far as he was concerned it was *about* time.

It would all be him and Mama now.

That was fine.

He thought all this as the food arrived and they ate—you might even say he savored it.

It was sure much easier to chew than the steak.

"I'd like to propose a toast," said Norman. His fork clattered noisily to his empty plate. *First one started, first one finished. Every time.* "You need champagne for this, little brother. Come on. Billy? Set my brother up, will you?"

"I don't drink champagne," said Howard. "Especially that stuff. You know that."

"One glass won't kill you. I want to make a proper toast here, all right? Gimme a break."

Norman was smiling, his lips still greasy from the eggs and fries, and flecked with crumbs of toast. It was amazing to Howard that his mother had given birth to something so repulsive.

He guessed he might as well go along with it, though. It was a holiday, right?

"Okay," he said. "One glass. You got anything better than that?" he asked the barman.

Billy shrugged. "I can give you a split of Korbel *Brut.*"

"Jesus. Yeah, okay."

The bartender popped open the bottle and poured, then freshened Mama's, Norman's, and Sonya's glasses with the Frexinet. Howard gulped the dregs of his Scotch, and they raised their glasses.

"To my brother," Norman said.

"Huh?"

"To you."

"It's Mother's Day. What's to toast me for?"

And then all three of them were smiling, looking at him.

Oh, cute, he thought. I got some kind of conspiracy going here.

"It's a surprise," said Norman. "Believe me, you're going to like it. Drink up. Cheers, everybody."

They drank.

Howard could already imagine the Korbel headache.

"Here's the story, little brother," Norman said. "You know that me and Sonya are getting married next month, right? Right. Okay, so the two of us have been talking, and then we talked it over with Mama, and ... well, the point is I'm not getting any younger, you know? Not that I'm all that much older than you are but the point is I'm not getting any younger, right? and Sonya and me, we're sick of the city. Crowds, hassles, dirt. Remember we were in Barbados last year? We keep thinking Barbados, Sonya and me. Now I know you've always wanted to run the business but Dad's will being Dad's will, it was always me who ran the business. But I tell you, I got plenty of money, I got plenty of investments, hell I'll be dead before I spend it all! So guess what, I'm giving it to you."

"Giving me ... ?"

"The business, you shmuck!" he laughed. "I'm giving you the business!"

"Isn't that *wonderful,* sonny!" said Mama. She leaned over and kissed him. Norman held out his hand.

"Congratulations, little brother."

Howard shook his brother's hand. His *dead* brother's hand.

He considered his options.

There weren't many.

There was no way to call off Castanza. He didn't even know where or how to reach the man. Norman's tickets were already paid for and short of Mama having a stroke or a heart attack right there at the bar, nothing anybody said or did—especially anything *he* said or did—was going to keep him and Sonya from climbing on that plane in four hours. Unless, of course, Howard were to admit to what he'd done.

If he admitted to what he'd done, he certainly wouldn't be getting the business. In fact, Norman was perfectly capable of having his ass thrown in jail. He wouldn't have blamed him.

His options were ... limited.

Sorry, Norm, he thought. Who'd have guessed you'd turn soft over a blonde after all these years of hardball.

"I don't know what to say," he said. "I'm ... I guess I'm overwhelmed, Norman. I can't believe it."

"Believe it, little brother. The transfer papers'll be on your desk in the morning. You're somebody's landlord now, buddy. Enjoy yourself."

Sonya came over and kissed his cheek.

She smelled of Tigress and fried eggs.

Mama gave him a hug.

"You'll do a wonderful job. I know you will, sonny."

"Thanks, Ma."

Over her shoulder he saw Norman check his Rolex.

"We better get going now, Mama," he said. "We got to get you packed up."

"Huh?"

Norman sighed. "Right, we forgot to tell you. Sonya's mom and dad are coming in tomorrow, her mother's sister's in St. Luke's. What is it, Sonya, colonostomy?"

"Colostomy."

"Colostomy. So anyway, Sonya can't go. So I invited Mama."

"You invited Mama? To Mexico?"

Norman laughed. "Sure, to Mexico. Where am I going, Hoboken? Mama's never seen it and I figured what the hell, it's either that or eat the tickets and why not."

"You'll have a *great* time," said Sonya.

"I'm sure we will," said Mama, smiling. "I haven't been anywhere with one of my boys in twenty years. Of course we will!"

Castanza doesn't know her, thought Howard. Not even a description. Castanza said the woman was *nada.* Just somebody traveling with Norman. Window-dressing.

My God, *Mama!*

Mama who had supported him, raised him, encouraged him. Who had, by marrying Nate forty-two years ago in the first place, then bearing two children in the second place, handed him his goddamn life!

He considered his options.

They were very much the same options he had considered when it was only Norman and Sonya he was worrying about. So it didn't take him long, just a moment or so while he pushed aside the half-empty champagne glass and signaled to Billy for another Dewar's rocks, one that he supposed would be the first of many—though it was still four hours to flight time, and he knew he'd have to be careful on the drinking.

He knew he shouldn't be too drunk when they boarded.

Norman wouldn't care.

But Mama would worry.

The Mother's Day Doubleheader

by Jon L. Breen

It's time somebody told the whole truth about that incident a few years ago at Grizzly Stadium in New Hopton and the murder that followed. Not just why my fellow ump Joe Whittlesy did what he did—that's the easy part—but the rest of it, too.

Joe is only briefly a suspect in the murder of Buckley Wilmoth, the loudmouth fan who was found stabbed to death in his apartment a couple hours after the last out. Joe has a perfect alibi. He's with me and the other umps (and assorted relatives) back at our hotel when Wilmoth buys it.

Still, it's understandable my old friend Sergeant Rojas of the New Hopton P.D. comes to talk to Joe because of what happened at Grizzly Stadium earlier in the day, and that's how yours truly, Ed Gorgon, winds up looking over another murder scene.

Let's start with a look at the calendar. Wilmoth is murdered on Mother's Day, the day of New Hopton's traditional doubleheader. Of all the changes to come about during my thirty-year-plus career as a major league umpire, I think the demise of the doubleheader is one of the saddest. Those two-game days are seldom scheduled on purpose anymore. Mostly they survive only as a way of making up a rain out. Ernie Banks, the Chicago Cub star who used to say, "Let's play two," belongs to a different era of baseball. And I guess old Ed Gorgon does, too.

In some ways, Mother's Day is the worst possible choice for a doubleheader. Think of all the kids who take their mothers to the ball game for a special treat, and their mothers make like they love it, even if they don't give a damn about baseball, because mothers are like that. Subjecting these poor ladies to one game isn't so bad. Forcing them to sit through two is cruel and unusual punishment.

But Sid Kramer, the sentimental owner of the Grizzlies, makes Mother's Day at the ballpark something special. The organist plays old tunes like "Mammy" and "My Mother's Eyes" all afternoon, and they have an Al Jolson imitator to sing the National Anthem, even if most of the mothers in attendance (let alone the kids) are too young to remember him.

The really special thing Kramer does is invite the mothers of the players to the game, paying all their expenses to come whether they live in Alaska or Rhode Island or the Dominican Republic. The first couple of times, he just invites the home team's mothers. Then, he starts inviting the visiting team's mothers. And finally this year I'm telling you about, all-heart Sid invites every living mother of everybody connected in any way with the game: the public address announcer's mother, the organist's mother—you get the idea. All the mothers get introduced in ceremonies between games.

Mother's Day always gives the Grizzlies their biggest crowd of the year, even if they're in last place at the time (and they usually are), but the added gate receipts can't possibly equal the expense of transporting all those mothers. I often think how Ma Gorgon would have enjoyed it.

The first game is a tight one. I'm working first base, and Joe Whittlesy is working behind the plate. Everybody seems happy, and all through the early innings, I'm hearing tributes to motherhood from the infielders, the base runners, the first-base coaches, even one of the managers who comes out pretending to argue a call.

In the bottom of the fifth, the big first base man of the L.A. Surfers says to me, "This is a great thing they do here, Ed. Men have a hard time telling their mothers how much they love and appreciate and value 'em, but on a day like this—" A ball whacks off a Grizzly bat, and he jumps up to spear it in his glove, setting the crowd to oohing, half in admiration and half in disappointment. Tossing the ball back to the pitcher, he finishes, "On a day like this, we can all show 'em, no matter how tongue-tied we might be." He looks toward the stands, where all the mothers are sitting together. "Did you see that, Mom?" he says softly.

In the late innings, things get really intense. Everybody wants to play well on Mother's Day, and everybody wants to win. I can tell Joe is working a good game, but he starts catching a lot of flack from both teams about his calls, and flack from the home players signals boos from the crowd.

In the bottom of the ninth, the Surfers lead 3–2, and the Grizzlies have the tying run on third with one out. The Grizzly shortstop sends a semi-deep fly ball to left. The Surfer left fielder is a guy with a great arm, but the man on third is a fast runner who tries to tag up and score. Both men go all out to impress Mom: the throw is perfect; the slide is perfect; and the play is as close as they come. Joe Whittlesy calls the guy out, and that's the ball game.

The crowd doesn't like it and lets Joe know.

In the umps' room between games, Joe is as even-tempered as ever. The guy is no hothead, believe me.

He just says, "It was a good call, Ed. You know they're gonna boo. It's part of the game."

We get a quick shower—it's a hot day—and hurry back down the tunnel to listen to the introduction of all the mothers in the stands. And the crowd is loving it. They're so glad to see all the mothers, they've all but forgotten how their team lost the first game. But one rotund guy in a third-row box seat on the first-base side—a real loud guy with shirt to match—hasn't forgotten. Joe tells me the guy's been on him all day.

This is the solid citizen we later find out is Buckley Wilmoth. And when he's murdered in his apartment, Sergeant Rojas gets a tip—one that anybody in the stadium or watching the game on TV could have given him—that Wilmoth had an altercation with an umpire earlier in the day. So he comes to the hotel to interview us umps, finding us in the middle of a family celebration that's somewhat clouded by Joe's problem. Once we satisfy him Joe couldn't have done it, he asks me to visit the crime scene with him.

"It's another baseball thing, Ed. You might see some angle I don't." It means I have to leave the family party, but there's no Gorgon family there anyway, so I go with him.

Wilmoth's apartment is on the third floor of an aging apartment building in the center of New Hopton. It's still a pretty nice address, if not as nice as fifteen years ago.

When we enter, a tall, thin, stooped guy in his late forties or early fifties is talking to the doorman. He gives me the kind of look real celebrities must get all the time but we very minor celebrities enjoy only occasionally—and probably enjoy a lot more. While Rojas is talking to the doorman, the other guy button-holes me.

"Ed Gorgon, right?" he says, pumping my hand. "I'm really pleased to meet you. I have to tell you

I've always enjoyed your work: decisive, not too flamboyant, but with a sense of real style."

"Thank you," I say, not used to this kind of lionization. "If umpires took out ads, I'd use that quote."

He laughs more than it's worth. "I don't suppose you can wait till I run up to my apartment, or better yet, come up and visit. I collect baseball memorabilia, and I have to get you to sign something out of my collection. I don't know what, though. What do you get an ump to sign?"

"Got a chest protector?" Rojas offers helpfully. He's through with the doorman and has joined us.

The guy guffaws again. He's a great audience. "Afraid not, but I'll think of something."

"Mister—what was the name?"

"Jim Atkins. I live up on two."

"I'm Sergeant Rojas, New Hopton Police Department. There's been a death in the building today."

Atkins turns solemn. "Oh yes, I know. It's all over the building. Buck Wilmoth."

"Did you know him?"

"Uh, yes, I knew him."

"We'll probably want to come around to talk to you later."

"Sure, great. I mean, you'll be very welcome. Is Mr. Gorgon—?"

"A friend of the family," Rojas says, whatever that means.

On the way up in the elevator, Rojas fills me in on his talk with the doorman, who swears nobody other than tenants entered or left the building between Wilmoth's arrival home and the finding of his body. In the Wilmoth apartment, Rojas shows me where the body was found, lying on its side in the living room. It's now represented by a chalk outline and a sickeningly wide bloodstain.

"What was the weapon?" I ask.

Rojas shrugs. "It looked like a stab wound. The weapon was something sharp, I guess. We haven't found it."

Next we go upstairs to meet the finder of the body, a distinctly dry-eyed widow named Sue. She's with her mother, who has an apartment on the fifth floor. Sue is a pretty lady of about forty who's kept herself in a lot better shape than her overweight husband. Inevitably, she's suspect number one.

"When did you last see your husband, Mrs. Wilmoth?" Rojas asks.

"Alive, you mean? This morning. Mom had come down for Mother's Day brunch with us. Buck scarfed his down in a hurry because he was going to the game. He liked to get there for batting practice."

"It's quieter then, and you can be more obnoxious," her mother put in. Mom's name is Christine Fordyce, and she's a sixty-year-old dead ringer for her daughter. Christine being closer to my age-group, I might find her attractive under other circumstances.

Rojas asks, "He didn't ask the two of you to go to the game with him?"

"No," says Sue. "Neither one of us cares about baseball, and Buck never missed a game. Had to renew his season tickets, even though I was out of work and he had to take a pay cut. Baseball came first."

"Were you angry with your husband for going out without you on Mother's Day?"

"I'm no mother," says Sue, "and I don't think you were ever sorry to see him go, were you, Mom?"

Christine shakes her head, smiling wryly.

"What about his own mother?" I put in.

"Dead twenty years. Not that he would have done shit for her if she was alive, you understand."

"Were you happily married, Mrs. Wilmoth?" Rojas

asks, a damn silly question he manages to deliver with a straight face.

"I guess not," says Sue, as though she's thinking about it for the first time. "We coexisted, never really thought about doing anything else. Habit, I guess."

"And you say you weren't angry with him today?"

"No, I didn't say that. I wasn't angry because he went to the game. But he took the car, even though he knew Mom and I wanted to drive up and see my brother this afternoon. He could have taken the bus easily to get to Grizzly Stadium, and trying to go to my brother's by public transportation would take till tomorrow. But that was typical of Buck. Inconsiderate of other people, especially when it involved baseball." She pauses. "Or basketball or football. Or hockey. Watching games always came first with Buck, and that was that."

I'm still looking for some emotion, any emotion in the recent widow. Maybe she's just in shock and will collapse in grief at any moment. Or maybe she's as indifferent to Buckley Wilmoth's death as she seems.

"Did your husband have any close friends he talked sports with? Somebody in the building, maybe?"

She laughs humorlessly. "Close friends, I don't think."

Christine Fordyce says, "You might talk to Jim Atkins down on two. He and Buck used to be pals anyway. They went to a lot of games together."

Sue Wilmoth shrugs. "Sure, you could talk to Jim. But they haven't seen much of each other lately."

Rojas turns to the mother-in-law. "Mrs. Fordyce, what did you mean when you said Mr. Wilmoth could be more obnoxious if he went to the game early?"

"He loved to ride people from the stands, and it was more fun with fewer people around. He knew the guys on the field could hear him, and his bon mots were reaching their target. Of course, he also ran the risk of somebody coming up and flattening him. I don't know if that ever happened to Buck. If it had, he might have thought twice."

It happened today, I reflect, but Buck Wilmoth didn't live long enough to profit by the lesson.

"You didn't like your son-in-law, did you, Mrs. Fordyce?" Rojas says, still poker-faced as Joe Friday.

She laughs. "Aren't you a hell of a detective? I told Sue not to marry him, but she wouldn't listen, would you, honey? And you found out I was right, didn't you? He was a loser, wasn't he?"

Sue just nods her head. She offers no objection to her mother's statements, and I don't think it's because she doesn't want to contradict her on Mother's Day.

Christine Fordyce goes on, "Buck was a good-looking devil in those days, I have to hand it to him, but I knew what kind of a guy he was from the first. Before they were married, Sue and her father and me went to a college basketball game with him. It's the only game I really enjoy—baseball's too boring, and football and hockey are too bloody. Buck was polite enough to us and attentive to Sue by his standards, but the way he approached the game showed me what he was really like. He picked out one visiting player who was having a bad night—a kid who wasn't complaining to the officials or playing dirty or being a bad sport or anything like that, just a kid who was inept, couldn't do anything right. Buck was all over him the whole night, calling him names, crowing every time he made a mistake. Always the needle, that was Buck."

Christine pauses for a breath, but she isn't done. She's just getting warmed up. "It was more than just being a boorish fan, though. He was a cruel person. He took pleasure from taking away from people whatever they valued, whatever was most important to them. Sometimes he was subtle about it, usually he wasn't."

"Mom, he wasn't that bad in a lot of ways," Sue says softly. "He made a decent living. He never ran around with other women. He never beat me."

Christine tells her daughter, "When all you can think of is negative virtues for somebody . . ."

"Mrs. Fordyce," says Rojas, "can you give me an example of what you mean?"

"Sure. I once saw him swipe a ball from a little kid who'd caught it at a game. Just swipe it from him when he wasn't looking. Not because he even wanted the ball—Sue told you he didn't care about that stuff. He just liked the idea of depriving some little kid he didn't even know of something that was important to him."

Sue says, "He wasn't that bad really." But Christine plows ahead.

"And what about your father's souvenir back scratcher, Sue? He broke that thing on purpose, you know he did."

"He was thoughtless sometimes."

"Most of the time! No, I'll take that back. He wasn't thoughtless at all. He thought of the rottenest thing he could do in a situation, and then he did it."

From there, Rojas works on the timetable. He knows from me that Buckley Wilmoth stays for the whole doubleheader—after the incident with Joe Whittlesy between games, I have reason to be conscious of him sitting in his seat on the third-base side, still getting in his licks, though Joe (understandably) has been given the rest of the day off. The second game ends at about five-thirty. Wilmoth's apartment is about twenty minutes from the stadium in the kind of traffic that follows a Mother's Day doubleheader, and the doorman reports he enters the apartment building at about six. Mrs. Wilmoth says she finds the body at eight, so he has to be killed in that two-hour period.

"Were you with your mother all day, Mrs. Wilmoth?" Rojas asks.

"Most of the day," she replies. "After Buck left, we watched a couple of old pictures on American Movie Classics. It was a kind of treat for us—Mom doesn't get cable, and when Buck's home, our set's never tuned to anything but sports. We called my brother and told him why we wouldn't be coming out. In the afternoon, about four, we came up here because we knew Buck would be coming home and neither of us were looking forward to seeing him. The rest of the time, we sat up here and ate and talked."

"And drank," Christine Fordyce puts in with a smile.

"That's right, I brought a bottle of champagne up to celebrate Mother's Day," said Sue.

"Maybe it's time to crack the second bottle," Christine says, a little too festively for the circumstances. "Can you gentlemen join us or—?"

"Of course they can't, Mom, and I just brought one bottle. I sure didn't want to share it with Buck after what he did, taking the car, I mean. I went down to get it out of our refrigerator at about five-thirty. I remember I was relieved Buck wasn't home yet, but I figured the doubleheader probably wouldn't be over. Mom and I were together all the rest of the time."

"Except when you went up to the roof," Mrs. Fordyce says.

"Oh, right, but that wasn't for long."

"About twenty minutes."

"Was it? It didn't seem that long. That was around seven, wasn't it, Mom?"

Mrs. Fordyce nods. "Yes, around seven." This means they don't conveniently alibi each other for every possible time of the murder. Should that make us more suspicious of them or less?

"Why the roof?" Rojas asks.

Sue Wilmoth shrugs. "I just like to go up there and think sometimes, look at the city. It's a real pretty view."

"You didn't want to go up and enjoy the view, too, Mrs. Fordyce?"

"No. Heights bother me."

"Did anybody see you on the roof, Mrs. Wilmoth?"

"I don't think so."

"And did you stay here in the apartment while Mrs. Wilmoth was gone, Mrs. Fordyce?"

"I sure did."

"Did anyone come to the apartment during that time, or did you talk to anyone on the phone?"

"Nope. Wish I had now. Wouldn't be a suspect." Christine seems to be enjoying the role.

After we leave the two ladies—to get on with their celebration. I can't help thinking, whether there's a second bottle or not—we go down to Jim Atkins's apartment. He answers the door immediately, like he's been hovering behind it and waiting for us.

"Come on in the den," he says and leads us in, jabbering every step of the way. He's nervous and overtalkative, but that may be his normal manner.

The den is full of sports memorabilia, mostly from baseball. Autographed pictures and scorecards in frames line the walls; bats and balls are exhibited museum style in all four corners of the room.

"I expected to see you, Sergeant—not you specifically, but police. I heard the sirens earlier, and like I said downstairs, it got around the building pretty quickly that somebody killed Buck. I had the game on the radio earlier today, and"—he turns to me—"you were working the doubleheader, weren't you? Well, of course, why else would you be in town? And an umpire went in the stands after a fan, and I remember thinking at the time—they didn't name who it was, of course, they wouldn't give that kind of publicity to an obnoxious fan, might encourage the bastard, wouldn't it? But I thought at the time, I wonder if it was Buck Wilmoth, and if it was, I hoped the ump—Joe Whittlesy, was it?—got in a few good licks before they pulled him off. What's going to happen to him, Ed? Bound to get a suspension, I guess, but I hope they don't kick him out of the league or anything. I mean, umpires are human, too. At least Buck can't sue him for assault now, huh? If it was Buck, that is. Was it?"

After glancing at Rojas to see if he wants to jump in, I nod. "It was Buck. And Joe did get in a couple of good licks, though not enough to remove your friend from his seat for the second game. But Joe Whittlesy didn't kill him."

"Oh, no, I'm sure not, I wouldn't accuse him—I mean, I wouldn't accuse anybody if I didn't have all the facts. Who did kill Buck anyway?"

"That's what we're working on, Mr. Atkins," Rojas says. "I need to ask you a few questions."

"Sure, fire away!"

"Do you live here alone?"

"No, but I'm alone today. My wife, Wanda's a sales representative for an electronics firm and has to travel a lot. Likes to travel a lot, actually. She's on a business trip in Phoenix. Well, it's mostly business, but she's also visiting our son and daughter-in-law who live out there, and I'm here because I couldn't get away from work and have no business there. In Phoenix, I mean."

"Have you been here all evening?"

"No, I got back about seven. I'd been to see my folks. They're in Golden Manor—you know, that retirement community out by the lake? I always get out there for Mother's Day. I believe in honoring mothers. Every day, of course, not just Mother's Day. I go other days, too, when I can, but Mother's Day is special. It was on my way there I heard a snatch of the game and wondered if it was Buck who the umpire went after—I guess I'm repeating myself, aren't I? I guess I'm nervous." He gave an uneasy laugh. "I'm not guilty, though, just nervous. I mean, a murder in the building is enough to make a person nervous, isn't it?"

"Did you see Buck Wilmoth at all today?"

"No, no, I hadn't seen Buck in quite a while. Weeks really."

"Were you friends?"

"That's hard to say exactly. I guess we were once, but not lately. We used to go to games together quite a bit. Wanda and I never got together with the Wilmoths as couples that much. Wanda likes Sue, but she never could stand being around Buck. I got to where I couldn't stand him anymore myself."

"Why?"

"He wasn't my kind of sports fan. When we went to games, I'd want to pretend I didn't know the bastard when he started getting on people. That's why when I heard about the ump going in the stands, I right away flashed Buck, Buck, Buck."

While they talk, I'm looking around at Atkins's collection. He has quite a few pennants on his wall, many out-of-town teams and all the local ones. But nothing for the New Hopton Grizzlies.

"Have you been collecting memorabilia for a long time?" I ask casually.

"Ever since I was a kid."

"Why no Grizzlies pennant? I see a perfect spot for one, right there between the Red Sox and the Yankees."

Atkins swallows nervously. "I used to have one. I've meant to get another."

"What happened to the one you had?"

"It just disappeared. I guess it was stolen."

"When?" Rojas asks.

"Oh, months ago."

"Who stole it?"

"I never figured it out."

"Could it have been Buck Wilmoth?"

Atkins shakes his head kind of jerkily, trying for calm and casual and not quite succeeding. "He wasn't into that kind of thing. When your sports interest is built on aggression and hate rather than team loyalty, you don't go in much for pennants, do you? But I guess you don't need me to psychoanalyze Buck."

"Who else had a chance to take it?" I ask. Rojas is looking at me funny, wondering why I'm making such a big deal over a missing team pennant. But he lets me carry on.

"Lots of people visit," he says. "But most of them are my wife's clients. It's very rare I get another sports buff in here, aside from Buck, and like I said, he doesn't often come any more."

"Did Buck's wife visit sometimes?"

"Why would Sue visit me?" he says sharply.

"I didn't say that. I thought maybe she visited your wife."

"Well, sure, sometimes. They were friends."

Ordinarily I wouldn't jump in with something at this point and risk putting my foot in my mouth. It's usually better I talk to Rojas later and let him handle things his way. But this time, I can't resist trying something dramatic, maybe because I know I haven't got much and it'll take a bold call to shake anything loose.

So I say casually, "Did you and Sue Wilmoth plan Buck's murder before you met on the roof today, or was it a spur of the moment thing?"

Atkins pauses just a beat, but he doesn't look as surprised as Rojas does. "Plan Buck's murder? You're crazy. All we ever did was talk." He laughs nervously. "It may sound corny, but my wife doesn't understand me. And God knows Buck Wilmoth never understood Sue." He thinks for a second and says, "Who saw us up there? I didn't see anybody, and I know Sue wouldn't have told you. Not that we have anything to hide, you understand . . ."

"What did she hand over to you up there on the roof?"

Rojas looks at me like I'm nuts, and Atkins's answer to my shot in the dark even surprises me.

"Ah . . . it was a loaf of French bread, that's all it was. There's this local bakery that makes this French bread we both like, and I can't always get over there . . ."

"What did you do with the weapon after you killed Wilmoth? Is it here in your apartment? The sarge's men can find it, you know. All they need's a search warrant." Rojas is still giving me funny looks but makes no move to interrupt.

Atkins looks at both of us in turn, sighs resignedly, and says, "Ah, the hell with it. How much do you know?"

What I don't want to tell him is I don't know much of anything, but I've been making some mental guesses, and every nervous reaction of his makes me think I'm right.

"I think you and Sue Wilmoth are lovers. I don't know if Buck Wilmoth knew it or not, but probably he stole that pennant from you. He liked to do things like that, take away something somebody really values."

Atkins nods his head. "Yeah, he sure did that all right." He turns to Rojas. "Tell me this. Can I keep it?"

His poker face back, Rojas says coolly, "Well, I don't know."

"What I mean is, can I have it back? Can I keep it in my cell with me? I mean, it can be made quite harmless."

"It's an unusual request," Rojas says. The sarge is

really good, but I can tell he doesn't know what the hell the subject of the conversation is, though I have an inkling. "But I'll see what I can do. No promises, but I'll try."

Atkins thinks that over, nods, then goes into the next room and brings out a New Hopton Grizzlies pennant. He holds it out to give to Rojas. "This is really quite valuable," he tells us. "It's from their first year in the league, the only one they ever made with the bear in profile."

But we aren't looking at the bear. We're looking at the end of the pennant's handle, covered with drying blood.

"Sue returned it to me today up on the roof, like you thought. But it wasn't her idea I kill Buck. It was all my idea."

"Who sharpened it to a point like that?" I ask.

"Well, I guess she did that, but she didn't suggest—"

"Didn't she even offer a little suggestion of what you might do with it? With Buck Wilmoth dead, you could divorce your wife, and you and Sue—"

"Are you nuts? I wouldn't divorce my wife." His outrage seems oddly genuine. "I wouldn't kill somebody so I could divorce my wife, especially on Mother's Day. Wanda is a mother, and I revere mothers."

"But you would kill Buck Wilmoth because he made Sue's life miserable, wouldn't you? And with him dead, she could use the car whenever she wanted to, and it would be even easier for you and Sue to get together during your wife's business trips, wouldn't it? You might revere your wife too much to divorce her, but not too much to get it on with one of her friends. It's easy to see how convenient your affair was—plenty of chances to get together without fear of being found out. You knew how long your wife would be away on one of her business trips, and the radio or

TV would tell you when to expect Buck Wilmoth back from the game."

"You make it sound really lousy, but it's not like that at all."

I know I should let Rojas take over, but I'm on a roll. "And didn't it give you a special pleasure to take that pennant and run through a guy who gave such a bad name to sports fans?"

"Sure, it did," Jim Atkins says, almost inaudibly. "And just because I couldn't divorce my wife to marry Sue, I could still kill Buck Wilmoth for her. It's the least I could do."

He looks at me like only I understand him. He adds in a somewhat stronger voice, "I just hope I can keep that pennant. I'd like to get Sid Kramer, the owner of the Grizzlies, to sign it for me: the pennant that was used to kill the kind of fan no team wants, the guy who ruined the Mother's Day doubleheader."

Later, Rojas asks me, "Ed, how in hell did you know all that?"

"I didn't know anything for sure. But I got some pointers when we talked to Sue Wilmoth and Christine Fordyce, and there had to be a reason Atkins was so nervous and why he reacted the way he did when you asked if Buck's wife ever visited his apartment. I didn't queer your case against him, did I?"

"What, with your Charlie Chan act? No you didn't, not the way he's cooperating with us. But you're lucky his lawyer can't keep him from pouring it all out like a dam that broke. But what were these pointers you talk about?"

"The main thing is that Sue Wilmoth didn't volunteer Jim Atkins's name. Her mother did, probably not knowing the significance of it. Sue also didn't mention her visit to the roof. Christine came up with that, too. Why wouldn't Sue think of either of those things before her mother did? And what was that stuff about another bottle? Sue obviously brought something else up from the apartment with her, maybe in another paper bag about the size of the one she had the bottle in. When Christine mentioned that, Sue got right off it. It wasn't a bottle. It was that pennant Wilmoth stole from Atkins. And until her mother talked about Buck's vicious pleasure in depriving somebody else of what they most valued, Sue was ready to tell the world what a creep Buck Wilmoth was. Then all of a sudden, she seemed to want to downplay it. That was the *only* time she expressed the slightest disagreement with anything her mother said about Buck. What her mother said came too close to what Buck did to Jim Atkins when he stole his pennant just because it was something Atkins loved. It came too close to what she'd used to motivate Atkins into getting rid of Buck for her."

"But he was ripe to be motivated, wasn't he. The guy's nuts. Atkins reminds me of that guy in the Hitchcock movie."

"Norman Bates in *Psycho,* you mean? I saw it when it first came out." With some other umps. But in what city I don't remember.

"Yeah. You think he really has parents at Golden Manor or has he got 'em stuffed in his back bedroom somewhere?"

That about wraps up the story, except for that uncharacteristic action of Joe Whittlesy that gets him in such trouble. Sure I know there's no excuse for Joe going into the stands after a fan, and so does he. But what would you do if somebody booed your mother?

Siblings

by Kathryn Ptacek

"Don't forget my medicine."

Rebecca Roberts tried hard not to grit her teeth at the hated sound of her brother's voice. "I wasn't planning on stopping at the pharmacy today," she said as she paused in the doorway of the den.

"Hmm." He eyed her belligerently. He scratched the white stubble on his rounded chin, then belched.

Though it was mid-afternoon, William Davidson, lounging on the sofa, was still clad in his pajamas. Most days he never bothered to dress, or sometimes he deigned to put on an old ratty T-shirt and baggy trousers that had been out of style a decade ago. There were half-empty bags of potato chips and discarded beer cans in a ring around his feet; an ashtray by his hand overflowed with half-smoked cigarettes, ashes were scattered on the couch, the floor, and on his pajamas; there were burn holes in the material of the sofa, which was only a year old. A glass partially filled with day-old milk sat on the table by him; a cigarette butt floated in the liquid. The television was on some game show, and the volume was turned up high.

William had perfect hearing, but she knew he cranked up the volume to annoy her.

"Thought you were. I need my medicine, you know." His face was beginning to turn red.

Rebecca sighed quietly. She knew he would work

himself up quickly if she didn't reassure him about his damned pills. And she wanted to escape from the house without a scene. Another scene, that is. Today she wanted it to be nice and quiet. It was a holiday; well, almost a holiday. It was Mother's Day, and that had always been special in their family. She and her mother and father had had certain traditions for each of the holidays and special days. Laughing, William had called them fools. Maybe, she thought, and maybe not.

"You have a whole bottle left, William."

"Took it already."

She tried not to sound exasperated. "You had a three-week supply left."

"Not anymore." He squinted. "You must have stole it, like you steal everything around here, you old bitch. It was full just the other day."

She pressed her lips together. It wouldn't do any good to argue with William; it never did, not in the entire ten years they'd lived together. As a child she'd looked forward to leaving home, getting away from her older brother, a bully even then. She married young, and had a good life with her husband for nearly thirty years. Then tragically he died of cancer. She had grieved for a long period, and had slowly been getting back to her own life when she had suffered a stroke.

It was mild and left her with no outward physical change, but she had to consider it a warning, the doctor said, and he prescribed medicine for her.

That had been excuse enough for William. Claiming he had to take care of Rebecca because she was his only family left—he had sponged off their parents until they had finally died, no doubt, she often thought, to escape him—he'd moved in. She'd come home from the hospital to find him in her house and hadn't been able to get rid of him since. At first she had welcomed the company; she soon came to regret that momentary weakness.

Eventually Rebecca had recovered, though with no help from her brother. She suspected the real reason he had decided to be so solicitous was that he thought she might be near death—and doubtless he thought he would stand to inherit her house and property.

What William didn't know was that she'd since gone to her attorney and changed her will. She had completely excluded her brother; everything she had would go to the local gardening club. That was a small victory to be sure. But it wasn't enough. She wanted to be rid of him.

He scratched himself, then slipped his hand down the front of his pajama bottoms. He knew she hated that; everything he did, she knew, was calculated to irritate her. "And you'd better get out into that garden today. It's a regular jungle with all those weeds. The neighbors are gonna call the cops on us."

"It's been so hot," she murmured.

"Lazy old bag."

She turned away. The garden was her only retreat. He refused to venture outside where he thought he might be pressed into some sort of physical labor, so she could spend many hours in peaceful solitude. She grew vegetables and herbs, and had an extensive flower garden—pansies, petunias, geraniums, lilies, foxglove, and marigolds, as well as all the usual spring bulb flowers. William told her flowers were a wasted effort; he whined about the water bill and cost of seeds. She ignored him; she would never give up gardening. And she always pretended that she didn't want to garden. If he found out she loved it, he'd probably be out there in a second, nagging at her. She shuddered at the thought.

"And don't forget my pills, if you don't want a thrashing."

That would be the day, she thought sourly. She closed the front door and breathed a sigh of relief.

William never moved from the sofa. She couldn't imagine him trying to hit her; it would require exertion on his part. She got into the car and rested her forehead against the steering wheel. She closed her eyes.

William was still a bully, though an elderly one now. He never had a kind word for her, and he always claimed to be ill, but if the truth be known she was the one who tended to get sick. True, he had to take pills for his high blood pressure, but that came from all the crap he put into his body, plus his smoking and drinking. She'd tried to get him to eat properly, to modify his bad habits, but he had simply cursed her, and she'd given up.

Given up ... except for one thing, that is. She wasn't sure when she first decided she had to kill him, but she knew the idea had been with her a long time now. She ought to feel some regret, shouldn't she? This was her kin, her only relative, but there was no regret. None. He had soured her last decade, years that should have been good ones. He badgered and cajoled her, threatened her with violence. She couldn't leave, wouldn't; this was her house, after all. And he never followed through with the violence, thank God. Except she'd never had any excuse to call the police.

Still, the threat was enough. And over the years the resentment and loathing had built up.

She glanced at herself in the rearview mirror. Tidy graying hair, bright blue eyes, not many wrinkles. She could have passed for a woman ten years younger. She wanted to enjoy her life without being bitched at. She wanted to have some semblance of a real life. William had driven away the few remaining friends she had. There wasn't much left, and she wanted to keep what *was*.

She had to do something. Soon.

She saw the curtain at the front window shift, and she knew he was spying on her. Frankly she was surprised he'd stirred his stumps. He was probably wondering what was keeping her.

She drove to the grocery store only a few miles away, and took her time shopping. Then dutifully she stopped at the pharmacy. She tried to make the errand take as long as possible, but finally she had to leave. She had to go home again. She could feel the anger and resentment building inside her as she pulled into the driveway and got out and began unloading groceries.

Once she was inside, she found William was in no better mood than when she left. And why should he be? she wondered. He was always in a foul mood. He came out to the kitchen to watch her put the groceries away—*never* to help—complaining that she'd bought the wrong kind of crackers, he'd wanted dill pickles and not sweet gherkins, that he was running out of beer so she'd better get right back in that car and go to the liquor store before it closed, and that he was hungry and why didn't she start dinner instead of diddling around all day?

She did not point out that he very well could have started dinner while she was gone. He would simply have stared at her as if she'd lost her mind. William ate, watched TV, slept and bitched, and that was the extent of his daily exertions.

When he had finally shuffled back to the den, she began dinner. She put the pork chops in the skillet to brown slowly, then went out to the garden to gather a few herbs. While she was there, she cut some flowers to arrange on the table. William always claimed that they made him sneeze, but she never gave in on this issue.

*   *   *

Close to an hour later, Rebecca called him to dinner.

"It's about time," he grumbled as he pulled the chair back with a nerve-wracking scrape. "What's this slop?" He pointed to the chops and a noodle casserole.

"It's your favorite, William. You've always liked it before." Actually, as far as she knew, he didn't have any favorite foods. He hated everything she cooked and always complained about it, whether it was a grilled cheese sandwich or a pot roast. But this recipe had been her mother's favorite. She had always cooked it for her on her special day.

He tucked the napkin into the neck of his T-shirt. "You make this junk all the damn time. Don't you think it's about time you learned to make something else? Decent food for a decent man?"

She bent over her plate, and said nothing.

Even though he complained, he ate quickly enough. He even demanded seconds.

Halfway through his second helping, William paused and looked up at her. "Why's this taste weird?" he demanded, pointing to the pork chops with his fork.

"Weird? I don't understand what you mean," she said mildly, blinking.

"Stupid cow. It tastes . . . different."

"I used some herbs from the garden, William. That's all."

It must not have been too bad, she thought, because he promptly polished off the remaining chop. He guzzled his beer, then stared across the table at her. The cut glass vase with the colorful blooms in it caught his attention for the first time. She noticed he hadn't sneezed once.

"What are these flowers?"

"Just flowers."

"Yeah? What kind?"

"Foxglove."

He frowned slightly, poked at the remains of the meat with his fork, then paled.

"Foxglove is poisonous."

"I know, William."

He blinked. "What did you put in the pork chops, Becky?"

"Nothing, William. Don't worry."

" 'Don't worry,' " he said sarcastically. His face was slightly flushed now.

"I just tried a different recipe. That's all. I thought it was time for a change."

"Bullshit. I know what you're doing. You're trying to poison me." He stared at her wildly, his face growing darker.

Carefully she patted her lips with the linen napkin; William didn't like the paper ones. He didn't think it was too much work for her to have to launder the napkins and then iron each one. "Don't be ridiculous."

"There was something in the chops."

"Herbs." She smiled sweetly.

"More than that." His chair crashed back as he stood. He pointed a finger at her. He saw it shaking uncontrollably, and he began weeping. "You're trying to poison me, I know it. And after all that I've done for you all these years, Becky." His lips trembled. Saliva trickled down his chin.

She smiled.

His face turned redder, and a moment later he began gasping for breath. His face contorted.

"You ... poisoned ..."

He lunged toward her and she moved quickly away.

William collapsed onto the tile kitchen floor, thrashed for a second or two, then was still. Rebecca knelt down and checked for his pulse. There was none.

She stood up, feeling her knees protesting with the

effort, then moved across to the wall phone and called 911. As she set the phone receiver down, she listened to the rise and fall of the ambulance in the distance.

The paramedics would be there soon, and it would be apparent to them, and to the doctor at the hospital, that William had suffered a fatal heart attack.

Poor William.

And when the paramedics found the pills scattered in William's bed—yes, he was right, she had been stealing them for a *very* long time—they would simply conclude that he'd abused his medicine, and a heart attack was the natural result.

She waited in the living room as the ambulance pulled into the driveway, and when the paramedics hastened into the house, she was crying. Not from sorrow, but rather from joy because she was still young enough to enjoy the sizable insurance money she would be getting from her brother's death.

She dabbed at her eyes as one of the attendants put his arm around her shoulders.

She had put the foxglove on the table because she knew what conclusion he would leap to. His high blood pressure had taken care of the rest.

William was wrong—dead wrong—she thought as she followed the white-clad men into the kitchen, you could do a lot with flowers.

Mommy Would Have Loved It

by Annette Meyers

She had dressed for the young man sitting across the butcher-block table, wanting him to like her so he wouldn't write anything bad about her. *The New York Times*. Finally.

Sweeney, who'd been sleeping on her lap, yawned and stretched, jumped onto the windowsill and cleaned his paws. The coffeemaker churned to a stop. "How do you like your coffee?"

"Black." His name, D. Schoenberg, was on the card he'd placed on the table when he sat down.

"I hope you don't mind sitting in here." She felt most herself in the kitchen.

"Not at all. I like kitchens." His eyes evaded her, skimming around the bright room, past the bottle of Irish Whiskey next to the coffeemaker, fixing on Sweeney. "Nice cat."

"That's Sweeney." Sweeney stared at them haughtily. "I write in here. Inspiration for my cookbooks."

"Your sour cream brownie pie is my favorite."

"Why, thank you, Mr. Schoenberg. I'm flattered that you're doing this piece," she said, pouring coffee into two cups. Actually, she thought this kind of recognition was long overdue. She'd been a best-selling writer of cookbooks for years, and her first novel had topped the fiction best-seller list for three months and showed no sign of wavering.

"I hope you can give me a couple of uninterrupted

hours." He was small-boned, poetic-looking, with fine, wispy hair.

"No one knows I'm back. I got in yesterday and still have a little jet lag. I've let the answering machine take care of my calls. Whiskey?" she asked, spiking her own coffee generously.

"No, thank you." Reaching into a briefcase, he produced a small lined notepad. "I won't keep you too long."

Her mouth was already tired of smiling, but she said, "What? No tape recorder?" She took an elephant-swallow of coffee, felt the warmth of the whiskey in her throat.

"I have a good memory. Photographic." He smiled at her tentatively.

"Have we met before?"

"I don't think so."

"Where would you like to start?"

"How did you meet David Belmont?"

"Is this about me or David?" She heard the testiness in her tone and so did he. Damn David. Every interview, it seemed, gravitated toward David Belmont.

"You, of course, but your connection to David Belmont is part of the story."

His smile was so earnest, she thought, why not? "It was when I was managing a bookstore on the Cape, way before he met Susan. His first play, *Ivy,* had opened and everyone was hailing him as the new Neil Simon. I was a lit major, a snobby sort just out of college, ready to write great novels. David offered me a job. He was such a charming man. You're too young to have known him, but oh, what a charmer he was."

Hearing her voice change, he looked up from his pad.

Surprised at herself for getting emotional about the

memory of the young David, she thought, I'm getting old and maudlin.

"He talked you into coming to New York and working for him?"

"Yes, and it was fun. I never regretted it . . . at least, not then." She took another sip of the brew and felt herself unwinding.

"Can you tell me what it was like working for him?"

"You are a sly one, getting me to talk about David."

"I thought I might gear the story from the time you went to work for him to the—"

"Oh, I get it. Appeal to many different audiences." She laughed cynically. "Did you have anything particular in mind?"

"The last summer," he said.

She toyed with her cup, turning it in the saucer. "In order to understand what happened, you have to start much earlier—"

"Start wherever you feel comfortable."

"Comfortable. My dear boy, what an interesting choice of words. Nothing was comfortable in their relationship. By the time David met the future Mrs. David Belmont, he was already a successful Broadway playwright. Productions of his plays were being done all over the world, and he was *the* sought after single man in New York. *Cosmo* kept listing him year after year as one of the most eligible bachelors."

"He was gay, wasn't he?" The young man was looking at her, waiting for her answer.

"I don't know, was he?"

"I'd heard . . . rumors . . ."

"David was of the generation who couldn't come out. He wanted a so-called normal life with wife and children." She pulled over the tin, opened it, and offered him almond *biscotti*. "I made them yesterday; they're in my new cookbook." He took one and set it in his saucer without eating it. "He told you he was gay?"

She laughed. "Never. There was Junior, of course."

"I was in London last week—" he blurted, then looked discomfited, as if he hadn't meant to tell her.

"Were you really? And did you happen to see Junior?"

He was watching the cat.

"How does he look? A lot like the pictures of his father? Gray, balding, going to fat?"

"He's just directed the new Andrew Lloyd Webber at the Drury Lane. It got wonderful reviews."

"Enough time has gone by, I suppose." She ran her hands through her hair. It was white now and fell in unruly waves to her shoulders. "I don't keep track of what goes on in the theater anymore."

"I've talked to the detective who covered the case. He's retired now. Ascenzo. He told me there was a lot of political pressure."

"I remember him. A little raven, pecking, pecking."

"That's a nice image. I'd like to use it."

"It's mine. I'm using it in the screenplay."

"You have a movie sale?" He looked surprised.

"Tri-Star." Had he been hiding under an oyster shell? The news of her movie sale was in all the newspapers. And he worked for the *Times*.

"Political pressure," he prompted.

"Yes. David's mother—Faun—is a Guggenhauser." She smiled. "I suppose you know she has Alzheimer's. Too bad. She would have given you an earful about Susan."

"Supposedly, she hated her."

"Understatement. Faun was one of those consuming mothers. David used to call her every day even after he was married and Junior was born. It was a constant source of conflict—one of many—between David and Susan." She was feeling mellow. "More coffee?" He shook his head. "Faun used to complain bitterly that when she visited them in Malta, they put her in the storage room, which was the coldest, and I might say ugliest, room in the house. She was always complaining to me about how they treated her."

His head was bowed over his notes, and she saw scalp through his pale hair. She refilled her cup, adding more whiskey.

He looked up and sent her a nervous smile. Why in the world, she wondered, was he so nervous?

"You were saying," he said, "you know—about starting earlier."

"Larry had a theory."

"Larry?"

"Larry Bronson. He was David's press agent. He lives in Provincetown now. We talk from time to time, but I haven't seen him in years." Ten years, in fact, she thought. She'd been on a tour for her big dessert book and had a drink with him at the Ritz in Boston. "Susan was a nice, attractive girl, a bit overweight— not much—and she turned into a world-class crazy bitch after they were married. Larry's theory was that David told her about his lovers on their wedding night, and she was going to make him pay forever."

"Were you and Susan friendly? You'd been David's secretary for um—"

"I was his assistant," she said sharply, "for seven years before he married Susan." The young man was staring at her, not writing. Slightly disconcerted, she said, "He hired me as his assistant because I could write, but I did everything for him. I was his third hand, you might say, his second head. Susan began treating me as if I were her slave." Old wounds, she thought, never heal, not even with time. Not even with whiskey.

"Can you give me an example?"

"Well, they decided after their fifth anniversary that

a personal checking account for Susan was not the answer."

He looked up from his notebook.

"You think that's mundane. Perhaps. You see, after they were married, Susan wrote checks for all sorts of things, clothing she never wore, classes she never attended, loans to her poor friends. She never paid attention to keeping a balance and was always over-drawn. And she ran up thousands of dollars in charges at all the department stores. Once she called David at rehearsals, said it was an emergency, screaming that she'd been humiliated at Bonwit's when they refused to accept her charge plate unless she paid the out-standing balance on her bill, then and there."

"What did David do?"

"He asked me to find her at Bonwit's and see if I could straighten it out. I did it reluctantly because it never pays to get in between married people. When I got to Bonwit's, they were about to call security to have her ejected. She was stamping around, yelling that she wouldn't shop in their smarmy store ever again and that she knew she was always welcome at Bendel's. I got her out of there, but she never forgave me for it. God, she kept screaming she was Mrs. David Belmont. It was awful." The memory made her queasy. She rose, a trifle unsteady, and busied herself straightening her obsessively orderly countertops, moving the Cuisinart a bit to the right, the knife box to the left.

"Are you all right?"

She turned back to the young man. Her skin shone white through her makeup. "It's okay. David tried to talk to her about it, but Susan became abusive and hysterical. She said all he ever talked about was money."

"Was she right?"

"I don't know. Maybe. I was never aware of it before they were married." She sat down opposite him again. "They were both in despair until Susan suggested they close out her checking and charge accounts and they try a traveler's check arrangement of three hundred dollars a week, which she assured him would more than cover all of her personal expenses. Since it was the first positive suggestion she'd made, David thought it was the solution. After all, she hadn't had any money when they were married. Her parents had divorced when she was thirteen, and she drifted between them for years. They were both actors, and there was never any money."

"How did David and Susan meet?"

"At a party. I don't remember who gave it, but they were each there with someone else. She was living in a studio with only a mattress on the floor, owned one black dress, a pair of jeans, and a black sweater. He'd been dismayed by the careless way she lived and had me send her a giant exotic fern."

D. Schoenberg smiled. "Just what she needed."

"You got it. Anyway, David had me set up the whole traveler's check thing. Every six months I would call the bank and order the traveler's checks in denominations of twenty. Then I would call Susan, and she would take a cab to the bank and go through the tiresome chore of signing all those checks under the staring eyes of the bank officers. She ranted at David that they knew she had been unable to control her checking account and they looked at her as if they didn't understand why he had married her."

"You have a very good memory, too."

"Yes. I also kept a detailed diary that proved very helpful when I wrote the book. Anyway, Susan was an earth mother type, and David really wanted children. After each of those sessions at the bank, she made David's life miserable. She claimed all he really cared about was his credit rating and that none of this would have happened if he spent more time with her. She knew he couldn't wait to get to his office and get away from her."

"Was she right?"

"Yes. She was like a child, bored, never able to amuse herself. He would tell her to do something constructive with her time. Study painting again. She'd once shown real talent at it. Or, go back to school. She'd dropped out of Bennington after one year because she said they couldn't teach her anything."

"She was a dancer."

"Something of the sort. Before he had met her, she'd been in the chorus of a short-lived Off-Broadway musical, but she never pursued it. She was chronically bored."

"And she traveled with him when his plays opened."

"She hated his trips. He'd ask her to come with him, but she refused, saying she couldn't leave Junior. Once, David was meeting with a major producer—Binkie Beaumont I think it was—in London, and she called and said it was an emergency. When David got on the line, she screamed at him that he was a selfish bastard and she would never forgive him for leaving her alone."

"I suppose that's why she was in therapy."

"She was in and out of therapy all the time. She'd torture David, saying that Junior had asthma because David was never home. Poor David, she was always loading him with guilt. But, you know something? The minute he left town, she would call all her friends—all of them poor so she would pick up the checks—and book every evening with theater, disco dancing, concerts, and ballet. She could talk to her friends, she claimed, and have late-night soul barings. When she tried to talk to David, he fell asleep."

D. Schoenberg's hand remained poised over his pad.

"Ah, yes, the great David Belmont fell asleep if he wasn't the center of the universe. Surprised?"

The young man merely smiled.

"The last time I dealt with the traveler's checks, David was in Washington and Susan had been going crazy trying to find someone to take in a movie with her. The housekeeper told me she had sent her out for magazines twice in two hours. Although it was afternoon, she had never even bothered to get out of bed. My bad luck, I called her to come down and sign traveler's checks. She left me hanging on the phone while she looked at her schedule. Can you believe it?"

He bit into the *biscotti,* had stopped taking notes.

"More coffee?"

He nodded. "This is delicious."

She smiled at him and filled his cup, and hers. "The President loves those. I make him a batch whenever I go to the White House. Where was I?"

"Susan was coming to the bank to sign the traveler's checks."

"Yes. She told me that they better be ready for her because she wasn't about to sit and wait. When she arrived at the bank, everyone began scurrying around to find her a comfortable place to sign the checks. She flopped down at a desk, and someone handed her a ballpoint pen, and suddenly she was up and screaming that she didn't use ballpoints. She slammed the pen down on the desk, and it bounced and skidded across the floor."

"God!"

"Someone handed her a felt-tipped pen, and she started to sign her name to the top of the check, stopped, and threw it down. It was blue and didn't they know she never used a blue pen? That's when she called me. She got me off another call because she said it was urgent and told me to bring a black felt-tipped pen to the bank immediately and to snap to it." She stopped and all the old fury came back to her. "Can you imagine? She told me to snap to it."

"What did she do when you got there?"

She smiled, remembering. "I sent our receptionist and when David came back, I told him that he would have to get someone else to deal with her or I would leave."

"And David?"

"He cried. It was pitiful. He begged me not to leave him." She got up and stared out at her garden. Sweeney stretched himself until his head was under her hand, and she scratched behind his ears. "I could never leave him."

"What about the last summer?"

"Wait till you see the house," David had said the first time, squeezing Susan's hand. "Just wait, you'll love it. I know you will."

They drove over an hour on a narrow, dusty road through blanched settlements that appeared suddenly on the very edge of the road and then disappeared even more suddenly. It was a countryside barren of vegetation, villages without sidewalks, houses like garages, dark, thin children just hanging about watching, and gaunt dogs. A couple of times a Vespa would *put-put* past them going in the opposite direction as they continued to drive, farther and farther inland. Inland. Wouldn't you know David would buy an inland house when he knew she wanted the sea? She wanted the Mediterranean at her feet, that was what she'd said often enough.

"Leave it to me, Susan," David had said. "I'll find something, and you'll love it." David always said that, and Susan never loved it.

So David plunked down three hundred thousand in cash, cash because there were no mortgages for Americans in foreign countries, for a villa perched on top of a sharp crater of a supposedly extinct volcano. And way, very far away, off in the distance, on a very, very clear day, you could actually see a speck of blue, Mediterranean blue, no doubt. And Susan was consigned to spend the rest of the summers of her life in David's marble villa, Villa Luna, as the natives called it.

"And it has a swimming pool," he had screamed excitedly over long-distance telephone. A swimming pool, indeed, about as big as a large bathtub, made only for dunking oneself when the weather got too hot, which was almost never. The truth was, the sun rarely came through the clouds that hung over Villa Luna.

"It's like living in a goddamn shroud," Susan said. "No wonder they call it Villa Luna."

That's when David sent to London for a brass sign that said "Villa Belmont," but the natives just laughed and Villa Luna it remained.

They were in their tenth summer now, and Susan was still revolted by the hand-hewn marble: "It's cold and it's damp"; the charming natives: "They cheat us blind"; the colorful little shops in the village below: "The pottery chips when you look at it"; and the quaint restaurants: "Ptomaine."

Susan refused to leave the villa, but David hated sitting around. He didn't read. He wanted to feel the atmosphere of the village. He wanted to feel part of it.

"Oh, come on, Mommy," he said, talking baby, and he always called her Mommy. He used to be able to cajole her down to the village in their first summers, but no longer. "You know you'll just love it . . ."

"Why do you think we have a cook?" Susan said, yawning loudly, thumbing the pages of the book as she read.

They were sitting in the living room, which Susan had done up in white wicker and a garish cotton fabric print of huge red flowers on a white ground, a purchase from the craft co-op in the village. The shutters were open to let the setting sun in, but there was no sign of the sun, just clouds. The butane heater had become another member of the family. It stood slightly off the center of the room, and would soon have to be lit.

David fidgeted, picked at his cuticles, sighed deeply. The big overhead fan creaked and spun slowly, *pha-toohm, pha-toohm,* doing its job of keeping the insects at bay. And there were insects, big flying beasts, that appeared the minute the fan stopped.

"God, David, why don't you read?" Susan said. "You're distracting me."

David's face took on that hurt look, which for some reason Susan had once found appealing. "Well, here, just look at the pictures," she said, handing him a magazine from under the coffee table.

Sofia stood in the arched doorway at that moment, carrying the chipped pottery coffeepot filled with hot water, the jar of Nescafé decaffeinated, and two chipped mugs on a rattan tray. She set the tray down on the glass top of the wicker coffee table, pushing away *Time* and *Vogue.*

Junior was right behind Sofia with the plate of cookies, munching and grunting, soggy cookie crumbs all over his mouth.

"Cover your mouth, Junior," Susan said. "It's disgusting." She put the book down, flat open. "Thanks, Sofia. You and Maria can go home whenever you're finished in the kitchen. Junior will bring the coffee things down later."

"Let me make the coffee, Mom," Junior wheedled, his hand on the Nescafé jar. "Can I? Please?"

Susan frowned. "We have to get those braces on your teeth as soon as we get home." She looked at David. "One Bugs Bunny in the family is enough."

"Aw, Mom," Junior said.

Susan went back to her book.

It was quiet, but for the click, click of Junior's measurements and the *pha-toohm, pha-toohm* of the fan. David got up and moved to the window. Dusk was falling, and in the village below the lights were coming on, one by one. It looked so warm and pretty. At dusk, the mist they lived in always cleared, and the view from their crater was lovely.

"I told the von Reichsteins we would have dinner with them at Cappello's tomorrow night," David said, turning from the window.

"Without asking me?" Susan's tone was cold and sharp. "Well, you can count me out."

Junior shivered. They were going to fight again. They had been fighting since the first day, when they found the weather was unusually cool and the house, uncomfortably cold.

"How I hate this place." Susan had stormed from room to room wrapped in sweaters. "Why aren't we on the Costa Brava or the Riviera, where the weather is always good? Why do you always do this to me? You promise I'll love it, and I always hate it."

"There are plenty of people who envy our life, plenty of people who would be grateful for all of this," David had countered. "Grateful for what you have."

"Well, they can have it, and you, too," Susan had screamed. She'd closed herself in the bedroom for the rest of that day.

Now David said, "But I thought you'd want to have dinner with the von Reichsteins," an ever-so-slight whine creeping into his voice.

"Why would I want to eat out anywhere in this country and get dysentery? You know how I feel about it. We have a perfectly good cook right here. Hedi and Max can just as well come here."

"But they always come here, and they want to take us out to dinner."

"No!" Susan went back to her book. "You go if you want to so much. I'll eat at home."

"But what will I tell them? I've already said we would go."

"Tell them the truth, David. You didn't ask me, did you?"

"You'll just call them and tell them yourself, Susan. You always put me in the position of making excuses for you."

"I'll do nothing of the kind. You accepted, and you can say whatever you want to say to them."

At an impasse, David paused to regroup. He took a sip of his coffee. The fan *pha-toohmed*.

"What do you think Mommy should do, sport?" David smiled at Junior, making light of it.

Junior grinned anxiously, looking from one to the other. His right eyelid twitched.

Susan stared daggers from her book. She waited.

"I think ..." Junior said haltingly, "... I ... think ... that you ... should have asked Mom before you said yes for her."

Susan's eyes glittered. She gave David a look of triumph and returned to her book.

"Okay, I give up," David said, furious. "I'll call them tomorrow and cancel, but this is very embarrassing."

"It's your own fault." Susan tucked her feet up under her and settled deeper into the sofa and her book.

The heaviness came again, the empty air, with only the sound of the fan, *pha-toohm, pha-toohm*.

David moved around the room restlessly. He straightened one of the framed posters on the wall. He wiped some light, almost invisible dust from the top of the piano. "Susan," he said, lightening up, "let's go down to the village for a nightcap."

Susan didn't look up, nor did she respond.

"Susan?"

"No," she said, still not looking up.

"Aw, come on, Mommy," David wheedled. "You know how nice it always is in the village after dinner with everyone out in the cafés in the square. You know you love it."

"No, David."

"Goddamn it!" David shouted, red-faced, stamping his foot. "What the hell kind of life is this? What are we—"

"I'll go with you, Dad," Junior said hastily, jumping up.

David froze mid-sentence, mid-motion. Then his face lit up. "That's great, sport," he said, clapping Junior on the back. "See, Susan, Junior's going with me."

Susan did not look up.

"We're going to have a swell time together, sport." David threw his arm around Junior's shoulders. "And Mommy will be sorry she didn't come with us," he added loudly.

They got into the Fiat and drove down the dark, winding road into the village, parking just off the square. The shops were shuttered. There were no people in the streets. Only the bars and cafés were open.

Early in the morning, every morning, the square held an outdoor market with farmers setting up stalls of fresh fruits and vegetables, homemade cheeses. At night the square belonged to the cafés that fronted it on all four sides. It was dimly lit by four street lamps, one on each corner, giving off a hazy glow. The cafés each had about a dozen bruised, round metal tables and assorted, not quite steady, chairs. All of the tables carried identical Cinzano ashtrays. Outside, under the street lamps, no café had any individual personality. It was just a café. The humidity and the pale yellow haze made the night air almost palpable. Harsh voices and laughter came from inside the cafés.

A couple replete with cameras and guidebooks were sitting at one of the tables arguing in German. No one else was in the square.

David and Junior picked a battered table in front of the Corsini Café, and David signaled for a waiter. Junior's chair rocked precariously. A boy about Junior's age, a half-smoked, wrinkled cigarette dangling from the corner of his mouth, slouched over to them. He wore an apron that said *Cinzano* in blue letters.

"One cognac," David said. "And one Coke, right, Junior?"

"Right, Dad." Junior's eyelid twitched.

The boy slouched away and into the bar area.

The voices from the café grew muffled, and as Junior looked around, they were alone in the square.

The boy brought their drinks on a cork and metal tray that also said Cinzano. He gave Junior a sly look.

"Grazie," David said, handing him some coins.

"Do not stay much longer, signor," the boy said. "There—"

"We'll stay as long as we like," David said pompously.

The boy shrugged and retreated. Laughter came from the café a moment later.

"Isn't this terrific?" David said. "Isn't this fun?"

"Sure, Dad." Junior rubbed his head. It was beginning to ache again, right behind his eyes.

One sad cube of ice lay melting in Junior's Coke, and it soon dissolved. The air grew thicker around them, and the haze turned sepia. A large, furry brown moth-like creature settled on their table, then another, and another. Junior's head throbbed. A brown moth spun around his head, drifted downward, and nestled in his Coke, drowning slowly in the thick, sweet liquid. He did nothing to save it. The effect was hypnotic. He wanted to be the moth drowning in the Coke. He looked up into the lamplight. The space was dense with the giant brown moths.

"Dad, come on, let's go home." Junior began shaking David's arm. He rubbed his aching head.

David rose woodenly, and they stood in a thick sea of hairy, flapping things, suffocating air, and diffused light.

"Let's go, Dad." Junior was frantic now, pulling David out of the aura.

They stumbled from the square, hardly able to see, waving their arms to keep the moths away. When they were near the car, Junior looked back. The square was deserted except for the insects that swirled and spun in the lamplight, covering everything.

They got into the Fiat and drove up the hill.

"Wasn't that fun, sport?" David said suddenly, cheerily.

Junior shrank down in the shadows. The little car bumped and twisted on the dark road. The Villa Belmont rose eerie against the night sky, a hulking specter.

"Yes," David said, smiling, "Mommy sure will be sorry she didn't come with us. She would have loved it."

"Afterward, people kept asking me if I'd known what was going to happen." Her eyelids felt weighted. "It's late," she said, "And I'm very tired. Is there anything else you wanted to ask me?"

"I'm sorry I've kept you so long." He put his yellow pad in his briefcase. "Just one thing more."

"Yes?" She needed desperately to be alone. This always happened when she talked about David. Hurry, she thought, hurry.

"It was murder and suicide?"

"Oh, my dear, it was never that simple. Are you rejecting robbery?"

Why wasn't he leaving? Go, she thought, go, please go.

His right eyelid twitched. "If it was robbery, why wasn't Junior killed also?"

"I found him lying in their blood." She poured whiskey into her empty cup.

"Unharmed. He could never remember what had happened."

"The mind can do that. And Junior was a strange one—something not quite right about him." Sweeney jumped up on the butcher-block table and rubbed against her arm, sniffed at the contents of her cup. "I arrived from New York the next morning. David had arranged for a car to pick me up." She was standing now. Get out, she thought.

"Your book is about them."

"My book is fiction."

He bent to put his pad in his briefcase. She saw the gleam of the blade only moments after he righted himself. Too late to stop its progress.

"David." She fell back against the butcher block, her hand on the shaft between her ribs. "David." The cup of whiskey shattered under her, but she no longer felt anything.

Sweeney arched his back and began to howl.

"Thank you for seeing me," Junior said. He closed the door behind him.

Nine Sons

by Wendy Hornsby

I saw Janos Bonachek's name in the paper this morning. There was a nice article about his twenty-five years on the federal bench, his plans for retirement. The Boy Wonder, they called him, but the accompanying photograph showed him to be nearly bald, a wispy white fringe over his ears the only remains of his once remarkable head of yellow hair.

For just a moment, I was tempted to write him, or call him, to put to rest forever questions I had about the death that was both a link and a wedge between us. In the end I didn't. What was the point after all these years? Perhaps Janos's long and fine career in the law was sufficient atonement, for us all, for events that happened so long ago.

It occurred on an otherwise ordinary day. It was April, but spring was still only a tease. If anything stood out among the endless acres of black mud and gray slush, it was two bright dabs of color: first the blue crocus pushing through a patch of dirty snow, then the bright yellow head of Janos Bonachek as he ran along the line of horizon toward his parents' farm after school. Small marvels maybe, the spring crocus and young Janos, but in that frozen place, and during those hard times, surely they were miracles.

The year was 1934, the depths of the Great Depression. Times were bad, but in the small farm town where I had been posted by the school board, hardship was an old acquaintance.

I had arrived the previous September, fresh from teachers' college, with a new red scarf in my bag and the last piece of my birthday cake. At twenty, I wasn't much older than my high-school-age pupils.

Janos was ten when the term began, and exactly the height of ripe wheat. His hair was so nearly the same gold as the bearded grain that he could run through the uncut fields and be no more noticeable than the ripples made by a prairie breeze. The wheat had to be mown before Janos could be seen at all.

On the northern plains, the season for growing is short, a quick breath of summer between the spring thaw and the first frost of fall. Below the surface of the soil, and within the people who forced a living from it, there seemed to be a layer that never had time to warm all the way through. I believe to this day that if the winter hadn't been so long, the chilling of the soul so complete, we would not have been forced to bury Janos Bonachek's baby sister.

Janos came from a large family, nine sons. Only one of them, Janos, was released from chores to attend school. Even then, he brought work with him in the form of his younger brother, Boya. Little Boya was then four or five. He wasn't as brilliant as Janos, but he tried hard. Tutored and cajoled by Janos, Boya managed to skip to the second-grade reader that year.

Around Halloween, that first year, Janos was passed up to me by the elementary teacher. She said she had nothing more to teach him. I don't know that I was any better prepared than she was, except that the high school textbooks were on the shelves in my room. I did my best.

Janos was a challenge. He absorbed everything I had to offer and demanded more, pushing me in his quiet yet insistent way to explain or to find out. He was eager for everything. Except geography. There he was a doubter. Having lived his entire life on a flat expanse of prairie, Janos would not believe the earth was a sphere, or that there were bodies of water vaster than the wheat fields that stretched past his horizon. The existence of mountains, deserts, and oceans, he had to take on faith, like the heavenly world the nuns taught me about in catechism.

Janos was an oddball to his classmates, certainly. I can still see that shiny head bent close to his books, the brow of his pinched little face furrowed as he took in a new set of universal truths from the world beyond the Central Grain Exchange. The other students deferred to him, respected him, though they never played with him. He spent recesses and lunch periods sitting on the school's front stoop, waiting for me to ring the big brass bell and let him back inside. I wonder how that affected him as a judge, this boy who never learned how to play.

Janos shivered when he was cold, but he seemed otherwise oblivious to external discomfort or appearances. Both he and Boya came to school barefoot until there was snow on the ground. Then they showed up in mismatched boots sizes too big, yet no one called attention to them, which I found singular. Janos's coat, even in blizzards, was an old gray blanket that I'm sure he slept under at night. His straight yellow hair stuck out in chunks as if it had been scythed like the wheat. He never acknowledged that he was in any way different from his well-scrubbed classmates.

While this oblivion to discomfort gave Janos an air of stoic dignity, it did impose some hardship on me. When the blizzards came and I knew school should be closed, I went out anyway because I knew Janos would be there, with Boya. If I didn't come to unlock the classroom, I was sure they would freeze waiting.

Getting there was itself a challenge. I boarded in

town with the doctor and his wife, my dear friend
Martha. When the snow blew in blinding swirls and
the road was impassable to any automobile, I would
persuade the doctor to harness his team of plow
horses to his cutter and drive me out. The doctor
made only token protest after the first trip: the boys
had been at the school for some time before we arrived, huddled together on the stoop like drifted snow.

Those were the best days, alone, the two boys and
I. I would bring books from Martha's shelves, books
not always on the school-board-approved list. We
would read together, and talk about the world on the
far side of the prairie and how one day we would see
it for ourselves. As the snowdrifts piled up to the sills
outside, we would try to imagine the sultry heat of
the tropics, the pitch and roll of the oceans, men in
pale suits in electric-lit parlors discussing being and
nothingness while they sipped hundred-year-old
sherry.

We had many days together. That year the first
snow came on All Saints Day and continued regularly
until Good Friday. I would have despaired during the
ceaseless cold if it weren't for Janos and the lessons I
received at home on the evenings of those blizzardy
days.

Invariably, on winter nights when the road was impassable and sensible people were at home before the
fire, someone would call for the doctor's services. He
would harness the cutter, and go. Martha, of course,
couldn't sleep until she heard the cutter return. We
would keep each other entertained, sometimes until
after the sun came up.

Martha had gone to Smith or Vassar. I'm not sure
which because Eastern girls' schools were so far from
my experience that the names meant nothing to me
then. She was my guide to the world I had only seen
in magazines and slick-paged catalogs, where people

were polished to a smooth and shiny perfection, where long underwear, if indeed any was worn, never showed below their hems. These people were oddly whole, no scars, no body parts lost to farm machinery. In their faces I saw a peace of mind I was sure left them open to the world of ideas. I longed for them, and was sure Martha did as well.

Martha took life in our small community with grace, though I knew she missed the company of other educated women. I had to suffice.

Just as I spent my days preparing Janos, Martha spent her evenings teaching me the social graces I would need if I were ever to make my escape. Perhaps I was not as quick a pupil as Janos, but I was as eager.

Lessons began in the attic where Martha kept her trunks. Packed in white tissue was the elegant trousseau she had brought with her from the East, gowns of wine-colored taffeta moiré and green velvet and a pink silk so fine I feared touching it with my calloused hands.

I had never actually seen a live woman in an evening gown, though I knew Martha's gowns surpassed the mail-order gowns that a woman might order for an Eastern Star ritual, if she had money for ready-made.

Martha and I would put on the gowns and drink coffee with brandy and read to each other from Proust, or take turns at the piano. I might struggle through a Strauss waltz or the Fat Lady Polka. She played flawless Dvorak and Debussy. This was my finishing school, long nights in Martha's front parlor, waiting for the cutter to bring the doctor home, praying the cutter hadn't overturned, hoping the neighbor he had gone to tend was all right.

When he did return, his hands so cold he needed help out of his layers of clothes, Martha's standard greeting was, "Delivering Mrs. Bonachek?" This was a big joke to us, because, of course, Mrs. Bonachek delivered herself. No one knew how many pregnancies she had had beyond her nine living sons. Poor people, they were rich in sons.

That's what I kept coming back to that early spring afternoon as I walked away from the Bonachek farm. I had seen Janos running across the fields after school. If he hadn't been hurrying home to help his mother, then where had he gone? And where were his brothers?

It lay on my mind.

As I said, the day in question had been perfectly ordinary. I had stayed after my students to sweep the classroom, so it was nearly four before I started for home. As always, I walked the single-lane road toward town, passing the Bonachek farm about halfway. Though underfoot the black earth was frozen hard as tarmac, I was looking for signs of spring, counting the weeks until the end of the school term.

My feet were cold inside my new Sears and Roebuck boots and I was mentally drafting a blistering letter to the company. The catalog copy had promised me boots that would withstand the coldest weather, so, as an act of faith in Sears, I had invested a good chunk of my slim savings for the luxury of warm feet. Perhaps the copywriter in a Chicago office could not imagine ground as cold as this road.

I watched for Janos's mother as I approached her farm. For three days running, I had seen Mrs. Bonachek working in the fields as I walked to school in the morning, and as I walked back to town in the dusky afternoon. There was no way to avoid her. The distance between the school and the Bonachek farm was uninterrupted by hill or wall or stand of trees.

Mrs. Bonachek would rarely glance up as I passed. Unlike the other parents, she never greeted me, never asked how her boys were doing in school, never suggested I let them out earlier for farm chores. She knew little English, but neither did many of the other parents, or my own.

She was an enigma. Formless, colorless, Mrs. Bonachek seemed no more than a piece of the landscape as she spread seed grain onto the plowed ground from a big pouch in her apron. Wearing felt boots, she walked slowly along the straight furrows, her thin arm moving in a sweep as regular as any motor-powered machine.

Hers was an odd display of initiative, I thought. No one else was out in the fields yet. It seemed to me she risked losing her seed to mildew or to a last spring freeze by planting so early. Something else bothered me more. While I was a dairyman's daughter and knew little about growing wheat, I knew what was expected of farm children. There were six in my family, my five brothers and myself. My mother never went to the barns alone when there was a child at hand. Mrs. Bonachek had nine sons. Why, I wondered, was she working in the fields all alone?

On the afternoon of the fourth day, as had become my habit, I began looking for Mrs. Bonachek as soon as I locked the schoolhouse door. When I couldn't find her, I felt a pang of guilty relief that I wouldn't have to see her that afternoon, call out a greeting that I knew she wouldn't return.

So I walked more boldly, dressing down Sears in language I could never put on paper, enjoying the anarchy of my phrases even as I counted the blue crocus along the road.

Just as I came abreast of the row of stones that served to define the beginning of the Bonachek driveway, I saw her. She sat on the ground between the road and the small house, head bowed, arms folded across her chest. Her faded calico apron, its big seed pocket looking flat and empty, was spread on the ground beside her. She could have been sleeping, she was so still. I thought she might be sick, and would have gone to her, but she turned her head toward me, saw me, and shifted around until her back was toward me.

I didn't stop. The road curved and after a while I couldn't see her without turning right around. I did look back once and saw Mrs. Bonachek upright again. She had left her apron on the ground, a faded red bundle at the end of a furrow. She gathered up the skirt of her dress, filled it with seed grain, and continued her work. So primitive, I thought. How was it possible she had spawned the bright light that was Janos?

I found Martha in an extravagant mood when I reached home. The weather was frigid, but she, too, had seen the crocus. She announced that we would hold a tea to welcome spring. We would put on the tea frocks from her trunk and invite in some ladies from town. It would be a lark, she said, a coming out. I could invite anyone I wanted.

I still had Mrs. Bonachek on my mind. I couldn't help picturing her rising from her squat in the muddy fields to come sit on Martha's brocade sofa, so I said I would invite her first. The idea made us laugh until I had hiccups. I said the woman had no daughters and probably needed some lively female company.

Martha went to the piano and banged out something suitable for a melodrama. I got a pan of hot water and soaked my cold feet while we talked about spring and the prospect of being warm again, truly warm, in all parts at once. I wondered what magazine ladies did at teas.

We were still planning little sandwiches and petits fours and onions cut into daisies when the doctor came in for supper. There were snowflakes on his beard and I saw snow falling outside, a lacy white curtain over the evening sky. When Martha looked away from the door, I saw tears in her eyes.

"You're late," Martha said to the doctor, managing a smile. "Out delivering Mrs. Bonachek?"

"No such luck." The doctor seemed grim. "I wish that just once the woman would call me in time. She delivered herself again. The baby died, low body temperature I suspect. A little girl. A pretty, perfect little girl."

I was stunned but I managed to blurt, "But she was working in the fields just this afternoon."

Martha and the doctor exchanged a glance that reminded me how much I still had to learn. Then the doctor launched into a speech about some people not having sense enough to take to their beds and what sort of life could a baby born into such circumstances expect, anyway?

"The poor dear," Martha said when he had run down. "She finally has a little girl to keep her company and it dies." She grabbed me by the arm. "We must go offer our consolation."

We put on our boots and coats and waited for the doctor to get his ancient Ford back out of the shed. It made a terrible racket, about which Martha complained gently, but there wasn't enough snow for the cutter. We were both disappointed—the cutter gave an occasion a certain weight.

"Say your piece then leave," the doctor warned as we rattled over the rutted road. "These are private people. They may not understand your intentions."

He didn't understand that Martha and I were suffering a bit of guilt from the fun we had had at poor Mrs. Bonachek's expense. And we were bored. Barn sour, my mother would say. Tired of being cooped up all winter and in desperate need of some diversion.

We stormed the Bonachek's tiny clapboard house, our offers of consolation translated by a grim-faced

Janos. Martha was effusive. A baby girl should have a proper send-off, she said. There needed to be both a coffin and a dress. When was the funeral?

Mrs. Bonachek looked from me to Martha, a glaze over her mud-colored eyes. Janos shrugged his skinny shoulders. There was no money for funerals, he said. When a baby died, you called in the doctor for a death certificate, then the county came for the remains. That was all.

Martha patted Mrs. Bonachek's scaly hands. Not to worry. We would take care of everything. And we did. Put off from our spring tea by the sudden change in the weather, we diverted our considerable social energy to the memorial services.

I found a nice wooden box of adequate size in the doctor's storeroom and painted it white. Martha went up to the attic and brought down her beautiful pink silk gown and an old feather pillow. She didn't even wince as she ran her sewing shears up the delicate hand-turned seams. I wept. She hugged me and talked about God's will being done and Mrs. Bonachek's peasant strength. I was thinking about the spoiled dress.

We worked half the night. We padded the inside of the box with feathers and lined it with pink silk. We made a tiny dress and bonnet to match. The doctor had talked the county into letting us have a plot in the cemetery. It was such a little bit of ground, they couldn't refuse.

We contacted the parish priest, but he didn't want to perform the services. The county cemetery wasn't consecrated and he didn't know the Bonacheks. We only hoped it wasn't a rabbi that was needed because there wasn't one for miles. Martha reasoned that heaven was heaven and the Methodist preacher would have to do, since he was willing.

By the following afternoon everything was ready.

The snow had turned to slush but our spirits weren't dampened. We set off, wearing prim navy-blue because Martha said it was more appropriate for a child's funeral than somber black.

When the doctor drove us up to the small house, the entire Bonachek family, scrubbed and brushed, turned out to greet us.

Janos smiled for the first time I could remember. He fingered a frayed necktie that hung below his twine belt. He looked very awkward, but I knew he felt elegant. Everyone, even Boya, wore some sort of shoes. It was a gala, if solemn event.

Mr. Bonachek, a scrawny, pale-faced man, relieved us of the makeshift coffin and led us into the single bedroom. The baby, wrapped in a scrap of calico, lay on the dresser. I unfolded the little silk dress on the bed while Martha shooed Mr. Bonachek out of the room.

"We should wash her," Martha said. A catch in her voice showed that her courage was failing. She began to unwrap the tiny creature. It was then I recognized the calico—Mrs. Bonachek's faded apron.

I thought of the nine sons lined up in the next room and Mrs. Bonachek sitting in the field with her apron spread on the cold ground beside her. Mrs. Bonachek who was rich in sons.

I needed to know how many babies, how many girls, had died before this little one wrapped in the apron. Janos would tell me, Janos who had been so matter-of-fact about the routine business of death. I hadn't the courage at that moment to ask him.

Martha was working hard to maintain her composure. She had the baby dressed and gently laid her in the coffin. The baby was beautiful, her porcelain face framed in soft pink silk. I couldn't bear to see her in the box, like a shop-window doll.

I wanted to talk with Martha about the nagging suspicion that was taking shape in my mind. I hesitated too long.

Janos appeared at the door and I didn't want him to hear what I had to say. Actually, his face was so thin and expectant that it suddenly occurred to me that we hadn't brought any food for a proper wake.

"Janos," Martha whispered. "Tell your mother she may come in now."

Janos led his mother only as far as the threshold when she stopped stubbornly. I went to her, put my arm around her and impelled her to come closer to the coffin. When she resisted, I pushed. I was desperate to see some normal emotion from her. If she had none, what hope was there for Janos?

Finally, she shuddered and reached out a hand to touch the baby's cheek. She said something in her native language. I could understand neither the words nor the tone. It could have been a prayer, it could have been a curse.

When I let her go, she turned and looked at me. For the barest instant there was a flicker in her eyes that showed neither fear nor guilt about what I might have seen the afternoon before. I was disquieted because, for the length of that small glimmer, she was beautiful. I saw who she might have become at another time, in a different place. When the tears at last came to my eyes, they were for her and not for the baby.

Janos and Boya carried the coffin out to the bare front room and set it on the table. The preacher arrived and he gave his best two-dollar service even though there would be no payment. He spoke to the little group, the Bonacheks, Martha, the doctor and I, as if we were a full congregation. I don't remember what he said. I wasn't listening. I traced the pattern of the cheap, worn linoleum floor with my eyes and silently damned the poverty of the place and the cold that seeped in under the door.

We were a small, depressed-looking procession, walking down the muddy road to the county cemetery at the edge of town, singing along to hymns only the preacher seemed to know. At the gravesite, the preacher prayed for the sinless soul and consigned her to the earth. It didn't seem to bother him that his principal mourners didn't understand a word he said.

Somehow, the doctor dissuaded Martha from inviting all of the Bonacheks home for supper—she, too, had belatedly thought about food.

As we walked back from the cemetery, I managed to separate the doctor from the group. I told him what was on my mind, what I had seen in the fields the day before. She had left her bundled apron at the end of a furrow and gone back to her work. I could not keep that guilty knowledge to myself.

The doctor wasn't as shocked as I expected him to be. But he was a man of worldly experience and I was merely a dairyman's daughter—the oldest child, the only girl in a family of five boys.

As the afternoon progressed, the air grew colder, threatening more snow. To this day, whenever I am very cold, I think of that afternoon. Janos, of course, fills that memory.

I think the little ceremony by strangers was a sort of coming out for him. He was suddenly not only a man of the community, but of the world beyond the road that ran between his farm and the schoolhouse, out where mountains and oceans were a possibility. It had been a revelation.

Janos called out to me and I stopped to wait for him, watching him run. He seemed incredibly small, outlined against the flat horizon. He was golden, and oddly ebullient.

Pale sunlight glinted off his bright head as he struggled through the slush on the road. Mud flew off his big boots in thick gobs and I thought his skinny legs would break with the weight of it. He seemed not to notice—mud was simply a part of the season's change, a harbinger of warmer days.

When he caught up, Janos was panting and red in the face. He looked like a wise little old man for whom life held no secrets. As always, he held himself with a stiff dignity that I imagine suited him quite well when he was draped in his judge's robes.

Too breathless to speak, he placed in my hand a fresh blue crocus he had plucked from the slush.

"Very pretty," I said, moved by his gesture. I looked into his smiling face and found courage. "What was the prayer your mother said for the baby?"

He shrugged and struggled for breath. Then he reached out and touched the delicate flower that was already turning brown from the warmth of my hand.

"No prayer," he said. "It's what she says. 'Know peace. Your sisters in heaven wait to embrace you.' "

I put my hand on his shoulder and looked up at the heavy, gathering clouds. "If it's snowing tomorrow," I said, "which books shall I bring?"

Loopy

by Ruth Rendell

At the end of the last performance, after the curtain calls, Red Riding Hood put me on a lead and with the rest of the company we went across to the pub. No one had taken make-up off or changed, there was no time for that before The George closed. I remember prancing across the road and growling at someone on a bicycle. They loved me in the pub—well, some of them loved me. Quite a lot were embarrassed. The funny thing was that I should have been embarrassed myself if I had been one of them. I should have ignored *me* and drunk up my drink and left. Except that it is unlikely I would have been in a pub at all. Normally, I never went near such places. But inside the wolf skin it was very different, everything was different in there.

I prowled about for a while, sometimes on all fours, though this is not easy for us who are accustomed to the upright stance, sometimes loping, with my forepaws held close up to my chest. I went up to tables where people were sitting and snuffled my snout at their packets of crisps. If they were smoking I growled and waved my paws in air-clearing gestures. Lots of them were forthcoming, stroking me and making jokes or pretending terror at my red jaws and wicked little eyes. There was even one lady who took hold of my head and laid it in her lap.

Bounding up to the bar to collect my small dry

sherry, I heard Bill Harkness (the First Woodcutter) say to Susan Hayes (Red Riding Hood's Mother):

"Old Colin's really come out of his shell tonight."

And Susan, bless her, said, "He's a real actor, isn't he?"

I was one of the few members of our company who was. I expect this is always true in amateur dramatics. There are one or two real actors, people who could have made their livings on the stage if it was not so overcrowded a profession, and the rest who just come for the fun of it and the social side. Did I ever consider the stage seriously? My father had been a civil servant, both my grandfathers in the ICS. As far back as I can remember it was taken for granted I should get my degree and go into the civil service. I never questioned it. If you have a mother like mine, one in a million, more a friend than a parent, you never feel the need to rebel. Besides, Mother gave me all the support I could have wished for in my acting. Acting as a hobby, that is. For instance, though the company made provision for hiring all the more complicated costumes for that year's Christmas pantomime, Mother made the wolf suit for me herself. It was ten times better than anything we could have hired. The head we had to buy but the body and the limbs she made from a long-haired grey fur fabric such as is manufactured for ladies' coats.

Moira used to say I enjoyed acting so much because it enabled me to lose myself and become, for a while, someone else. She said I disliked what I was and looked for ways of escape. A strange way to talk to the man you intend to marry! But before I approach the subject of Moira or, indeed, continue with this account, I should explain what its purpose is. The psychiatrist attached to this place or who visits it (I am not entirely clear which), one Dr. Vernon-Peak, has asked me to write down some of my feelings and im-

pressions. That, I said, would only be possible in the
context of a narrative. Very well, he said, he had no
objection. What will become of it when finished I
hardly know. Will it constitute a statement to be used
in court? Or will it enter Dr. Vernon-Peak's files as
another "case history"? It is all the same to me. I can
only tell the truth.

After The George closed, then, we took off our
make-up and changed and went our several ways
home. Mother was waiting up for me. This was not
invariably her habit. If I told her I should be late and
to go to bed at her usual time she always did so. But
I, quite naturally, was not averse to a welcome when
I got home, particularly after a triumph like that one.
Besides, I had been looking forward to telling her
what an amusing time I had had in the pub.

Our house is late Victorian, double-fronted, of grey
limestone, by no means beautiful, but a comfortable
well-built place. My grandfather bought it when he
retired and came home from India in 1920. Mother
was ten at the time, so she has spent most of her life
in that house.

Grandfather was quite a famous shot and used to
go big game hunting before that kind of thing became,
and rightly so, very much frowned upon. The result
was that the place was full of "trophies of the chase."
While Grandfather was alive, and he lived to a great
age, we had no choice but to put up with the antlers
and tusks that sprouted everywhere out of the walls,
the elephant's foot umbrella stand, and the snarling
maws of *tigris* and *ursa*. We had to grin and bear it,
as Mother, who has a fine turn of wit, used to put
it. But when Grandfather was at last gathered to his
ancestors, reverently and without the least disrespect
to him, we took down all those heads and horns and
packed them away in trunks. The fur rugs, however,
we did not disturb. These days they are worth a for-

tune and I always felt that the tiger skins scattered across the hall parquet, the snow leopard draped across the back of the sofa and the bear into whose fur one could bury one's toes before the fire, gave to the place a luxurious look. I took off my shoes, I remember, and snuggled my toes in it that night.

Mother, of course, had been to see the show. She had come on the first night and seen me make my onslaught on Red Riding Hood, an attack so sudden and unexpected that the whole audience had jumped to its feet and gasped. (In our version we did not have the wolf actually devour Red Riding Hood. Unanimously, we agreed this would hardly have been the thing at Christmas.) Mother, however, wanted to see me wearing her creation once more, so I put it on and did some prancing and growling for her benefit. Again I noticed how curiously uninhibited I became once inside the wolf skin. For instance, I bounded up to the snow leopard and began snarling at it. I boxed at its great grey-white face and made playful bites at its ears. Down on all fours I went and pounced on the bear, fighting it, actually forcing its neck within the space of my jaws.

How Mother laughed! She said it was as good as anything in the panto and a good deal better than anything they put on television.

"Animal crackers in my soup," she said, wiping her eyes. "There used to be a song that went like that in my youth. How did it go on? Something about lions and tigers loop the loop."

"Well, *lupus* means a wolf in Latin," I said.

"And you're certainly loopy! When you put that suit on I shall have to say you're going all loopy again!"

When I put that suit on again. Did I intend to put it on again? I had not really thought about it. Yes, perhaps if I ever went to a fancy-dress party, a remote enough contingency. Yet what a shame it seemed to waste it, to pack it away like Grandfather's tusks and antlers, after all the labour Mother had put into it. That night I hung it up in my wardrobe and I remember how strange I felt when I took it off that second time, more naked than I usually felt without my clothes, almost as if I had taken off my skin.

Life kept to the "even tenor" of its way. I felt a little flat with no rehearsals to attend and no lines to learn. Christmas came. Traditionally, Mother and I were alone on the Day itself, we would not have had it any other way, but on Boxing Day Moira arrived and Mother invited a couple of neighbors of ours as well. At some stage, I seem to recall, Susan Hayes dropped in with her husband to wish us the "compliments of the season."

Moira and I had been engaged for three years. We would have got married some time before, there was no question of our not being able to afford to marry, but a difficulty had arisen over where we should live. I think I may say in all fairness that the difficulty was entirely of Moira's making. No mother could have been more welcoming to a future daughter-in-law than mine. She actually wanted us to live with her at Simla House, she said we must think of it as our home and of her simply as our housekeeper. But Moira wanted us to buy a place of our own, so we had reached a deadlock, an impasse.

It was unfortunate that on that Boxing Day, after the others had gone, Moira brought the subject up again. Her brother (an estate agent) had told her of a bungalow for sale halfway between Simla House and her parents' home and it was what he called "a real snip." Fortunately, *I* thought, Mother managed to turn the conversation by telling us about the bungalow she and her parents had lived in in India, with its great colonnaded veranda, its English flower garden and its peepul tree. But Moira interrupted her.

"This is *our* future we're talking about, not your past. I thought Colin and I were getting married."

Mother was quite alarmed. "Aren't you? Surely Colin hasn't broken things off?"

"I suppose you don't consider the possibility *I* might break things off?"

Poor Mother could not help smiling at that. She smiled to cover her hurt. Moira could upset her very easily. For some reason this made Moira angry.

"I'm too old and unattractive to have any choice in the matter, is that what you mean?"

"Moira," I said.

She took no notice. "You may not realize it," she said, "but marrying me will be the making of Colin. It's what he needs to make a man of him."

It must have slipped out before Mother quite knew what she was saying. She patted Moira's knee. "I can quite see it may be a tough assignment, dear."

There was no quarrel. Mother would never have allowed herself to be drawn into that. But Moira became very huffy and said she wanted to go home, so I had to get the car out and take her. All the way to her parents' house I had to listen to a catalog of her wrongs at my hands and my mother's. By the time we parted I felt dispirited and nervous, I even wondered if I was doing the right thing, contemplating matrimony in the "sere and yellow leaf" of forty-two.

Mother had cleared the things away and gone to bed. I went into my bedroom and began undressing. Opening the wardrobe to hang up my tweed trousers, I caught sight of the wolf suit and on some impulse I put it on.

Once inside the wolf I felt calmer and, yes, happier. I sat down in an armchair but after a while I found it more comfortable to crouch, then lie stretched out, on the floor. Lying there, basking in the warmth from the gas fire on my belly and paws, I found myself remembering tales of man's affinity with wolves, Romulus and Remus suckled by a she-wolf, the ancient myth of the werewolf, abandoned children reared by wolves even in these modern times. All this seemed to deflect my mind from the discord between Moira and my mother and I was able to go to bed reasonably happily and to sleep well.

Perhaps, then, it will not seem so very strange and wonderful that the next time I felt depressed I put the suit on again. Mother was out, so I was able to have the freedom of the whole house, not just of my room. It was dusk at four but instead of putting the lights on, I prowled about the house in the twilight, sometimes catching sight of my lean grey form in the many large mirrors Mother is so fond of. Because there was so little light and our house is crammed with bulky furniture and knick-knacks, the reflection I saw looked not like a man disguised but like a real wolf that has somehow escaped and strayed into a cluttered Victorian room. Or a werewolf, that animal part of man's personality that detaches itself and wanders free while leaving behind the depleted human shape.

I crept up upon the teakwood carving of the antelope and devoured the little creature before it knew what had attacked it. I resumed my battle with the bear and we struggled in front of the fireplace, locked in a desperate hairy embrace. It was then that I heard Mother let herself in at the back door. Time had passed more quickly than I had thought. I had escaped and whisked my hind paws and tail 'round the bend in the stairs just before she came into the hall.

Dr. Vernon-Peak seems to want to know why I began this at the age of forty-two, or rather, why I had not done it before. I wish I knew. Of course there is the simple solution that I did not have a wolf skin

before, but that is not the whole answer. Was it perhaps that until then I did not know what my needs
were, though partially I had satisfied them by playing
the parts I was given in dramatic productions? There
is one other thing. I have told him that I recall, as a
very young child, having a close relationship with
some large animal, a dog perhaps or a pony, though
a search conducted into family history by this same
assiduous Vernon-Peak has yielded no evidence that
we ever kept a pet. But more of this anon.

Be that as it may, once I had lived inside the wolf,
I felt the need to do so more and more. Erect on my
hind legs, drawn up to my full height, I do not think
I flatter myself unduly when I say I made a fine handsome animal. And having written that, I realize that I
have not yet described the wolf suit, taking for
granted, I suppose, that those who see this document
will also see it. Yet this may not be the case. They
have refused to let *me* see it, which makes me wonder
if it has been cleaned and made presentable again or
if it is still—but, no, there is no point in going into
unsavory details.

I have said that the body and limbs of the suit were
made of long-haired grey fur fabric. The stuff of it
was coarse, hardly an attractive material for a coat, I
should have thought, but very closely similar to a
wolf's pelt. Mother made the paws after the fashion
of fur gloves but with the padded and stiffened fingers
of a pair of leather gloves for the claws. The head we
bought from a jokes and games shop. It had tall prick
ears, small yellow eyes and a wonderful, half-open
mouth, red, voracious-looking and with a double row
of white fangs. The opening for me to breathe
through was just beneath the lower jaw where the
head joined the powerful grey hairy throat.

As the spring came I would sometimes drive out
into the countryside, park the car and slip into the

skin. It was far from my ambition to be seen by anyone, though. I sought solitude. Whether I should have cared for a "beastly" companion, that is something else again. At that time I wanted merely to wander in the woods and copses or along a hedgerow in my wolf's persona. And this I did, choosing unfrequented places, avoiding anywhere that I might come in contact with the human race. I am trying, in writing this, to explain how I felt. Principally, I felt *not human*. And to be not human is to be without human responsibilities and human cares. Inside the wolf, I laid aside with my humanity my apprehensiveness about getting married, my apprehensiveness about *not* getting married, my fear of leaving Mother on her own, my justifiable resentment at not getting the leading part in our new production. All this got left behind with the depleted sleeping man I left behind to become a happy mindless wild creature.

Our wedding had once again been postponed. The purchase of the house Moira and I had finally agreed upon fell through at the last moment. I cannot say I was altogether sorry. It was near enough to my home, in the same street in fact as Simla House, but I had begun to wonder how I would feel passing our dear old house every day yet knowing it was not under that familiar roof I should lay my head.

Moira was very upset.

Yet, "I won't live in the same house as your mother even for three months," she said in answer to my suggestion. "That's a certain recipe for disaster."

"Mother and Daddy lived with Mother's parents for twenty years," I said.

"Yes, and look at the result." It was then that she made that remark about my enjoying playing parts because I disliked my real self.

There was nothing more to be said except that we must keep on house hunting.

"We can still go to Malta, I suppose," Moira said. "We don't have to cancel that."

Perhaps, but it would be no honeymoon. Anticipating the delights of matrimony was something I had not done up till then and had no intention of doing. And I was on my guard when Moira—Mother was out at her bridge evening—insisted on going up to my bedroom with me, ostensibly to check on the shade of the suit I had bought to get married in. She said she wanted to buy me a tie. Once there, she reclined on my bed, cajoling me to come and sit beside her.

I suppose it was because I was feeling depressed that I put on the wolf skin. I took off my jacket, but nothing more of course in front of Moira, stepped into the wolf skin, fastened it up and adjusted the head. She watched me. She had seen me in it before when she came to the pantomime.

"Why have you put that on?"

I said nothing. What could I have said? The usual contentment filled me, though, and I found myself obeying her command, loping across to the bed where she was. It seemed to come naturally to fawn on her, to rub my great prick-eared head against her breast, to enclose her hands with my paws. All kinds of fantasies filled my wolfish mind and they were of an intense piercing sweetness. If we had been on our holiday then, I do not think moral resolutions would have held me back.

But unlike the lady in The George, Moira did not take hold of my head and lay it in her lap. She jumped up and shouted at me to stop this nonsense, stop it at once, she hated it. So I did as I was told, of course I did, and got sadly out of the skin and hung it back in the cupboard. I took Moira home. On our way we called in at her brother's and looked at fresh lists of houses.

It was on one of these that we eventually settled

after another month or so of picking and choosing and stalling, and we fixed our wedding for the middle of December. During the summer the company had done *Blithe Spirit* (in which I had the meager part of Dr. Bradman, Bill Harkness being Charles Condomine) and the pantomime this year was Cinderella with Susan Hayes in the name part and me as the Elder of the Ugly Sisters. I had calculated I should be back from my honeymoon just in time.

No doubt I would have been. No doubt I would have married and gone away on my honeymoon and come back to play my comic part had I not agreed to go shopping with Moira on her birthday. What happened that day changed everything.

It was a Thursday evening. The stores in the West End stay open late on Thursdays. We left our offices at five, met by arrangement and together walked up Bond Street. The last thing I had in view was that we should begin bickering again, though we had seemed to do little else lately. It started with my mentioning our honeymoon. We were outside Asprey's, walking along arm in arm. Since our house would not be ready for us to move into till the middle of January, I suggested we should go back for just two weeks to Simla House. We should be going there for Christmas in any case.

"I thought we'd decided to go to an hotel," Moira said.

"Don't you think that's rather a waste of money?"

"I think," she said in a grim sort of tone, "I think it's money we daren't not spend," and she drew her arm away from mine.

I asked her what on earth she meant.

"Once you get back there with Mommy you'll never move."

I treated that with the contempt it deserved and said nothing. We walked along in silence. Then Moira began talking in a low monotone, using expressions from paperback psychology which I am glad to say I have never heard from Dr. Vernon-Peak. We crossed the street and entered Selfridge's. Moira was still going on about Oedipus complexes and that nonsense about making a man of me.

"Keep your voice down," I said. "Everyone can hear you."

She shouted at me to shut up, she would say what she pleased. Well, she had repeatedly told me to be a man and to assert myself, so I did just that. I went up to one of the counters, wrote her a cheque for, I must admit, a good deal more than I had originally meant to give her, put it into her hands and walked off, leaving her there.

For a while I felt not displeased with myself but on the way home in the train, depression set in. I should have liked to tell Mother about it but Mother would be out, playing bridge. So I had recourse to my other source of comfort, my wolf skin. The phone rang several times while I was gambolling about the rooms but I did not answer it. I knew it was Moira. I was on the floor with Grandfather's stuffed eagle in my paws and my teeth in its neck when Mother walked in.

Bridge had ended early. One of the ladies had been taken ill and rushed to the hospital. I had been too intent on my task to see the light come on or hear the door. She stood there in her old fur coat, looking at me. I let the eagle fall, I bowed my head, I wanted to die I was so ashamed and embarrassed. How little I really knew my mother! My dear faithful companion, my only friend! Might I not say, my other self?

She smiled. I could hardly believe it but she was smiling. It was that wonderful, conspiratorial, rather naughty smile of hers. "Hallo," she said. "Are you going all loopy?"

In a moment she was down on her knees beside me,

the fur coat enveloping her, and together we worried at the eagle, engaged in battle with the bear, attacked the antelope. Together we bounded into the hall to pounce upon the sleeping tigers. Mother kept laughing (and growling too) saying, what a relief, what a relief! I think we embraced. Next day when I got home she was waiting for me, transformed and ready. She had made herself an animal suit, she must have worked on it all day, out of the snow leopard skin and a length of white fur fabric. I could see her eyes dancing through the gap in its throat.

"You don't know how I've longed to be an animal again," she said. "I used to be animals when you were a baby, I was a dog for a long time and then I was a bear, but your father found out and he didn't like it. I had to stop."

So that was what I dimly remembered. I said she looked like the Queen of the Beasts.

"Do I, Loopy?" she said.

We had a wonderful weekend, Mother and I. Wolf and leopard, we breakfasted together that morning. Then we played. We played all over the house, sometimes fighting, sometimes dancing, hunting of course, carrying off our prey to the lairs we made for ourselves among the furniture. We went out in the car, drove into the country and there in a wood got into our skins and for many happy hours roamed wild among the trees.

There seemed no reason, during those two days, to become human again at all, but on the Tuesday I had a rehearsal, on the Monday morning I had to go off to work. It was coming down to earth, back to what we call reality, with a nasty bang. Still, it had its amusing side too. A lady in the train trod on my toe and I had growled at her before I remembered and turned it into a cough.

All through that weekend neither of us had bothered to answer the phone. In the office I had no choice and it was there that Moira caught me. Marriage had come to seem remote, something grotesque, something that others did, not me. Animals do not marry. But that was not the sort of thing I could say to Moira. I promised to ring her, I said we must meet before the week was out.

I suppose she did tell me she would come over on the Thursday evening and show me what she had bought with the money I had given her. She knew Mother was always out on Thursdays. I suppose Moira did tell me and I failed to take it in. Nothing was important to me but being animals with Mother, Loopy and the Queen of the Beasts.

Each night as soon as I got home we made ourselves ready for our evening's games. How harmless it all was! How innocent! Like the gentle creatures in the dawn of the world before man came. Like the Garden of Eden after Adam and Eve had been sent away.

The lady who had been taken ill at the bridge evening had since died, so this week it was cancelled. But would Mother have gone anyway? Probably not. Our animal capers meant as much to her as they did to me, almost more perhaps, for she had denied herself so long. We were sitting at the dining table, eating our evening meal. Mother had cooked, I recall, a rack of lamb so that we might later gnaw the bones. We never ate it, of course, and I have since wondered what became of it. But we did begin on our soup. The bread was at my end of the table, with the bread board and the long sharp knife.

Moira, when she called and I was alone, was in the habit of letting herself in by the back door. We did not hear her, neither of us heard her, though I do remember Mother's noble head lifted a fraction before Moira came in, her fangs bared and her ears pricked. Moira opened the dining-room door and walked in. I can see her now, the complacent smile on her lips fading and the scream starting to come. She was wearing what must have been my present, a full-length white sheepskin coat.

And then? This is what Dr. Vernon-Peak will particularly wish to know but what I cannot clearly remember. I remember that as the door opened I was holding the bread knife in my paws. I think I remember letting out a low growl and poising myself to spring. But what came after?

The last things I can recall before they brought me here are the blood on my fur and the two wild predatory creatures crouched on the floor over the body of the lamb.